"God of my ancestors! What—"

The night air was rent wide by a hellish wolf-yelling that rose from many throats, and the moonlight outlined the forms of many dark, squatty men, with broad, protruding foreheads and shocks of black hair that were bound with silver fillets.

"Picts," Cormac snapped, brushing past Ceann. "They shriek when they attack; it's supposed to strike terror in the hearts of their prey, and render them stone-still with fear!"

The next Pictish cry Ceann Ruadh heard was not a challenge to battle, but a shriek of bloody death as Cormac's Viking sword ripped the warrior open. The short dark attacker went falling in a spray of blood from a wound that would empty him in minutes; it was too huge for coagulation.

Sword against dagger, spear against shield, man against Pict . . . Ceann was sure he and Cormac were outnumbered and underarmed. But even the most ferocious Picts could not out-fight the

SWORD OF THE GAEL

THE SWORD OF THE GAEL

ANDREW J. OFFUTT

SF
ace books
A Division of Charter Communications Inc.
A GROSSET & DUNLAP COMPANY
51 Madison Avenue
New York, New York 10010

An ACE Book

First Ace printing: April 1981
Published Simultaneously in Canada

2 4 6 8 0 9 7 5 3 1
Manufactured in the United States of America

to
Mary Josephine McCarney-McCabe Offutt
until further notice

Foreword

This novel is the result of a couple of love affairs.

To begin with, I have been a fan of the work of Robert E. Howard for a long time. I don't expect to "outgrow" that, and Cormac son of Art of Connacht is a Howard character.

Next, while reading over a million words in research and taking thousands of words of notes, I fell hopelessly in love with the Emerald Isle, whether it be called Eirrin or Erin or Eire or Ireland. That me grandmither was an O'Driscoll has nothing to do with it — I think. Nor even—I think—that I once married a woman whose name strings out as Mary Josephine McCarney McCabe Offutt. Or maybe that's O'ffutt . . .

It is astonishing how little we know of history or "history," other than Roman, before AD 800 or so. Open your encyclopedia to Scotland or Ireland or any part of Britain and see when they seem to think history began. Even at that I was unable to get hold of all the material I needed (whether I knew of its existence or not), and shall as a consequence probably catch it from some of the Eirrin-born.

Consider this: We think stirrups were unknown in the west at this time (about AD 490). Stirrups made possible chivalry (from *cheval*, horse) and knighthood, for they made possible combat on horseback. Try sitting even a standing horse without stirrups, and swinging your arms strenuously. Revelation can be painful, even without a heavy sword or ax in hand, much less while weighted with helmet, armor, and buckler!

Some will note that the history shown here is accurate — but that the history books show different royal names in the late fifth century. This is *fiction*, and I *wanted* people such as Prince Ceann to exist, and Samaire, and Feredach the Dark. Also . . . Howard held ever an awareness or belief in *continuity*, both in the history of this planet and among races and nations. Does racial memory exist? Howard thought so. It is obvious from his work that he carried the same awareness/belief as regards *individuals*.

But I think that belongs in an article I will probably write, some day. Meanwhile: Things are not always as they seem, even when we have "historical records." (Tell me about a contemporary —?— of Cormac, King Arthur, and then go look him up. The Mayaguez incident of modern piracy is history, and we can lay it all out neatly from start to finish — or can we?)

Finally there is this.

I have avowed being a fan of Robert E. Howard; we even collect *Conan* comics at my house. I am extremely, often painfully, aware of REH's shortcomings, too. I *studied* Howard before I wrote this book, and while I wrote it, too. His Cormac stories I read four times over before I even began to write, and I made notes. (Don't tell me Howard said Cormac had been in exile fifteen years or more, while I say twelve. It was twelve. Maybe Cormac dissembled to Howard as he did to Wulfhere, hating to be so young — while so bright and competent.)

Nevertheless, I have not attempted to copy Howard. Where is the worthiness in that?

Howard was like Burroughs in that people can and do make themselves feel superior by making fun of his cardboard characters and purple prose. (Building oneself up by tearing others down is a favorite game — because it is so easy.) Yet, like that of Burroughs, Howard's work lives and has grown increasingly more popular. Simply put, REH, like ERB, had the Magic. Whether we are fans or imitators — there are lots of those — or emulators or choke-gasp critics, we all sort of wish we had that Magic, too. If I've got hold of some of it, wonderful!

7

You can pat my back if you're of a mind to and my hand will be right there with yours.

In addition, though, I was completely charmed by the language of Augusta Gregory's 1892 translation of the great Irish folk-cycle, *Cuchulain of Muirthemne* (see Pronunciation Guide). I copy no one, consciously. Let's say though that I have been ever conscious and most mindful of both Howard's style and of Lady Gregory's "Old Gaelic" way of telling Cuchulain's story, while I told Cormac's.

That's enough. All I started off to do was tell you about the lack of stirrups, and what a great joy and sheer *fun* this has been for me, and to assure you that all I have done here is with love of Howard's work and what little I know of old Eirrin.

Maybe the publisher will let me write another Cormac story. It's fun.

Afterword to the Foreword: 1981 edition

"They're building Zamboula just outside of Madrid."

Those staggering words came to me not by rolled parchment, but on the phone from my literary agent, who also represents the Robert E. Howard interests, Conan Properties Inc. One afternoon in August of 1980, after I had written two Conan novelettes and a novel, I was advised that Conan's Zamboula was being constructed in Spain, and that in January, 1981 the cameras would begin to roll. Conan lives in books, and comics, and black-and-white "comics" I call illustrated journals, and in the imaginations of millions of us . . . and now Conan will live on film, with the massively constructed Arnold Schwarzenegger playing the Cimmerian.

Meanwhile, I did get to write more Cormac tales, and no one ever wrote to chastise me for my slips—and I did make some!—and fans all over this country and in others continue to ask me when "we" or that ubiquitous "they" are going to make a Cormac movie.

Beats me. The books are visual, but that is not the criterion for spending millions on a film!

Meanwhile, I have revised *Sword of the Gael* (which was always simply *Cormac mac Art,* to me), and with love and enjoyment. It was the first I wrote, and yet it is not first in the cycle; chronologically first. As a matter of fact neither is Howard's *Tigers of the Sea!*

Cormac's youth is chronicled in *The Mists of Doom,* and of course that is Cormac mac Art #1. Next comes *The Tower of Death,* written with Keith Taylor (an Australian I have never met). Strangely, it will be the last to be published! Its direct sequel is *When Death Birds Fly,* which culminates with the Battle of Soissons. Cormac and Wulfhere just missed it. Unless someone elects to resume the series—the novel outlines are ready!—the book that chronologically follows *Death Birds* is Howard's *Tigers of the Sea.* That gives way naturally and obviously to this one. Thus I have written on both sides of Robert Howard's four Cormac mac Art stories.

This novel's direct sequel is *The Undying Wizard,* in which Cutha Atheldane returns—in a way, along with my all-time favorite villain, Thulsa Doom. (He was Kull's nemesis, but the Conan moviemakers like him as well as I do. Skull-faced Thulsa Doom—who may be reincarnated now as Marvel Comics' Doctor Doom—is or was slated to appear in the Conan movie.) *Sign of the Moonbow* is about as direct a sequel as a novel can be; it begins about ten minutes after *Undying* ends. (Not only did I write *Moonbow* without the word "The" before "Sign," I wrote it alone. The appearance of Keith Taylor's name on the flyleaf of the November '80 edition is an error, though neither of us minds much.)

And that is the story behind the Cormac mac Art story. I am sorry I didn't get to correct all the typographical errors and dropped lines in *Mists* and *Moonbow,* which were injected by the first publisher's ingenious typo-injection machine. Now we'll see if this is the end of the Cormac mac Art story. I, darn it, am still waiting for someone to let me write about Kull of Atlantis. Or to write a novel around the cover painting on the British edition of *Sword of the Gael!*

Andrew Offutt
Kentucky, U.S.A.
24-Feburary-'81

Patrick, enquire of God
Whether he recollects when Cormac was alive;
Or hath he seen, East or West
A man his equal, in time of fight.

—from "Cormac the Gael,"
by Ceann Ruadh, the "Minstrel-king"

Chapter One: The Wrath of Manannan MacLir

"I pray that we reach the land of Eirrin, those who are riding upon the great, productive, vast sea:

That they be distributed upon her plains, her mountains, and her valleys; upon her forests that shed showers of nuts and all fruits; upon her rivers and her cataracts; upon her lakes and her great waters; upon her spring-abounding hills:

That they may hold their fairs and equestrian sports upon her territories:

That there may be a king from them in Tara; and that Tara be the territory of their many kings:

That noble Eirrin be the home of the ships and boats of the sons of Milesius:

Eirrin that is now in darkness, it is for her this oration is pronounced:

Let the learned wives of Breas and Buaigne pray that we may reach the noble woman, great Eirrin.

Let Eremon pray, and let Ir and Eber implore, that we may reach Eirrin."
— *Prayer of the poet Amergin for the coming of the Celts to Eire*

Like a demon from the darkest Plutonian hell of the fallen Romans, the wind shrieked and howled in its sudden attack.

It was a vicious wild thing bent on the destruction of sailcloth and timber and human flesh, and men of the *Wolfsail* went hurtling from the frail vessel to their deaths. Their screams were unheard above that of the slashing wind.

The deckless little ship spun and careened. Its single mast was cracked and had fallen, to carry with it two good men amid striped squaresail of Nordic weave. Down went *Wolfsail*'s starboard, till she lay flat with her port side to the darkling sun. Her keel rose like a low wall from the brine. In that sudden sideward lunge more men met their weirds with wails of horror and black death.

The hugest of those desperate seafarers held fast the jagged stump of the ruined mast. To his great broad swordbelt clung one of his men; to his knotty calf in its soaked leggings hung another, fearful of being swept off the ridge of the world. The huge man gripped the mast as though it was his beloved. He it was who bellowed out to Father Odin and his son The Thunderer, for they had escaped the dread whirlpool off these nameless little isles of unpredictable elements only to fall prey to this demon-shrieking gale.

One-eyed Odin and his son heard not — or if they did, were steadfast in their resolve to punish their sometime servant for his many sins. Nor durst he relinquish his grip even so long as to draw steel, that he might die as befit his people, with sword in ruddy fist.

The little ship spun, swung, tipped, and spun again. It hurtled headlong. Islands flew by, shod and crowned with jagged rock. Cordage creaked and wood groaned as if in mortal agony. Men moaned, or prayed, or shouted — or screamed and went to their fathers.

One among their number was silent, and him alone.

He was a man apart in other ways, his armour different and his hair a swatch of the midnight sky. Grim, stolid with the insouciance of a fighting man who expects neither reward nor punishment but takes what may come from gods and men, his mouth was tightpressed and his scarred face almost impassive. He had nailed himself to the dying craft with his own great sword.

Full two inches into the ship's wood just aft of the

dragon headed prow he had driven that oft-gored blade. Around its hilt he had secured his swordbelt, and to belt and gunwale he clung, with hands like the vises in a smith's smoky domain.

This man's slitted eyes were grey as the steel of the blade by which he bound himself aboard. In those eyes there was no fear, no horror — nor yet acceptance, either. Only a certain sadness as his Danish companions died for nought but god-whim, and a waiting. He remained alert and ready to release his iron handed grips and hurl himself into those waves like walls, should the craft break or be driven down into airless realms.

Between two craggy little isles no bigger than the dun-keeps of rich men the frail craft was swept.

Rocky walls rushed by. Instantly the force of the dread gale was quartered by intervening granite. Ten men, left of nineteen, heaved sighs of relief —

But *Wolfsail's* mindless speed was great. She burst from that rock-shadowed lee into the open waters once more. Again the angry wind attacked as with a scarlet battle fury. The vessel lurched twenty feet to starboard as if shoved by the hand of a callous giant.

"Ah, NO!" a man cried out, and his nails dug into the ship's seasoned timber so that the fingers bled. "Pray to your people's sea-god, Gael! It's in his domain we're wind-captured, sure, not the All-father's!"

The grey-eyed man regarded him without change in his set features. He recalled the seagod of the blue-hilled land he'd long since left, a fugitive. His lips formed that ancient name, though not in prayer, for this descendant of Milesian Celts begged of neither human nor immortal.

"Manannan MacLir," he murmured.

And then his teeth clamped, hard, for the ship was dashed against the offshore rocks of another isle

13

and wind-rammed up an unknown beach, and *Wolfsail* had her death therefrom, in a terrible scraping and tearing and splintering of wood.

Strong men flew like dolls clad in glittering steel onto that nameless shore, and were still.

The wind relented and returned to whatever dark lair housed it between the times it drove howling forth to express contempt and hatred for the sons of men.

Like new gold a summer sun burst its cloud-bonds. Sand sparkled on the strand of an unknown island well off the southwestern coast of abandoned Britain. Wind-driven water vanished in vapourous shimmers and the sand paled as it dried. The airy shimmer hovered, too, above the forms of nine prostrate men. Prone or supine or pitifully curled, they lay strewn along the shore where they'd been flung.

The scales and links of battle-scarred armour dried, and heated in the sun. Prostrate men sent back a steely scintillance.

Nine men, lying still.

All were flaxen or red of hair, save the one whose dark mane tumbled from beneath his scarred helmet. All wore armour of good scale mail, save only that one, whose chainmail was forged and linked in the way of Eirrin and Alba to the northeast. All were believers in and followers of One-eyed Odin and his hammer-wielding son Thor or Thunor — save only that one, whose superstitions lay with those of the Druids: The Sidhe of green-cloaked Eirrin, and Agron and Scathach, Grannus and Morrigu the Battle Crow and cu Roi mac Dairi, and Behl of the sun for whom burned the Behl-fires . . . and great Crom, god of an Eirrin older even than Behl's power.

All, too, were of the cold land of the Danes, save

only that one, and he of Eirrin — and an exile.

It was he who first awoke.

The Gael wakened to the familiar salt scent of the sea. A gull screeked. Lying still, the black-haired man twitched his nostrils in the manner of a wary wolf. He scented nothing of that which was all too familiar — raw blood. Blinking against the flaming sun and the lingering grogginess of unconsciousness, he squinted open his eyes.

"Blood of the gods," he muttered. "This be no afterworld, surely — I live!"

Slowly, alert to the flashing pain of broken limb or back or neck, he sat up. There was no flash, but only twinges from a body badly used by the wind. He was whole. Those twinges might have brought moans and lamentations and supine confinement to other men. To him, they were but the boon companions of weapon-men. He was whole; it was enough.

He looked about.

Strewn around him were his companions, lying as they had fallen along a stretch of beach that would have enclosed the house of one of those self-proclaimed "kings" of Britain since the Romans left. A tiny smile tugged at his mouth when he saw the rise and fall of the great barrel that was the chest of Wulfhere Skull-splitter. The giant lived also. Slitted eyes roved; assured their owner that so did all breathe — though there were but seven others.

Before the gale, they had been one and twenty.

He swallowed. There was thirst on him. With a grunt he rose, saw the gleam of his sword, and retrieved it. He wiped it again and again on his sun-hot trews before returning it to the sand; a watery sheath was no more trustworthy than a crowned man.

As he unbuckled belt with pendent sheaths, he looked around himself the more.

Of their ship there was no sign. *Dragged back by the wind*, he mused grimly, *and chased on to be*

15

*buried in the sea. We are stranded here, then. And
. . . where is "here"?*

The sweet sandy shore was a lie. This was a
barren and inhospitable speck on the waters, and it
would offer little comfort to man or beast. Only the
fowls could come and go at will, for ayé there were
ugly-voiced gulls, and he heard the honk of wild ducks
or geese.

And all around: stone. Granite and basalt,
igneous rock like petrified sponge, and the sand to
which some of it had been worn, by wind and sea with
the aid of uncaring time.

He saw how the beach ran up bare and desolate,
strewn with drifts and gravel and fragments of rock.
Then rose, towering, steep and gloomy ramparts of
natural rock, deep-hued basalt. Its somberness was
cut here and there with veins of paler lipartite and
studded with twinkling quartz, set like jewels against
the dark and brooding background.

The Gael compressed his lips. The island was like
a great rock wall or giant's castle, surrounded by shore
and a coast that was mostly rocky and precipitous,
and then by an enormous protective moat: the domain
of Manannan MacLir, the unending sea.

Then a voice rumbled up from a massy chest.
"There's a great drouth in my throat. If this be
Valhalla, where be the cup-bearers?"

The Gael was forced to chuckle. He turned to
look at the big man, Wulfhere Hausakliufr, who was
in the act of sitting up. Already he scratched in his
beard.

"I see no cup-bearers, and a Valkyrie I am not,
bush-face."

Wulfhere looked at him. "Cormac! We live!"

The Gael nodded. "We do. And all the others
breathe."

Even as he spoke, another stirred. Like
Wulfhere, he scratched at the salt encrusting his chin

16

deep within his vermilion beard. "Where are we?"

Wulfhere's reply was a snort. "Ask the gulls, Ivarr."

The Gael named Cormac said, "Where are we? Here."

Ivarr sighed, twisted, shoved himself erect with a palm against the sand. He gazed around himself.

"Ugh and och! *Here*, is it? I'd rather be *there*."

"Ahh . . . methinks my arm be broke."

"You are lying on it, Guthrum," Cormac told that waking Dane. "Stir yourself. It's a nice sleep we've had: the little death. An we find not water, and that soon, it will be the big sleep on us all."

Another man moved, with first a grunt and then a curse. "Water! Hmp — it's *food* this snarling belly wants!"

Cormac was removing his sleeveless tunic of linked chain. "Food! *That*, Half-a-man, we'll have, for there are tasty gulls —"

"Arrgh," Halfdan Half-a-man growled, and he made a face.

" — and wild geese or ducks," the man of Eirrin went on. "And it's their blood we'll be drinking, Wulfhere, and proclaiming it the fairest quencher of thirst on the ridge of the world!"

On his feet, Wulfhere poked a finger into his scarlet beard to scratch. He nodded, a giant with breast muscles that bulged like a brace of shields beneath his corselet of scalemail. He grunted when he stooped for his great helmet. With that on his head ne was even more formidable and giant-like.

"Ummm," he agreed in a rumbling grumble. "We shall not die of thirst or starvation, then. And meanwhile — what do we *do* here?"

"Care for our armour," Cormac advised. With his removed, he folded his legs and lowered himself to the sand. He commenced a meticulous wiping of each of the many links of good small chain, to rid it of salt

17

and rust-bringing water.

Thirst and rumbling bellies were ignored as one, then three, and at last eight others followed his example. A man could stand his hunger and his dry throat. Arms and armour, though — on those his life depended. Despite the fact that this island was surely abandoned by the gods, and unpeopled by the sons of man so that it might be home now in both life and death, the nine survivors of *Wolfsail* sat, and squinted, and rubbed and picked and polished.

As he had begun first and had no scales to lift, it was Cormac who first finished and rose. As though he might at any instant meet an army of attackers, he doggedly fastened armour and arms about his lean, rangy form. Wulfhere glanced up.

"Whither?"

"You've more armour to see to," Cormac said, with that small sardonic smile of his. "I think I'll take a walk."

"Aye, with care. Halfdan will follow you, Cormac mac Art — he has less steel to see to."

Halfdan-called-halfman said nothing. He was built low to the ground, too, but like an ox. Thus the name jestingly given him meant naught to the short man, who could lift and hurl the likes of Cormac and who had sent many taller men to their fathers, and them longer of arm.

Cormac mac Art set off walking, along the shore to the eastward. He angled his steps inland to the rocky wall that stood between him and — whatever dark secrets this grim land housed, back of its lifeless shore.

Halfdan — and Knud the Swift as well — were just on their feet and clad in well-inspected armour when their Gaelic comrade called.

"Ho! A divide splits the rock here, and winds inland."

Then he walked on past it, rounding a granitic

spur that ran down to the very water. Around it Cormac peered, and shook his head, for there was only more rock, and the sea, which ran out and out to turn dark and melt against the farther sky.

Water to the end of the world, the son of Eirrin mused without cheer, and he turned back to meet the others.

They straggled up the sand, huge Wulfhere still buckling on a swordbelt like an ox-harness. Knud limped a bit on a turned ankle, and Hakon Snorri's son had wiped face and left arm clear of patches of skin on the sand in his violent sliding along it. Hrothgar swung his right arm, wincing, whilst he constantly worked the fingers of his left.

Twelve men had died, and nine had been blessed of their gods. All could walk, nor was there break or sprain among them. Cormac's lower back nagged; he gave it no more heed than had it been a hangnail.

In dented helmets and steely-rustling mail over leg-hugging trews that bulged over the winding of their footgear, the little band entered the narrow declivity Cormac had found. Natural walls loomed high on either side, no farther apart here than the length of two men, as though in some time long gone a giant had carved out this entry to the interior with two swift wedging strokes of an ax the size of the father of all oak trees.

They walked.

And they walked the more, while barren cliffs brooded over them and chilled them in grim shadow. The declivity widened, then narrowed. It widened again, and still again drew snug, while it turned a half-score times like a road that followed a cow's meandering path. Nor did the nine men see aught of man or animal, not even the wild fowls they had heard.

Then they rounded another turn in that winding corridor roofed with sky and walled with somber

19

basalt, and they came to a halt, and every man stared.

"Odin's eye!"

"By Odin and the beard of Odin!"

"It — it be a jest of Loki, surely!"

"It's to Valhall we've come for all that, and still no cup-bearer in sight!"

Thus did those stout weapon-men make exclamation, while they stared.

Before them the slash in the rock widened into a canyon. The canyon became a valley, dotted with fallen rock ranging in size from pebbles to great deep-set chunks large as houses. The expanse of the valley itself was such that they could discern no details in the great dark wall of glowering basalt at its far end. But it was not that natural wall that gave them pause and filled them with awe.

Here were man-made walls.

Between the lofty natural fortress and the stranded sea-rovers, incredibly, stood no less than a castle, a towered and columned palace of spectacular porportion.

Chapter Two: The Castle of Atlantis

> *Great were their deeds, their passions,*
> *and their sports;*
> *With clay and stone*
> *They piled on strath and shore*
> *those mystic forts,*
> *Not yet o'erthrown . . .*
> —D'Arcy McGee, *The Celts*

"Not in all my years of wandering have I seen the like of this," Wulfhere said, and not without awe. "Cormac?"

The Gael shook his head. "I have seen the palace of Connacht's king, and served a king in Leinster and another in Dalriada, and it's the halls of their keeps these feet have trod. But that man-raised mountain would hold all Leinster's palace . . . aye, and a tenth of the kingdom of King Gol of Dalriada in Alba as well!"

There was nervousness in the voice of Knud. "Who . . . raised this mighty keep — and why here?"

"No man alive," Cormac mac Art said, very quietly.

Slitted of eye, the Gael was studying the lofty and massive pile of carved stone blocks with its weathered carvings and bronze trim. Broad was its entry and finely arched, the product of science and skill. Arched windows were impudently wide, in scorn of possible attackers.

"Nor was this set here," Cormac mac Art said into their awed silence, "by those Romans who thought they were the chosen of the earth. Those carved decorations . . . it's from the Celts we Gaels sprang, and from the men of long-vanished Cimmeria the Celts sprang, and from the rulers of the world time out of mind that the Cimmerians came — the world-spanning Atlanteans. Aye. Atlantis . . ."

The Danes looked at him curiously.

He was staring, as though seeing the throngs of golden men in their other-land garb, the stalwart folk of that long-ago land now gone forever.

"The great serpent," he murmured, and the hair of more than one man bristled on his nape.

This was not the first time the scarred, sinister-faced Gael had seemed to slip away from them in this wise, as though he saw what they saw not, as though he spoke of a dream composed of pictures painted on the walls of his mind, and none other's. His glacial eyes were invisible within their deep, slitted sockets as he stared at the visions of high civilization and artifice before them, and spoke on, quietly, in a droning voice.

"Kull," he murmured. "Kull . . . An this great keep was not devised by the men of Atlantis and their slaves that were taken from the men and women of all the world, I am . . . not the son of Art na Morna, of Connacht, and him not the son of Conla Dair, son of Conal Crimthanni of the Briton wife of that Niall who was High-king over all Eirrin and gnawed at the heels of the Romans even so far as the land of the Gauls . . ."

"Cormac."

" . . . and him the descendant of those world-spanning giants of old who sailed their high-prowed craft over all the seas of the world and came even here to . . ."

"Cormac," Wulfhere repeated.

22

The murmuring Gael twitched, then jerked as though aroused from sleep. His hand dropped automatically to sword-pommel. He looked at the big Dane, and Cormac blinked.

"Why stand we here, when someone time out of mind has put this nice little house here for the cooling of our heels?"

The nervous men about him over-reacted by laughing uproariously.

They started forward, with Cormac suggesting, in a mutter that hardly disturbed the compression of his lips, that they stay not bunched. In that he was right, for when they were within fifty paces of the towering pair of columns flanking the door of that ancient keep, the arrows came.

Bow-loosed shafts came singing like angry wasps, but it was from the roundshields and surrounding stone they rattled, all save one. Wulfhere stared down at the slender stave that stood from his chest.

Then he laughed, and yanked it free of his mail, nor did blood come with it.

"Odin's good eye," he grunted, "the man who sped this feathered toy has the strength of a child of the Briton weaklings!"

More arrows whirred, but the little band was well scattered and ready now. They took what cover the terrain afforded, for after the long-dead men had erected the castle, boulders and stones and flattish shards of rock had come slithering and bounding down the cliffs to dot the plain.

Guthrum and Ivarr Ivarr's son had their bows, and what few arrows they had saved from the greedy sea. They unlimbered bows, nocked feathered shafts, and glanced at Wulfhere. Each man squatted behind a tumbled boulder partially embedded in the earth, and held his bow sidewise. With a confident grin, Wulfhere muttered that he would rise to draw arrows — and reveal thus the positions of their speeders.

Ivarr had picked up an enemy arrow; Wulfhere tossed his to Guthrum.

"Wulfhere."

The voice was Cormac's. Wulfhere turned questioning eyes on the Gael, who squatted behind a pile of shaly rock that had once been clay.

"Knud," Cormac said, and when that man and the giant leader were looking at him: "When the arrows come, Guthrum and Ivarr will both give them back a few. And Knud — you and I are the fleetest of foot. Shall we pretend demons are on our heels and run straight to the door of that keep, you to the leftward pillar?"

Knud grinned. "Aye," he said, and inspected his buskins' straps.

All were ready, and after a moment Wulfhere rose confidently to his feet, his legs protected by the massy boulder behind which he'd ducked. He waved his great ax so that the sun caught its silvery head and splashed dazzle-fire from it.

"HO-O-OH!" the Skull-splitter bellowed, and back rolled his voice from the canyon's walls. "We've seen how your CHILDREN loose arrows — be there MEN among ye too?"

Aye, and an arrow sounded *ting* and rattled off his huge helmet ere he'd bellowed the last few words. More came, and he struck one so hard with his shield that the little deathstick snapped in twain.

All saw now that there was more than one floor within that lofty castle of old, and that it was from two high windows the keening shafts came. Ivarr and Guthrum joined Wulfhere in standing, and strings thunked as they sent arrows into those same windows.

Like runners in one of the races at the Great Fair of Eirrin, Cormac mac Art and Knud the Swift went racing castle-ward. Knud ran straight , trusting to his well-known speed afoot; Cormac wove a bit, for he was none so fleet of foot as the leggy Dane to his left.

24

Brave or foolhardy, one of the defenders exposed himself to speed an arrow at the Dane and, in a swift movement of hand to waist and back to bow, another at the runner. Cormac felt the arrow strike his belt or the armour there. He grunted and continued running. The castle rushed closer to him, while Wulfhere continued his madman's bellowing — and from ahead and above came a scream of horror and pain.

Cormac grinned wolfishly. An arrow from Guthrum or Ivarr had paid the defender for his temerity, then, and in steely coin!

Cormac mac Art reached the castle. Despite his efforts to slow his headlong pace, he slammed a shoulder into the pillar. It was strangely white despite its age, and iron hard. No more than a grunt escaped the Gael, who met Knud's eyes across a distance of several feet. Knud was there first, naturally enough, and himself not winded. Now the two found that the doorway's width was full the length of a man. Too, it was open. The door itself, massive and ironbound, hung by one huge hinge-strap. It had been chopped well by several axes.

The defenders within did not belong here, Cormac reasoned, but had found this prodigious keep the same as he and his companions, and had hacked and smashed their way inside.

"They've left the door open in welcome," Knud said, showing the other man his drawn steel.

"Shields low and sword ready and in, you to the left."

They entered thus, in crouching movements that emanated from their toes, both men poised to wheel, run, duck, or drop.

A blank wall of well-cut stone met them. To either side a stone stairway ran up to a landing, turned, and vanished behind a wall. A nice way to greet invaders, Cormac thought; *were I on those steps and others entering, I'd hold the place for a day and a night and cover the steps with bodies and gore!*

The two men exchanged a look. With a nod they went each to a separate stairwell. Cormac went up cautiously, close-pressed to the inner wall, step after step with sword out and ready. Knud, who was left-handed as well as fleet as a deer, ascended the other stairway in the same manner.

At the landing, Cormac gathered himself and took a deep breath. He bounded all the way across the platform, into the far corner. By the time he alighted there, his eyes were turned upward and his shield covered his crouching body from collarbones to crotch. He'd had experience with bow-men, and good ones, and knew they seldom drove shaft at the more difficult target of head or throat, but at the midsection or below; a man with an arrow through his leg was more likely than not completely out of any fight.

But he was staring up an empty stairwell, and Knud had not been so clever.

Cormac heard him scream, but could not see the other landing. He soon saw the Dane nevertheless, for he came bumping and rolling back down the stairs. An arrow stood from his guts. He struck the floor face down, and a tent appeared in the back of his mailcoat as the weight of his own limp body against the floor drove the arrow all the way through him.

Without a sound, Cormac mac Art bounded up the second set of narrow stone steps. Passing a corridor to his right, he charged straight ahead. On the floor, in a shaft of sunlight from the broad window, a man lay still, with an arrow through his throat. Ivarr or Guthrum had shot well, at a man who had shown them only head and shoulders!

Another archer, crouched by that same window, was already whipping around and loosing a feathered shaft at the charging invader.

Cormac spun his left arm, trusting to the shield to

26

find the rushing arrow. He was rewarded by the sound of ironshod wood ringing off ironbound buckler. Then his right arm came whipping around in a grey blur. He had a vision of enormous blue eyes beneath a small cap of a helmet, and then eyes and the face in which they were set leaped high and were gone, as his blade sent the head flying from its shoulders — and out the window.

There was no time for so much as a grim smile at the sound of an exultant cry from his comrades outside.

"COMMMMMMME!" the son of Art of Eirrin shouted, and then he was slamming his shoulder against a wall. From it dangled dusty tatters of an eons-old tapestry that had once lent beauty to these somber basaltic halls. From the corner of his eye Cormac had seen the appearance of another man, at the top of the steps at the far end of the broad corridor.

He wore a dark helmet of iron and he held a bow with arrow nocked. The string snapped home and the arrow came too fast for Cormac to see it, at this close range. His shield was angle-held, and the arrow was deflected with a ring and a rap of its tail that was followed instantly by the sound of its glancing off the wall to his left.

Already another arrow was being fitted to string.

Only an idiot charged an archer at such proximity. Had he been a bit closer, only an idiot of a bow-man would have tried to stop attack with an arrow. As it was, the other man had the better of it, and Cormac adopted an uncoventional defense and attack — born of desperation.

With all his might he hurled his sword at the archer.

At the same time, he lunged wildly leftward, toward that gaping window. Even then he was mindful of keeping his buckler betwixt him and the enemy.

27

It was unnecessary; the disconcerted yeoman sent his shaft on a wild upward angle, in his attempt to dodge the flung sword. He did not succeed, nor did it do him harm. But in the seconds he took to recover from that ridiculous "attack," his foe covered yards of stone floor.

Cormac's shield smashed into the other man's breast and face and the Gael's dagger drove into his belly, its impact heightened by the speed of his charge and muscles so powerful that mail parted like paper. The dagger's hilt clanked against steel scales.

With a deliberate twist of his wrist, Cormac jerked the blade back and swung the shield straight up, away from the clawing hand that sought to grasp it.

Nose smashed and belly gutted, the wide-eyed, fast-dying bowman staggered back one step, then two. The third time his foot came down not on floor, but on empty air, and then the topmost step.

The man Cormac recognized as of the Norse went tumbling and clattering and clanging down the stone stairwell.

"What's this?" a great voice came bellowing up. "Cormac sends us a gift of welcome?" And there was a *chunk*. That, the Gael knew, was Wulfhere's ax, and they'd never know which of them had slain Knud's slayer.

Knotty-legged Wulfhere rounded the corner of the landing, and then Hakon and Ivarr, and from behind himself Cormac heard others of his Danish companions, who had come by the steps he had chosen. For the space of several seconds, all stood in that ancient corridor and stared at each other, in wondering silence.

A great castle the size of a Roman circus and the height of an oak lofty enough for the highest Druidic rites — and but three men to defend?

Aye, for by the time the sun had moved across the

28

sky the length of two joints of Cormac's finger, the eight men had assured themselves that the castle was empty of life other than their own. But not of other things . . .

"It be the hiding-hie and treasure-keep of a band of rievers," Cormac muttered, as they stood to stare with greed-bright eyes at what they'd found. "And them off a-roving. They came upon this place as we did, and made it theirs, and left three of their number as guards. Against nothing, for we should not be here but for that treacherous wind."

"And they've gone a-raiding again," Wulfhere murmured.

They gazed at the large room piled and strewn with bales of fine fabric and cloaks, and arms, and gold and gems that gave off their dull light in the dimness, and they nodded.

"Touch," Wulfhere said, and stepped past the Gael. His word was a warning and assurance that he meant not to grab for himself.

The bearded Dane scooped up and held aloft a string of shining pearls the colour of milk and the size of large peas. There were full thirty on the strand. He brandished them, shaking his head.

"From far and far came *these* beauties, by Odin, and it's a ship and arms they'd buy, and two women for a month as well!"

"Find me the women!" Ivarr called.

"Find me the ship," Cormac said darkly, and the laughter died.

So too had Knud died, and the three men from Norge, nor could they be sent their way properly into the world of grim shades or high joy. Their laden bodies were removed to the sunlight, each wrapped in rich cloth from the booty. With more of that dear fabric that was surely for the cloaks and robes of kings and their women, the Danes and their Gaelic comrade wiped and mopped up the blood. Wulfhere was

29

unyielding: no disporting of themselves until the dead were away. And so all of them carried those four in their purple and scarlet wrappings back along the valley, and along the narrow defile that opened into it, and far down the beach. And on their return, despite their anxiousness, they obliterated their own tracks.

Then did the eight return to that magickal castle from a time long gone, for they had found other booty there as well: food, and ale. There was even a small quantity of wine. And the fabulous room that might have contained an army of hundreds.

In it, their voices echoing, they ate, and drank. There was many a growled admonition from Wulfhere and Cormac against gluttony in the matter of wine and ale, for those who had first found this unlikely place might return at any time. Nor would their number be so few as eight.

Eeriness struck among them. Seconds after he drank of the ale, Snorri Evil-eye groaned, and his wayward eyes bulged, and he gasped and rattled deep in his throat. Then he fell. He was dead.

Men who had faced death and slain, and that bloodily and often, stared at him and at each other, and their flesh crawled.

"Sorcery," Halfdan whispered, for his mind was of such a bent more than his companions'.

"It's the sorcery and the power of the Druids I've believed in all these years," Cormac mac Art said quietly, "but never have I seen its evidence."

Others looked at him, hopefully. Then Wulfhere spoke.

"Call it then the displeasure of the gods, and the delayed death I have seen afore with these eyes. It was within himself that poor old Evil-eye took some injury, when the sea flung him upon the strand. But he knew it not, and felt nothing of it — until now, when he sought to drink. Any man knows that inward injuries may leave no sign upon the body — and later

30

bring such results." He gazed down at their dead companion.

"Aye," a voice said in relief, and a ruddy-haired hand went out for a pothern of ale.

"Mayhap," Cormac said. "But it's none of that strong drink I'll be tasting."

Widened eyes fixed upon him, and his words did more to protect their sobriety than all Wulfhere's grousing, though Cormac was as sure as the huge Dane that it was unknown internal injuries had slain Snorri thus.

Striding to the grand old throne of ironwood that sat imperiously on its dais, Guthrum whipped from its base the bale of purple, shot through with cloth-of-silver. Ivarr had placed it there as a joke: an offering to the invisible king of this land. With the cloth, Guthrum now covered their dead companion, and wound him about.

They had been one and twenty, and then nine, and then eight, and now they numbered but seven.

Slowly they returned to the business of filling their bellies, but with less noise and jubilation. Cormac would have liked to be in the magnificent dome overhead, and it set with a cyclopean eye that must have been the size of his shield. For he knew how ridiculous they must look, so few in this vast hall.

Into it could have been fitted the house and entire grounds of Gol, King of Dalriada on the coast of Alba, in whose service Cormac had borne sword until the king did treachery on his fellow Gael, for kings must see to their daughters.

Supported by a double row of lofty columns thrice the thickness of Cormac's body or twice Wulfhere's the room was; the length of two men separated the pillars of that colonnade, and in each row there were five and twenty. Round about them the walls were etched and carved with decorative swirlings and scrollwork and stylized representations of the sea, and

31

ships on its breast.

In addition the walls told a story in pictures scratched into their surface with fine tools, and Cormac walked to read it.

Men had come here in great ships that could have carried within them three or four such as *Wolfsail*, strong and mighty men, bronze of body and them in clothing and armour that were both strange and rich.

Across the broad sea we came, Cormac thought, and shuddered. *And to this place, and here we met the fathers and grandfathers of the serpent-people who ruled the world, above and within, ere Kull wrested Valusia's crown from Borna. And there was war upon us, and I struck and struck and slew and was sore injured . . .*

The wall pictures showed those mighty serpents, prodigiously large and surely exaggerated — but Cormac mac Art knew without knowing how he knew that this wall was history, and without embellishment. The sons of men met in battle those who had preceded them and were loath to give up the world they had so long ruled. There was a great war, and the golden skinned men of Atlantis prevailed.

Then did we set about the erection of this great keep, as a monument to Man, with all its corridors straight and broad that there might be no resemblance to the tracks and lairs of the serpents.

Cormac blinked. He jerked his head from side to side, looked up and around. *We? I must be losing what mind I have! What dark sorcery sends into my brain these memories that cannot be memories, for full a thousand lifetimes separate me from Atlantis!*

But . . . was I here? Have I been here, in each of those lifetimes, ever the warrior, ever slaying so that I must come back, and back, and . . .

Again he shook his head, sharply and more than once. And he was again Cormac, son of Art of Connacht in Eirrin, and nothing crowded his head but the present, and his own memories of this short lifetime — memories that were entirely enough, and bad enough.

He studied the wall, biting his lower lip to make sure he was not distracted into some dreamish world he could not explain and thus resisted with all his sanity.

Unless he missed his guess, those islands the engravings showed the ancients exploring were Britain, and beside it Eirrin, narrow to the north, and above it Alba that the Romans called Caledonia. Strange beasts had roamed their soils then, Cormac saw, and serpents too. He smiled a little, for surely this triumphant etching showed why it was that green Eirrin was free of serpents but contained only toads and a few trifling lizards: the ancient sea-roamers and palace-builders had slain the serpents on that soil, every one.

And I was with them . . .
No!

A new feeling came over him, and he liked it no better than the remembering that was surely false. As though sorcerously drawn out, his finger went forth to touch a certain portion of the isle he thought must be Eirrin. Connacht, western home of the Shannon's source. Green Connacht with its long ragged hills that were blue in the distance, its fens and plains and slopes and its bogs. Connacht of Eirrin; here it was that the son of Art had been born, and raised, until . . .

Cormac turned away from the wall and the story it told.

No longer was he interested in that tale of ancient triumph, or either in food, or the companionship of his Dane-born fellows. If the wall there past the throne showed what had happened to take away these great seafarers and builders, long long centuries agone, he was not interested. No matter what they had recorded,

33

and builded here, it was exiles they'd been. So too was Cormac mac Art exile, and it came down on him now, in the great hall of what must have been his ancestors of a thousand or ten thousand years ago. What matter how long?

Eirrin.

Corn and nuts up to the knees at every Behl-smiling harvest, he thought helplessly, with his eyes full of pain. *And the good trees bending with the weight of their fruit, and the Bueis and the Boyne full of salmon and trout, and the sun of Behl shining on his own land with ever smiling brightness and favour.*

Before his eyes he saw the face of his father. And then again, but changed, for these were the blue eyes Cormac had last seen, and them fixed in death. The son of Eirrin gritted his teeth, for it was no natural death his father had got, and his dangerously-named son just at the age of manhood at the time, fourteen winters and thirteen summers old . . .

Cormac swallowed. He flicked his gaze to his fellows. Wulfhere was staring at him.

"Has it come upon you again, old friend?"

Cormac stared at him.

"The remembering?"

Cormac's face was expressionless. "We be vulnerable as sea-dogs in their mating season," he said gruffly. "I'm for scaling one of the cliffs outside — the westward looked to have handholds enow — and keeping a seaward watch. It's a bow and two arrows I'll be taking, for a warning if need be."

"Cormac — "

But the Gael, his eyes bleak and his shoulders seeming somehow less broad and confidently set, was leaving them. He said no more, nor did he look back.

"There be an enchantment on that man," Wulfhere said, and he heaved a sigh. "Some say we have trod this world before, all of us. Cormac knows it."

34

"Aye." Ivarr nodded. "Know you what he dreams of, when he goes away thus, and him still with us?"

"A yesterday he cannot possibly know."

"And —"

"Eirrin."

"We shall lose his sword and companionship some day," Hakon said, staring fixedly as he ruminated, for it came not easily upon him, the thinking.

"Aye, and his counsel, that crafty calculating warrior's brain of his!"

"And it's not to sword, or arrow or spear we'll lose Cormac mac Art."

Again Wulfhere nodded, and again he uttered the single word: "Eirrin."

Chapter Three: Vikings!

> *Never until now have I met,*
> *Since first I saw sun's light,*
> *Thy like in deeds of battle —*
> *Never in my life, O Cormac!*

—from "Cormac the Gael"
by Ceann Ruadh, the "Minstrel-king"

As Cormac mac Art ascended, the sun went down. The Gael climbed in the dusk-light with great care, his buskins thonged to his belt. He completed his scaling of that looming natural wall of brooding stone in the gloom of last dusk.

From the summit, a long and nigh flat mesa, he watched, hardly seeing, while the sun died. The fat orange half-disk squatted on the far reaches of the ocean. Crimson fingers of its light came reaching out along the waters, seeming to bloody the surface, as if the sun were desperately trying to hold on with breaking nails. Failing, it slid off the edge of the world, which was plunged into darkness. The million eyes of the night sky appeared, presided over by the moon's cold light.

Cormac sat. He was high above the hidden valley now and above even the highest tower of the castle that should not have been there. He re-laced his buskins.

The son of Art of Connacht thought: about Eirrin, about Connacht where he was born and Leinster where he'd taken service, and about Dalriada in Alba where he had also served at arms, before the years of outlaw raiding along those same coasts. "Riever" was the word of his people; "Scoti" was the Romans' word that meant the same, and before they had withdrawn from their Briton sword-land they had commenced calling Alba "Scot-land" as well as Caledonia.

A riever he was still, with Wulfhere and the crew of Danes. Or had been, until this day of dark portent.

Art's son of Connacht was an exile from Dalriada; an exile from Connacht and Leinster. He was an exile from Alba . . . and from his own Eirrin. The name given him by his father had made even more nervous a High-king who sat his throne unsteadily, ever in fear of being toppled from it. By means of that High-king's machinations Cormac had foolishly, youthfully let himself be goaded until he had fought, and slain the man he knew not was in royal pay, and that during the Great Fair.

That youthful Cormac had broken the King's Peace at Fair-time, and death was the penalty. He had not waited for it to come seeking him.

Not in twelve years had he set foot on his native soil, though he claimed it to have been longer. Cormac was more thoughtful and less reckless than Wulfhere, who was older. Cormac pretended to be older, out of regard for his friend and fellow riever. He who was the descendant of kings had the vision and the wisdom of a king — though no regard for them, for by two crowned heads he had been betrayed.

He wondered, as he kept his brooding seaward watch, if the monarchs of old had been different.

Nigh onto three hundred years agone, a usurper had slain Art the Lonely, King over the kings of Eirrin. Not long did the murderer sit the throne of the *Ard-righ*, the High-king, in Tara of Meath. For the son of Art the Lonely slew that man and claimed his father's throne. It was he who gave his people the safety of peace, and the sea-laws, and too their Book of Rights. Too, he caused to be builded magnificent structures at Tara, and a new dignity was born to the high crown.

"He was the greatest king that Eirrin ever knew," Cormac's father had told the boy. "In power and eloquence, in the vigour and splendour of his reign, he had not his like before or since. In his reign none needed bar the door, no flocks need be guarded, nor was anyone in all Eirrin distressed for want of food or clothing. For all Eirrin that wise and just king made a beautiful land of promise. His grandfather was Conn of the Hundred Battles; his father was Art; and he was King Cormac. Like you, son, for I have given you the greatest name in the history of our land: Cormac mac Art. And you of Connacht as well."

He had told the bright-eyed boy Cormac had been how that other Cormac resigned his office in his old age, and after that there ruled other High-kings. Then came Niall of the Nine Hostages, who raided the Picts in Alba and the Romans in Britain — and even into Gaul of the Franks. One wrongful deed Niall had done. He it was who brought home to Eirrin a slave from Britain, who was to return decades later with a new name and a vocation other than the shepherd he'd been, up in Antrim.

Now he was styled "Patricius" by the chief priest in Rome, and Padraigh by the Gaels of his adopted land. He it was who preached the new faith — which Cormac despised as being unworthy of men and particularly of men Eirrin-born. It was that same "Patrick" who threw down the great gold and silver statue of the ancient chief-god of the Celts who came so long ago to Eirrin: Crom Cruach, on the plain of Magh Slecht near Ballymagauran.

38

Atop the basalt cliffs on the island with no name, Cormac stood, and stretched, and turned to gaze norwestward, into darkness. For there lay Eirrin. And he reflected on his heritage.

It was trouble King Niall had with Leinster, as did all the High-kings over the matter of the Boru Tribute, which chafed the Leinstermen hide and spirit and soul. Eochaid son of Enna King of Leinster slew Niall then, these six and eighty years gone, and that from ambush, with an arrow.

Many sons Niall left, who scattered to found kingdoms whilst his brother's son succeeded to the high throne. He too died across the water west of Britain, in the land of the Franks. And his son Ailill was High-king, and none of Niall's get. Nor were they at rest under their helmets.

Time came when those descendants of Niall, the *ua-Neill*, gave challenge. With Leinster's king they met Ailill in great battle at Ocha, and Ailill was overthrown. He was the second High-king of all Eirrin from Connacht — and now Connacht's power was broke.

"Perhaps he was the last son of Connacht to sit enthroned on Tara Hill and preside over the assembled kings at *Feis-mor*," Cormac's father had said, with his eyes on his stout son who was so proficient with weapons — and with his brain. "And . . . perhaps not."

Cormac had known what he meant, even then. He dreamed.

Now, exiled and marooned dreamless on this nameless isle so many years later, that son gave a sardonic smile to the heedless moon. Turning his back on the northwest, he resumed his seat on a round-smoothed stone. He stared morosely at the sea, which reflected the moonlight now as if it were a plain all of brass. Cormac wrestled with his restive mind; stubbornly it returned to his heritage.

After Ailill, Niall's son Laegair ruled, and he it was who sat the throne when Padraigh came back on his infernal mission. Once the strange "bishop" with the spear-pointed staff had converted both Laegair's wife and chief adviser to belief in his selfish *Iosa Chriost* — who brooked no other gods at all — Laegair gave Padraigh permission to preach throughout the emerald isle. Incredibly, the new religion gained and began to supercede the ancient faith of the Celts. The power of the bishops rose. That of the Druids declined. But not in the household of Art of Connacht, or in the mind of his son.

Art of Connacht, Cormac thought, and amused himself darkly by framing it in his mind as the seanachies and poets might style it:

"And in the time when Laegair's son Lugaid was Ard-righ on Tara Hill, Art mac Comal, a member of the Bear sept of the powerless clan na Morna in Connacht and kinsman of the *ua-Neill*, got a son on his wife, and it was after the great king of old they named him: Cormac mac Art."

That same Cormac mac Art snorted.

"King Cormac," he muttered, and his scarred face was not pleasant in the pearl-light of the moon. "Good night on you, subjects all," he muttered, and he lay back, and went to sleep, a marooned exile.

Cormac awoke at dawn, squinting. He resumed his watch and his reverie — but not for long.

It was shortly after dawn that the ship came. Lying prone, he watched it approach the island. When the striped sail vanished from his ken beyond the stern brow of the mesa's shoreward cliffs, he rose. Cormac ran along the mesa heedless of his snarling stomach, until he found a vantage point for unseen observing.

From the towering cliffs above them he watched

40

the ship's crew drag her onto the beach. They were bearded, ruddy men in helms of the Norse style, men from Norge — Vikings! Though from the northlands like the Danes, those were no friends of his comrades.

He watched as they fetched their cargo up the beach: sword-gained booty in sacks and two chests, and two captives as well. The watcher's deepset, narrow eyes narrowed the more as he gazed on those two.

Both wore sleeved white tunics that were dirty and bedraggled, and leather leggings and soft buskins of leather: riding togs, and not peasantish. They were a man and a woman, slim and seemingly young, and them orange-red of hair.

More booty, Cormac mused, *for those be worth ransom, surely.*

Among the Norsemen was also a man lean as a reed rising from the fen and long of silvery beard, with a robe on him. A Nordic Druid, dark-robed and tall and with hair just past his shoulders, as his beard lay on his chest. Cormac saw that he was well deferred to, that slim old man. He wondered at his powers, for he who said the Druids were without powers beyond those of other men was a fool on the face of the earth.

The Norsemen came up the beach. Without choice, the captives were meek enough about it.

Cormac waited only long enough to assure himself of what he already assumed: these men knew where they were going. They it was who had found the ancient palace of this island afore him, and left behind the men he had slain. The Vikings, with their Druid and their booty and their prisoners, were bent for that castle now.

Narrow-eyed, the Gael looked longingly at their dragon-prowed ship.

Then backing like a river crayfish until he was sure he could not be seen afoot, he rose and sped back

41

along the mesa. His route was far more direct than that circuitous one through the defile.

The arrow he sped through a window of the palace brought forth his companions soon enough. When they emerged with drawn sword, faces upturned, he motioned them into hiding. Wulfhere nodded and signaled back; the six Danes concealed themselves.

Cormac waited.

When the Norse Vikings at last appeared, he counted them as they wended their way onto the valley of the castle. The corsairs from the northlands numbered one and twenty. They entered the castle, and long Cormac waited for their reaction to the disappearance of their sentries. A strangeness: they made no outcry, nor did any man emerge to call. He did hear the sounds happy men make when they begin to let ale glide down their throats to cool the belly and warm the mind.

He had known it to happen before, particularly when leadership was not strong or clearly defined. Weary and triumphant from a successful expedition, even good weapon-men had been known to ignore all in their eagerness to relax with food and drink.

Cormac waited long, then waved Wulfhere and the others to cross the valley. They did, making use of all possible cover. Soon, within the shade-darkened defile, the seven held discourse.

Wulfhere Hausakliufr was for attacking the Vikings at once, but listened as ever to Cormac's quietly voiced logic.

"It's doling out their sword-gains and celebrating they'll be, old friend. Let those happy men slake their thirst with all that ale we . . . saw." A smile twisted Cormac's lips. "They'll be easier foemen for it."

They did not mention or consider the prisoners the Norsemen were having such a care with. No sensible man made attempt to "save" a woman from

42

whatever her captors chose to do with her, and despite the impetuous nature of Wulfhere Skull-splitter, he was a sensible man.

Pragmatism prevailed. Having brought both food and drink out with them, the Danes would abide just within the side-cleft of the main defile; they had noted it before, and passed it by. Cormac, meanwhile, would check the strand, and that with care. He would soon know how many guards had been left with the small Viking craft with its striped sail.

"A good craft for us," Wulfhere said darkly.

"So it will be," the Gael said. "We will do nothing until night cloaks this land then . . . agreed?"

"A long wait."

Cormac ignored the petulant tone, said only, "aye."

Wulfhere gazed at him and at last gave him a brief nod. Cormac returned it and went away over the mesa again.

A spire-like chunk of granitic rock remained where weather had washed away that around it. In its lee, Cormac settled himself. He had doffed his helmet to cool his black mane, and laid aside swordbelt against its possible clank. Now and then staring briefly out to sea to re-adjust his eyes, he took up his watch on the beach where lay the Viking ship. And its scalemailed guards with their ferociously big beards and droopy mustachios.

At last he was certain: there were four. Restless they were, and surely not happy to be left behind whilst the others adjourned within the shady palace and betook themselves of ale and wine — and perhaps of their captives as well.

Cormac had tossed the bow down to Wulfhere and the others; Guthrum and Ivarr were better with those far-killing weapons, while Cormac had not his match with sword and shield and dagger. Too, the business of fighting and reddening another's body was

43

to him a personal one. He liked not the bow, or the great siege engines that hurled stone or spear or fire. The world would be an ugly place, Cormac felt and had said, and men the less for it, if ever the time came when wars were fought impersonally, from a distance. For then truly all would be up to the old and unskilled, sitting back in high places while others did their blood-work for them.

He waited, and watched the men on the beach.

When it is dark, Cormac mac Art decided, *I will carry death among those four.*

He waited.

He had waited before, and was little troubled by it. There were gulls to watch, and clouds and their changing shapes, and the shifting of the sea and the occasional flashing appearance of one of her dwellers. And there were the activities of the men below. Them, however, he watched but little. He was not eager to know the men he must soon go among, carrying steel death.

The sun dragged across the sky.

Cormac waited.

Slowly the sun settled, and Cormac moved when the shade changed, so as to remain in shadow. He had spotted the place where he would make his descent, and that unseen by the men with the ship.

He waited, considering the mystery of the great palace built here so long ago. Into his mind came the words of a dying priest of the new god, over in Britain.

"The serpent-man," he had gasped out, "the last of that race that preceded humanity in dominion over the world. King Kull slew the last of his brethren with the edge of the sword in desperate conflict, but the Dark Druid survived to ape the form of man and hand down the Satanic lore of olden times."

Mayhap it was not all those serpentish men Kull of Valusia slew in Atlantis herself, Cormac mused, remembering the wall-etched pictures he had studied yesterday. Then his heart thudded the harder within him, and he fought to thrust castle and wall and pictures and Kull and . . . "memories" from his head.

"This temple," the old priest had got out before his death, "is the last Outpost of their accursed civilization to remain above the ground — and beneath it rages the last Shoggoth to remain near the surface of the world. The goat-spawn roam the hills only at night, fearful now of man, and the Old Ones and the Shoggoths hide deep within the earth . . . "

Cormac mac Art hoped the man had been right. He and Wulfhere had slain raving obscenities in form and ferocity on that occasion, and he was content to confine the edge of his sword to men, not monsters. A frown came onto his face as he thought of the palace back in the valley.

But no; six men had spent the previous night there, and others had doubtless nighted there many times. The Norsemen would not return here had they seen aught of serpent-men or worse!

Of course, he reminded himself, *they have with them their Druid!*

As on the afternoon before, the dying sun bathed the westering sea in blood from horizon to shore, and Cormac prepared himself for the descent.

It was then that the four Vikings emerged from the defile, having come from out the castle, and debouched onto the beach. Cormac froze.

Two of the newcomers were none too steady on their feet, and they carried the reason in a leathern ale-sack. They were greeted enthusiastically by the quartet already there — but that, Cormac saw, was because the four newcomers comprised a relief watch. They remained; the others bent their feet castleward for food and drink, nor were they laggardly about it.

45

Wolf-grinning, Cormac donned helmet and buckled on sword. Then he moved across the lip of the mesa to the sloping talus where rock had slid and fallen. Down he went, and onto the loose rock below. His feet made noise, but the four on the beach made more. They had not, he noted, built a fire.

No. They'd not be wanting others to find this isle-haven!

In the darkness, he walked along the sand toward them.

He was perhaps a ship's length from them when one cried out in alarm. With his sword naked in his fist, Cormac charged.

He rushed upon them in deliberate silence, knowing that would strike fear and confusion into these loud-mouthed men of the north far more than the most bloodcurdling battle-scream.

Three had drawn swords and lifted shields; one, in the act of rising, had slipped and fallen in the darkness. Him Cormac passed up, for it was his way to attack the strongest first, rather than be set upon by that one while he wasted time and strength on a lesser foe. The strongest generally made himself known . . . and did now.

"It's only a man!" a burly Norseman in a great visored helmet called, and he came forward in a crouch, shield and sword up and ready.

Cormac never slowed.

He charged the braver man, and struck at his sword with shield rather than merely catching the vicious sideward cut. At the same time Cormac swung, low. It was not a tactic the Viking was prepared to meet.

Even as his sword struck sparks off the metal rim of his attacker's shield with a frightful clashing clang, hard-swung steel was biting away most of his right leg below the knee. Blood pumped in spurts and the man fell with an awful cry. Cormac was already

46

sweeping his blood-smeared brand viciously back to shear away the blade that came at him from another direction — and that second man's wrist with it. The Gael's buckler seemed to leap out of itself to smash back the sobbing Norseman.

The third man of ice-girt Norge made his try from behind, sure of his prey when the latter was busy with two others.

But Cormac was no longer busy.

Whirling, he interposed his buckler to catch another crashing sword in a new burst of firefly sparks. At the same time, he kicked banefully up under the lower edge of the other's buckler, and crashingly slammed his shield into that one.

The man's cry was ugly, a sound of dreadful pain and gut-sickness. Both pain and cry were ended by the swishing steel blade that sent his helmeted head rolling over the sand. Blood gouted and splashed warmly up Cormac's arm. Without pause he chopped down at the man bent on daggering him in the leg; it was he whose leg the Gael had ruined. Better than dying of blood-loss, surely, Cormac thought, while he swung away to drive his foot up under the chin of the Viking in the act of rising from the sand: the man with no right hand. Jagged jarring pain to his toes made Cormac wince. There was a loud cracking sound and the man, straightened nearly to his feet, flopped sidewise. His head lolled from a broken neck.

Four men had become one.

The fourth, miraculously sobered by the sudden whirlwind ferocity of the attack on these men known for the sudden whirlwind viciousness of their attacks, came a-running with ax and shield. The ax circled the air with a heavy *whoosh* and came rushing down.

Cormac did not ruin his shield by thrusting it up to meet that descending blade, which was hand-broad and long as his head. Instead, he charged into it, and past. The ax was far too heavy for its wielder to change

47

its course. Passing the last guard on his left, Cormac chopped him deeply in the side before the Norseman could recover from the overbalancing effect of chopping mightily into the sand. The man sank down, releasing the ax, clapping a hand to his side.

"It's Wulfhere's choice of weapons that is, and he a man mighty enough to wield it," mac Art muttered to the man writhing on the sand. "Ye'd have done better with a sword."

"O — Odin's name . . . *slay me!*"

Cormac was no barbarian to delight in letting a man die slowly and in terrible pain. Nor had the mindless berserker rage come upon him in this brief conflict. He obliged the Viking.

Then Cormac whirled and set off at the run to rejoin his comrades.

Chapter Four: Cutha Atheldane — Sorcerer

> *The Druid's altar and the Druid's creed*
> *We scarce can trace,*
> *There is not left an undisputed deed*
> *Of all your race . . .*

> —from "The Celts"
> by D'Arcy McGee

Once he'd done railing at mac Art for having slain four without allowing him the pleasure of joining in, Wulfhere, predictably, was for taking the ship and going at once a-roving.

"There's booty here, man," Cormac told him. "And the captives may well be worth more, in ransom. Prisoners, after all, are kept alive only for the use of men's lusts or if they are valuable — and I remind you that the *male* was kept alive."

The conclusion was obvious, and Wulfhere sighed. Then he nodded: the two red-haired captives of the Norse were of value, to someone, somewhere . . . and thus surely to himself and his men. Now the giant was for carrying attack on the men in the castle . . . .

Again, he acquiesced to Cormac's proposal. But

it was not without grumbling that they all trekked back to the beach. There they shoved the ship off into the shallows and guided it carefully along the moonlit surf. Well down the strand and out of sight of its previous beaching, they again pushed and pulled the craft ashore.

Grumbling still, all trekked back to the defile, and along it to the palace. Cormac remonstrated. There were too many Norse, and but a few of his and Wulfhere's band. They could all use some sleep. Perhaps on the morrow the Vikings could be tricked, divided . . . .

This time he did not prevail. All were for attacking, now. The time to strike was when the Norsemen were slowed by full bellies and ale-dulled brains, they insisted. The Gael gave in, because he must, and immediately began counseling caution, a silent attack.

"Those we find must be silenced swiftly, and quietly," Cormac pointed out, as the seven men approached the castle in the wan moonlight.

"And permanently," Wulfhere whispered — loudly enough to have been heard ten yards distant.

"Who's that?" a voice immediately demanded, from the shadows beside the broad entry of that towering pile of stone. "Rane? Olaf?"

"Sh-h," Cormac instantly hissed to his companions. Then he groaned, and pushed a staying hand behind while he continued to move forward.

The man ahead muttered. Another voice answered. Cormac frowned. *Come out of those thrice-damned shadows,* he bade them mentally, *that I may see your number.*

As though the unspoken words carried a command, two un-helmeted but spear-armed men stepped from beside the leftward pillar and came his way, hesitantly. "Olaf? Skel? What's happened? Be ye hurt?"

"By Odin, these two are not yours alone, you selfish son of a selfish Gaedhil pig-farmer!" The angrily grunted words, miraculously not bellowed, emerged from Wulfhere's throat. Deliberately he elbowed Cormac — as he charged past him.

Steel flashed in the moonlight. The two sentries died within seconds of each other, with Wulfhere neither scratched nor winded. He gave the Gael a leering grin.

"Ye'd have done for them both yourself wouldn't you, ye selfish baresarker!"

"I'd have laid them to rest more quietly," Cormac drily assured him. Then, with finger to lips, he bade the giant hush.

In silence, they waited. None came forth from the palace, however, in response to the swift sounds of combat and death. Only loud and jocular voices wafted forth. Unaware of the red doom that had stalked and taken six of their number and was now moving somberly on them, the Vikings laughed and joked, sang and celebrated the success of their latest raid.

"The ale be good — but where's the sorcerous Cutha Atheldane gone to," a Norseman demanded rather plaintively, "with that nice little morsel of Eirrin-born wench? It's not by ale alone that a man lives and recreates himself!"

"The Druid said he hath business with her," another Viking answered, "above stairs. Amuse yourself with her pretty brother, there!"

There was raucous laughter. Cormac and Wulfhere exchanged grim looks.

"They've all gathered in the great hall," the man called Skull-splitter muttered. Their companions had drawn about them now, listening to the revelry within.

"Aye," Cormac snarled, "all save the robed Druid — it's him I'd be going after!"

Wulfhere snorted. "It's the *wench* ye'd be going

51

after, Wolf!"

Cormac earned the sobriquet *an Cliuin*, the Wolf, in his pre-Wulfhere rieving years. Now he gave the other man a challenging look, but the Dane was smiling.

Wulfhere turned to the others. "They are nineteen now, and we six to fall upon them. There will be thirteen in seconds, an we do our work properly. Fear we those odds?"

"Ye should," Cormac tried one last time, but the grim-faced men made assurance that they did not.

"Then Halfdan," Wulfhere said, "do you cut loose the captive first off, an he be tied. Mayhap he knows how to wield sword or ax, and we'll be seven. Cormac goes above, to the simpler work of dealing with an old man."

Cormac shot him a look. That was all; again, Wulfhere's teeth flashed in his broad grin.

They gathered themselves and entered the keep, doom-shadows in the pallid moonlight. The Gael touched two men; they went with him up the leftward stair, whilst Wulfhere and the others mounted by the far steps. The two little parties were soon gazing down the long corridor at each other, having met no sentry. The noises of the merrymaking Vikings had got louder.

Wulfhere was right, Cormac mac Art knew. The Norsemen, one less now than a score in number, were disporting themselves in the sprawling main hall, through that central doorway and down the steps. Doubtless they lay luxuriously about, their bellies stuffed with food and the ale they still quaffed. Surprise would surely give the attackers just what Wulfhere had said: six less foes in the initial onslaught. For Cormac there would be only the light work of despoiling the old Druid of his captive.

It's back with them I'll be, he thought, *ere sword and ax have stopped drinking Norse blood!*

"Give me a small bit of time," he muttered, and

52

set off along the corridor that ran directly back from the stairs,

His goal was easily seen: every ancient door was closed or rotted away to expose the black entry to a dark empty room — save one. Halfway down the corridor, light spilled from an open doorway. Toward that glim Cormac hurried, on feet that moved as silently as he could will them.

Then he heard the old voice, dry as blowing leaves in autumn.

"Then, my dear Lady Samaire, ye'd wear a chaplet on your head among the Norse, and be far better off than were ye in the household of your murderous brother!"

Samaire, Cormac thought. A daughter of Eirrin. And with the same name as his . . . friend, of many years past. *And he offers her wedlock to some Viking — one of those below, or be there treachery in the heart of this Cutha Atheldane?* He heard the captive woman's reply:

"And my brother?"

"He will live," the Druid said, and Cormac stepped into the doorway.

The room was partially restored, looking warm and comfortable with stolen drapes. A torch stood from a sconce bracketed to a wall of paneled wood. There was a table, with the remains of a good meal and a brace of ale-jacks, and a chair. In it sat the woman, her hair loosened and aflow now, and so golden red as to be orange. She yet wore the dirty white tunic or shirt, since it was sleeved, and the leather leggings that vanished into short boots.

Over her stood the tall, reed-thin Druid, his beard six shades of gray and white; his flowing robe of mauve, and a rich fabric as well.

Four eyes stared at the man who had come silently upon them, and him with a naked sword.

"Samaire!"

The familiar face, older now and even better to look upon than when she'd been but a girl and he a boyish soldier in her father's employ, disconcerted Cormac mac Art.

The Druid availed himself of the pause, and that swiftly. He stared, catching and then holding the warrior's eyes, and dolmen-sleeved arms moved in slow gestures. The old man's lips were invisible within his mustache and beard, but they moved as he murmured . . . .

Knowing some ensorcelment was being prepared, Cormac twisted his mouth and swung his sword into line for a swift thrust. He started forward — and there facing him was his old friend and comrade-at-arms, Wulfhere Hausakliufr of the Danes!

Staring, seeing the familiar smile that was ever nigh-mocking, Cormac felt his arm growing heavy. The point of his sword lowered . . .

It was the young woman's scream of warning that shook the hypnotic mist of Druidic power from the eyes of Cormac mac Art. With a blink, he saw that "Wulfhere" was the tall robed man of the Norse — and that he had filled his hand with a glittering dagger. Already he was stabbing — and Cormac hurled himself desperately out of the path of that downrushing blade. It swished past like a striking cobra. The thwarted sorcerer snarled in disappointment.

The intended victim had no time to choose the direction of his sideward lunge. The table was there to meet him; with a crash, man and table went to the floor. Cormac's buckler slammed down noisily on one side and his sword on the other. His feet flew high, and the shock of his backside's hitting the floor sent pain-shock up into his brain. Darkness eddied before his eyes. Even so his warrior's reflexes were drawing him together, and he went a-rolling to avoid a killing blow.

There was none. Cutha Atheldane spurned or durst not risk another attempt. One long bony hand snatched the torch from its sconce, another clamped the girl's wrist. Cormac knew the man's strength, then, for she screwed up her face and writhed in pain.

The sorcerer's shod boot thumped into the paneled wall — and a narrow doorway opened for him, the wood swinging away into a dark passage beyond!

The musty odour of ages gone poured into the room to assail Cormac's nostrils. He was still on the floor when Cutha Atheldane and his captive vanished into the space behind the wall — and the slim door of thick wood began to swing shut.

Chapter Five: The Power of Cutha Atheldane

> *The Bochanach and The Bachanachs*
> *And the witches of the deep vales*
> *Shriek'd from the rims of the shields*
> *And keen'd from the blades of the swords.*

— "Cormac the Gael," Ceann Ruadh

Cutha Atheldane and his captive vanished into some dark passage, taking the only source of light; the narrow door commenced to close behind them; Cormac mac Art heard the yelling, clanging eruption of his companions' attack on the Vikings in the great hall of the old castle.

He paid them no heed. His business lay beyond the wall. In desperation, he kicked out both legs with all his strength. His feet thudded into the overturned table, which was catapulted toward the small doorway in the wall. The table groaned and one of its legs broke, but it wedged itself into the opening. The door's closing was blocked.

Gaining his feet, Cormac sprang across the room. It was well he had done his job, so well that he had to lay aside his sword to wrest the table from the small doorway. Within the passage, he leaned the sword against the wall while he made sure the table was again wedged in place. Then, with sword and buckler, he turned to chase down the fleeing Norse Druid like a hungry wolf on the scent-trail.

The passage was dark, and narrow, and dusty. Why it was dark when he should have seen the glimmer of the other man's torch, Cormac soon learned — by running squarely into the wall with a clang and clash of shield and sword. Sparks seemed to dance in the darkness, but he knew they were behind his eyes, not before.

He made a cross of himself, extending his sword-arm one way and his buckler the other. Sharp-edged brand struck wall; buckler plunged through emptiness. That emptiness was floored, and Cormac turned leftward.

Three steps took him into another wall, and he cursed volubly as he turned to his right.

A grin without mirth pulled at his mouth: ahead he saw a flicker of torchlight, already around still another bend in this serpentine passage. He hurried after it. His extended sword apprised him of that turning. Three steps beyond, the dark corridor swung still again.

Were these walls not so smooth, the Gael thought angrily, *I'd think this circuitous trail was hollowed here by a man both blind and drunk—and led by a lazy serpent!*

He knew otherwise. The passageway was of course an ancient escape-route, its turnings designed to baffle and slow pursuit. Cormac was slowed, right enough, though he refused to be baffled. Then the dusty floor beneath his feet changed, and he nearly fell headlong.

The shaft angled downward, a sloping ramp that dipped steadily, rather than stairs. Shield and sword ready, Cormac mac Art descended.

And descended.

His feet scuffed through dust so that he blew through his nostrils like a tracking hound, to clear them. Already he was sure that he was below the level of the palace entry, which was on a level with the valley's floor. A way to the sea? Probably. He tried, with care, to speed his steps. The darkness absolutely forbade running.

Down and down he went the further. The passage turned now and again, but twice after sufficient distance to enable him to see the flicker of his quarry's torch, well ahead. The pursuer dared not race after it; while Cutha Atheldane's glim would show him any traps this dusty floor might hold, Cormac was in darkness, and forced to a warily slow pace.

Dust lay instep deep on this downward angling floor, where no feet had trod for uncounted centuries. With his shield out to warn him of another blank wall and his sword close to his hip, ready to drive forward in a skewering thrust if he came upon lurking ambush, Cormac descended the somber trail into the earth. Now and again the floor leveled for a space, then angled down once more. All was silence; he heard only the susurrant hissing of his feet through dust older than time.

Samaire!

Gods of Eirrin, he'd not set eyes on her for a half-score and two years, long years of blood-splashed exile! Another time rose up in his mind . . . .

The young Cormac had been a sturdy boy, and that and his auspicious name attracted him notice. Too much notice: High-king Lugaid was a fearful man whose ancient crown rested shakily on his head. And so time came when Cormac's father was mysteriously slain. Nor did Cormac mac Art tarry for blood-feud, even in his own land of Connacht!

Large for his age, well trained at arms and in letters as well by the old Druid Sualtim, Cormac vanished from his homeland.

None knew him or his true age, when he took warrior-service in Leinster, using the name Partha mac Othna of Ulahd. He was too young in years even

58

for that, but a good and sturdy soldier was Partha, who kept his counsel as a "man" apart. Soon he had a secret friend who was then a lover: the king of Leinster's own daughter Samaire, but a year younger than himself. Forfeit would have been his head, had His Majesty known of Cormac/Partha's off duty activities!

Came the day when the young weapon-man well represented Leinster in the fighting over Tara's collection—with the sword, as usual—of the hated Boru Tribute. The aged High-king in Tara soon knew that the hero was Partha mac Othna, a warrior so accomplished that some compared him with the legendary hero Cuchulain of old. And then the High-king learned the real name of that Partha. His gold it was that brought to an end that era of Cormac's life, at the Great Fair when he was deliberately goaded into slaying. After that his choice was simple: flight or death.

Cormac mac Art fled Eirrin.

Samaire of Leinster had wept, and assured him that she loved him . . . .

Samaire!

What strange whim of the capricious gods of old Eirrin sent her now into his life, after so many years, and her as Viking captive and central in some Druidic plot to gain . . . whatever ends it was Cutha Atheldane hoped to gain, by seeing her wed to a Norseman.

She did not even recognize me, Cormac thought, and blundered into a wall, which meant another turning.

Cursing the wall and himself equally, he turned, and four paces after he made the usual second turn.

Then his pursuit down that dim corridor beneath the earth was arrested by a vision, and he stared in astonishment.

Before him stood a woman, beautiful, and she having the appearance of a queen. Yellow plaited hair

59

like new corn she had, and folds of fine silk, purple
and silver, draped soft skin white as the foam of a
seaborne wave. A cloak of gold-worked green silk
swung from her shoulder, and sandals of white bronze
protected her feet from the tunnel's dusty floor.

Cormac stared. The sword was forgotten in his
hand.

"All good be with you, warrior of Eirrin."

Her softly spoken words roused him—partially.
Though his heart raced and his temples pounded, he
made sure he'd got a good grip on his sword.

"How . . . came you here?"

Her pleasant expression did not change. "I swear
by the gods my people swear by, O warrior, that ahead
lie Midir and his son the man you seek, Cutha
Atheldane, and with him three times fifty men, and
the victory will be with them. Pursue and it's your own
father you'll be seeing this night, and him in the other
world."

Cormac drew breath. "Who are you, who tells me
of that yet to come?"

"One who wishes only good, and no burial-
keening, to so noble a warrior of Eirrin born!"

"Swear it then—on my sword!"

But the queenly vision shook her head, and
smiled. She stretched forth her snowy arms through
the folds of her gown. "I will not, but beg you to put it
from you, handsome warrior, and tarry here with me
in activity less warlike."

"Two things I know," Cormac bit out through
clenched teeth. "That I am not handsome, and that
Druid-sent demons cannot abide iron! Be ye shade of
the Sidhe, or demon of the Northlands, or yet again
this Cutha Atheldane in a new guise, you're no woman
born of woman, and it's the colour of your blood I'd be
seeing!"

Lunging forward with the swiftness of those
things called serpents he had first seen in Britain

60

Cormac plunged his long sword between the breasts of the most beautiful woman he had ever beheld.

But he did not see the colour of her blood, for she vanished on the instant. Nor was the dust disturbed, where she had stood.

Blinking and shaking his head violently to clear it of the Druid-sent vision of temptation, Cormac went on. Ancient dust puffed up about his feet. Along that thrice-old corridor he went, on silent feet, with good steel ready in his fist and his ears sharp as five senses for the sound of his quarry. Around a bend in that dim tunnel he moved, close to the far wall—and he brought up short.

A trio of war-girt men blocked his way, staring at him from feral eyes. Their knuckles were pale as they gripped the pommels of their naked swords.

Cormac gazed at them and they stared. Then did his brows rise, and he felt the prickling of his skin. These men who barred his way where the floor's dust was disturbed only by the footsteps of Cutha Atheldane and his captive . . . he knew them!

The big one with the blond beard and evil eyes and horn-sprouting helm—it was Sigrel of the Norsemen. He it was who had recognized the son of Art and called down attack on him, months ago in Alban Dalriada. And that one—he was Arslaf Jarl's-bane with his broken nose, follower of Thorwald Shield-hewer of little Golara . . . and that other, the Pict . . . .

Cormac knew them all. His sweeping sword had parted Sigrel's head from his shoulders, and that a year ago; and into Arslaf's throat had bloodily plunged Cormac's point but a few months gone, to send the man to his people's Valhalla; as for the short, dark Pict, Cormac knew not his name but recognized the stocky man by the Roman belt he wore—and had worn nigh two years ago, when Cormac had sliced away his sword-hand and sundered the Pict's heart

61

with his dagger.

They . . . are all dead! These be dead men, to have their second chance with me!

Cormac's skin prickled anew, and his black mane stirred as his nape writhed; for a moment his bones sought to become unbaked dough. But he shook it off with a jerk of his head and a hunch and twist of his shoulders. Up came his sword.

"Ha, Sigrel! Long since we met, son of a wanderlust mother, and how is it you have set your head again on your craven shoulders?"

Sigrel did not answer the challenge with words, but laughed hollowly—and rushed the Gael, sword swinging aloft.

Rather than stand his ground to await that ferocious charge, Cormac rushed forward to meet it. His sword he held extended, rather than broad-cutting. Its point plunged, with a grating of its flat on the buckle of the man's broad belt, into Sigrel's belly. At the same moment Cormac's left hand rushed up. The edge of his shield caught the other man's swift-descending wrist with bone-cracking impact.

With his sword wrist broken and more than a hand's length of steel in his belly, Sigrel was brought to a halt. But again he vented that hollow laugh that sounded as though it came from the pits of the Hel of his people.

It did, Cormac realized, and he knew then that the purpose of the woman had been to slow him; so too, was the attack of these three. For they were all dead men, and what he saw were only Cutha Atheldane's illusions, sent to terrify or, failing that, to slow his pursuer.

Cormac laughed. "Och! Get hence and back to the land of eternal shade, all of ye—I have business beyond you!" And he charged, to and through and past them.

Nor did he glance back to see them vanish.

Dust flew and the slap of his footsteps resounded

from those walls hewn from stone time out of mind, as he raced down that dreary hallway. Whence came its twilight he did not know. Nor did the insouciant Gael question that there was light, however dim. He knew the power of the Druids, and he was no sneering "civilized" Roman to scoff at the preternatural. He knew of its existence.

Where was mighty Rome now, but beneath the heels that followed those of its Gothic sacker, Alaric?

The appearance of the huge green serpent slowed him, even brought him up short. But it struck no terror to his heart, though its size was prodigious. Its jaws, when it opened them to emit a hiss that was like that of a green log on a hot fire, gaped wide enough to encompass his head. Far behind, its tail twitched.

"By the blood of the gods! *Another* one!"

It angered the Gael that he felt sweat in his palm, and he flipped his sword to his shield-hand. Wiping his right hand on his trews, he returned the gaze of eyes that were black slits set vertically in gleaming pupils like new flax.

"So now it's a serpent the length of three Cormacs and thick as his arm, is it!" he called, and the sound of his voice was good. Sweat and gooseflesh evaporated together. "Well, shade-creature, illusion born . . . get hence! It's your master I've business with!"

The snake was ahead and leftward. Cormac strode forward, breaking into a run, past the outsized reptile on its right.

Thus did Cormac lose his iron-bossed shield, and very nearly the arm that held it.

As it was, that arm was wrenched and sore-bruised. It jerked up with the automatic response of a fighting man, when the serpent moved. It lunged at him, a streak of sleek seagreen hide. The whipping, whirling loop of its body it threw to envelop the man slammed against his interposed shield, and with more

63

force than a man-swung ax.

The shield was ruined, badly bent. Its owner was hurled against a wall of earth hardened by centuries to the consistency of stone. His shield-strap had badly gouged his arm, which quivered violently and sent pain-messages on crimson trails to his brain.

Another message, too, his brain registered: this time his foe was no illusion!

A second sweeping loop of that very real attacker's body came flipping sinuously at him, with rushing speed. Wallowing in the floor's dust against the wall, Cormac again whipped up his shield. A groan was torn from his throat as the stout buckler was wrested from him—and the leathern strap tried to slice through his arm. Then the leather gave, and tore. The shield went flying with a clatter.

An instant later, Cormac's sword-arm was pressed close to his body by a tubular coil of reptilian muscle that looped around arm and chest. The coil was thick as the man's upper arm, and just as powerfully muscled. It was prehensile as well, a great curling crushing rope of flexible steel. It tightened. Another loop took his right leg when he tried to kick. It tightened.

Just as the woman-illusion had said, Art of Connacht was about to be joined by his son Cormac in the afterworld—and that but seconds hence.

There was no time for thinking. It was warrior's reflexes that forced Cormac's lungs full of air and expanded his chest many inches; that strained his right arm away from his body with all his might—though it moved not a centimeter; that sent his left hand rushing to his hip. There hung his dagger, a seax-knife he had of a dead Saxon.

In less than a half-minute, the desperate man drove his dagger seventeen times into the column of muscle that was the serpent's body. Its blood spurted over him, and it was cold to his skin. Since the days of the serpent-men that preceded Kull's reign over Atlantis and sought his red death, the warm-blooded rulers of the earth had abhorred snakes and all their ilk. No exception were the men of Eirrin, where no serpent had ever wriggled. Cormac's shudder was completely involuntary, an ancient atavistic reaction. He stabbed.

The tightening coils forcing his arm into his body and the air from his lungs, Cormac mac Art began to die.

Even then, weirdly, he wondered why the sons of men ever said that one attacked or slew or died *in cold blood*. For only here, in this abhorrent thing that had owned the earth before was spawned the race of man, only in its monster body did the blood run ever cold.

He stabbed. He stabbed the more. His mailed arm flashed up and down like the wing of some giant hummingbird. Steel bit, and drank deep, and serpentish blood oozed and spurted, and splashed—and the last six feet of that body lashed wildly.

Agonized, pain-crazed, the creature sought to gulp its prey even before it crushed him to the easily-swallowed red pulp it preferred. The head flashed down. Great jaws gaped.

Cormac's arm, whipping up for another stab, slammed up under the creature's jaw. The arm and its momentum were powerful enough to knock that fearful head aside, with jarring pain to attacked and attacker. Then attacked became attacker. Twisting his wrist, Cormac drove his dagger up into that lower jaw with such force that the point of the blade ripped bloodily through the upper jaw, between the creature's eyes.

The son of Art hardly knew what happened, then.

It was as though the world was quake-shaken. Cormac was jerked upward. He lost all equilibrium, all sense of up and down as he was whirled in air. A

65

heavy groaning grunt escaped him when his back was slammed, not against the wall but the *ceiling* of that tunnel made by man and ruled by reptile. Yet that he'd been able to grunt was a gaining; the serpentine grip had loosened!

Whirled aloft in the massive snake's throes of pain and desperation, Cormac was released. There was a wind in his ears, and he sought with all his concentration to curl his body as he flew through the air—

Amid pain and clouds of dust, he struck the tunnel's floor, and he rolled.

The wall stopped him. His bones creaked. His head felt as if it would be snapped off. The world spun and the heaven-lights of a clear winter's night seemed to dance and race before his eyes. He wallowed on the corridor floor, in the dust, which clung to the reptile's blood on him.

When he was sure of floor and ceiling, and the lights had gone out before his eyes, the aching Gael set hand to wall and dragged himself to his feet.

He was coughing; the corridor was full of the swirling dust of centuries. Nor would it soon abate, he saw, for the monster reptile was still writhing and hurling itself wildly about. Between its jaws gleamed Cormac's dagger. The serpent made no sound. Only the heavy thump of its lashing body against the floor. and walls of the tunnel sounded its agony and terror-madness.

For a moment Cormac stood staring, blinking, coughing.

Then he saw the glint of steel in the dust, and he went forward. Dodging sidewise to avoid a sweeping rope of arm-sized green that slammed into the wall, he darted into the center of the corridor.

He paused only long enough to crouch, and snatch steel, and then he was running to be out of the way of a death-dealing hurricane in serpent form. He

66

had his sword back, and he was past. He had no care whether the creature died now or later. Its body's juices were being forced from it by its own violent lashing. At hand was the business of following Cutha Atheldane, and Samaire. Already he'd been too long delayed, and nearly killed for being fool enough to assume that because A was equal to B, so would C be. Temptress and attacking men had been illusions; the serpent was unconditionally, prodigiously real!

"Fool I, to make such assumption," he chastised himself. And he ran.

He limped, and he gripped his belt on the right with his left hand, that the aching arm could be kept from swinging. He'd had ribs cracked in his stormy life, and knew that such was not the case this time. Nor were bones broken. The arm would be all right. Heedless of possible traps now, Cormac ran.

The limp went first, and then the left arm began to feel as if it might be worth keeping. He ran.

Ahead were Cutha Atheldane and Samaire, and Cormac had not found her again after twelve years to have his first love, his first woman—though then she'd been but a budding girl—carried off by an illusion-spawning mage from the cold lands of the Vikings!

He plunged along the dark and dusty corridor, strangely twilit now, and odoriferous of a time remotest in the womb of Chronos. He knew he was far beneath the earth. This subterranean burrow must lead to the shore, he thought.

Ahead he saw a wall, and in addition to the eerie lighting of the tunnel itself there was the glimmer of a torch. Cormac's lips parted in a grim smile of satisfaction. Around that turning then, and he'd be upon them, and it was not as captive he wanted Cutha Atheldane of the northlands!

Three running steps from the turning he heard a scraping, a blow, and a throaty gurgle from a human throat. Then he was there, and swinging leftward again, and he was upon them.

Cutha Atheldane stared at him, but the man made no move to attack or make a gesture of ensorcelment. One hand hung limp. The other scraped along the wall beside him, dragging downward as it tried to support his body. Nails tore and knees cracked as the Druid dropped. Behind him stood Samaire of Leinster, also staring at Cormac. In her hand was a dagger he recognized as the Druid's. Its blade was darkened, and it dripped.

Cutha Atheldane lurched forward and lay still in the dust between the two Gaels.

Bending to snatch up the dropped torch, Cormac let the woman see his smile.

"So, dairlin' girl, it's warrior ye've become, after twelve years! And robbing me of the pleasure of gaining this Viking slime his death, too."

She stared at him in silence, looking shocked. Cormac swallowed, knowing she still did not recognize the man the smooth-cheeked boy had become—a man of scarred and sinister face beneath his dented helm.

"A plucky woman indeed. Aye, and a true daughter of Eirrin, whose women have for centuries gone to the warring with their men-folk! But come, dairlin' girl—it's a smallish pack of wolves I had with me, and they may well be hard put to account for all your captors!" He sheathed his sword and extended his hand.

"P-Partha? Cormac?"

"Aye, Samaire. Partha and Cormac, both at once, but it's my own name I've used these past few years. Now—"

But she had taken his proffered hand, and the willowy woman with the loosened mane of sunset-coloured hair clamped it tightly enough to let him know it was no •weakling had slain Cutha Atheldane.

68

"Partha!" she cried, and gripped his other arm. "I mean, Cormac—" And she burst into joyous laughter that wavered on the brink of hysteria. "God in heaven, you be so—so—oh, Cormac!"

There was woman-scent in her hair, and woman-feel in her, even when it was against his steely mailcoat she pressed herself, with both arms around him.

Cormac stood awkwardly. Twelve years had passed, and no daughter of a king remained unwed—and there was business, elsewhere. Heaving a great sigh, he filled his hand with the softness of her hair . . . but clenched his teeth. He pulled back.

"It's later we'll greet and talk, Samaire," he told her. "There are my companions . . ."

She shot him a look from eyes green as a cat's, and nodded. In a sinuous movement the mannishly-dressed woman scooped up the dropped dagger.

"Aye, then, Cormac! Hurry then, and let's reap a red harvest among those sneering Norsemen—and call me what you did of old, not Samaire, or it's this blade I may be tempted to slip betwixt your links!"

Laughing a great laugh, Cormac swung an arm around her, turned, and lofted his torch to light their long way back.

"A king's daughter," he called, "and she talking of bloody slaying—and wanting to be called 'dairlin' girl' as a boy of Connacht once called her? Och, it's a strange world Eirrin's become since my leaving of it!"

"Faster," she urged, striding out in leatherclad legs. "And aye, and careful with your tongue, Cormac mac Cuchulain, for it was no boy to whom I gave my girlhood in Carman-on-the-sea, what seems a century ago!"

Laughing, Cormac strode back the way he had come.

Chapter Six: Treachery of a King

> *My mind is upon Eirrin,*
> *Upon Loch Lene, upon Linny,*
> *Upon the land where the Ulstermen are,*
> *Upon gentle Leinster and upon Meath.*

> —Ceann Ruadh, the "Minstrel-king"
> (from *Voyage of the Exiles*)

Their rapid pace and the circuitousness of tha
subterranean burrow prevented Cormac mac Art and
Samaire from exchanging many words. He did learn
that the other prisoner was her brother Ceann, and
that their father was dead nigh two years.

No inimical serpent awaited them in that dusty
and echoic corridor. The vast reptile was dead when
they came upon him, though Samaire was frightened
enough. Cormac was both surprised and troubled to
learn that she had seen no sign of the snake, ere now
Had it erupted from some side passage he had failed
to note, then, last survivor of an ages-agone war? Or
— had Cutha Atheldane possessed even more power
than suspected, and Samaire slain a sorcerer of
considerable note?

The snake had thrashed until the lethargy of
death overcame it, and left a lake of blood they must
walk through. Cormac was more than happy to sweep

70

his "dairlin' girl" up in his arms and carry her across to dry dust, though she railed at him.

"I be no weak mewling girl who must be sheltered from the hint or sight of harm and carried like a babe across a mere bit of blood!"

"Oh," he said.

He walked three paces on, into the dust, and dropped her. Dust flew up and she groaned, but he was already turning back. He retrieved his Saxon dagger from the serpent's mouth, calmly enough, and he took up his ruined shield too, to show the others he'd had no easy time of it and had not been a-womanizing whilst they faced stern blades against his counsel.

"I suppose," Saimare of the flaming hair said when he rejoined her, and her standing, "that I am committed and cannot now put bad words on you for having dropped me, and me both a woman and a king's daughter."

"I suppose not," Cormac said.

They went on, ever upward. After a time he glanced at her face in the torchlight, and she looked up at him. They grinned together, and then they laughed.

"Barbarian," she snapped. "Cu Roi mac Dairi!" There was laughter still, in her voice.

"Warrior-woman," he retorted, grinning. "Morrigu and Agron all in one, ye are!"

Laughing, they went on. She had named him that god who was master of sorcerers and great traveler; he who had done conquest all over the world, but had never reddened his sword in Eirrin; it was apt enough, saving only that one man Cormac had slain, at the Great Feast twelve years ago. He in his turn had called her by the name of both the goddesses of war and of slaughter. He hoped there was no aptness in her case: a prophetess, Morrigu the Battle Crow was not unknown for treachery done on the sons of men.

71

At last they re-entered the room where Cutha had sought to bargain with her, and thence they went around and down into the castle's main chamber.

It was a charnel house.

The reek of gore was in the air, and somewhere Morrigu must have been licking her lips. Blood was splashed everywhere and pooling the floor around the corpses of slain men. A great battle had taken place here, and Cormac and Samaire found but two survivors. Both men dripped blood.

One was a red-bearded giant, taller even than Cormac, and hugely built. He leaned on a great gore-smeared ax, and his fierce eyes gleamed with the joy of battle and having done to death every man of his foes. His thrice-dented helmet lay on the floor, and now it sprouted but one horn.

The other man was built more as Cormac was; lean and lithe and catlike, with a rippling sinuousness. Fire and sunset his hair was, and his face had been smooth-shaven; now it sprouted the gleaming growth of a seven-day or so. He was not so tall as mac Art and was in truth considerably better looking, without Cormac's several scars and slitted eyes. Rent blood-soaked was his once-white shirt, and there was blood too on his chin and many dark spots and lines marked where it had splashed his leather leggings and boots. This man, not yet thirty, sat on the floor with his right hand clamped around his left arm at the elbow, where blood trickled.

"Ceann!" Samaire cried. "You're hurt!"

"Aye." He nodded. "It's the edge of a dagger I caught here, but it's hardly my death I'll have from it. The dagger is still clenched in the hand that wielded it — see?"

She followed the direction of his nod. "Ugh," she said rather than groaned, for the dagger-clenching fist was several feet from any arm. Wulfhere laughed aloud.

"This great warrior had the fellow's hand apart from his body and his entrails plopping forth with two slashes so swift I could not have swung my ax once in the same space! It's a fellow son of Eirrin we've liberated from the Norse, Cormac. And by Odin and the blood of Odin, he himself liberated several of their spirits from their bodies in the doing!"

"Cormac!" the young man said, and he stared at the man who had returned with his sister. She had already ripped and slashed a great long strip of cloth from a tumbled bale of purest white, and anointed his arm with wine as though it were plentiful as water. Now she was binding up his wound.

Cormac's blue eyes met the seated man's strangely pale, blue-green ones. "Aye, Ceann mogh Ruadh mac Ulad, Cormac, whom you knew as Partha mac Othna."

"And who my sister knew all too well!"

"Still your body and your tongue, darling brother," Samaire snapped, "or I'll pull both ends of this cloth till your arm drops off! He has just followed me miles underground, and him in the dark, and forced to face too the grandfather of all serpents — which he slew with so much blood as to redden the Boyne for a week!"

Cormac blinked at the fierceness of Samaire's tone, and her poetic exaggeration. It was Wulfhere who spoke.

"Ho! So that's the way of it — methought perhaps you bent your shield so in falling over your own feet, Cormac!"

With a swift, small smile, Cormac hurled the ruined shield at him. Wulfhere batted it away negligently, though in truth another man might have been bowled over.

"So it's all old friends you Gaels are, then. Ceann Red-hair I have already exchanged names with. And this be his sister, Samaire?" The hulking Dane smiled

73

upon her. "It's nice heads of hair ye both have — I be partial to red!"

Samaire looked about that great hall. "So," she said, "I see. There, Ceann, and try to keep yourself quiet a time, that the wound has time to close. Does it hurt, brother?"

"It hurts. Seeing the waste of that good wine hurts the more, though!"

"A warrior indeed!" Wulfhere called out, amid a burst of laughter. "An all the men of Eirrin were as you twain, Cormac and Ceann, it's straight for Dane-mark I'd set my sail, to avoid getting my death at the hands of such ferocious heroes as ye both be!"

Ceann stood up. "It's in your debt I remain now, Parth — Cormac mac Art."

Cormac nodded. "I lay no claim," he said. "Now suppose we take up a bit of food and enough ale for ten —"

"Twenty, an I'm to have aught!" Wulfhere interrupted.

"— and get ourselves elsewhere, away from the smell and sight of blood. It's sword-companions Wulfhere and I have lost this night, and a man deep in ale has no memory."

Immediately, after the manner of Eirrin, Samaire set up a keening. Wulfhere glanced at his comrade.

"She does us honour, keening our dead," Cormac told him. "It is our — it is the way of Eirrin."

Wulfhere nodded. He walked to the lamenting young woman, scooping up two leathern sacks of ale as he went. His hand on her shoulder covered it from throat to upper arm.

"With thanks, friend of my friend. But let's away from this slaughterhouse and shriek in our minds."

Well laden, the quartet departed the reeking scene of red horror and destruction, and went along the corridor none of them had traversed. There they found two rooms, one after the other, spread with stolen cloths and cloaks — of Gaelic manufacture, Cormac noticed — and tables. The arrangement of cloth and furs showed that the Vikings had slept here. The only four occupants of that palace great enough for a thousand entered, and sat and drank. And Samaire and Ceann told their story.

Ulad Ceannselaigh, king of tribute-laden Leinster, had died of a sudden, and without blood. Naturally he left his throne to his firstborn, Liadh. That elder brother of Ceann and Samaire sat the high seat well, and retained most of his father's advisers, creating his brother Feredach his high minister. Her father had long since wed Samaire to a prince of Osraige, which to everyone but its king was a part of Leinster, along the western border. Aiding the southern Munstermen in resisting a Pictish incursion into their lands, Samaire's husband took an arrow in the chest. He died even as he was being carried back to Osraige. Childless and in difficulties with her husband's mother, Samaire returned to Carman in Leinster. She had an honoured place in the household of her kingly brother Liadh, along with Ceann, whose wife had died in the bearing him of their second child.

Then Liadh was slain, and him less than a year on the throne.

"There was little secret," Ceann Ruadh said bitterly, "and no doubt in the minds of many: it was our brother Feredach had him murdered."

Cormac sighed, but only nodded. It was the way of royalty in all lands. An a king had but one heir, the succession was endangered by but one fragile life. An he had several sons, to insure the continuity of his clan on the throne, each was in danger of the other.

"Feredach Ruadh-lam!" Samaire whispered viciously through clenched teeth, calling her brother the Red-handed.

And so Feredach was crowned in Leinster. Nor was he popular, a mean grasping man who suspected

75

everyone of plotting as he had ever done. Nervous he was of the popularity of his own younger brother Ceann — and Ceann's confidante, Samaire, four years widowed and returned to the keep of her family.

"We knew it not then," Ceann said, with ugliness in his pleasant tenor voice. "But our brother thought it was plotting we were, in the time we spent together."

"Poor fearful Feredach feared us!" Samaire put in, and Cormac knew that was as incredible as her voice and manner indicated; she and Ceann were not of such a bent.

"I see the light as of dawn," Wulfhere Skull-splitter said, holding aside his alesack long enough to speak. "Ye two fell into the hands of Viking-raiders, and while you were out for a ride, from the looks of you. This Feredach did treachery on you, I'm thinking."

He had indeed. In a scurrilous bargain with the Norsemen just slain, Feredach had his younger brother and sister carried off, that there might be no claim on this throne but his own.

"And it's well paid his hirelings are after being," Cormac said snarling, in a castle peopled by ghosts and the crimsoned corpses of slain kidnapers.

None of them knew aught of this place and Cormac assured them it was of Atlantean origin — Wulfhere looking nervous, lest his companion go away into his strange *remembering*. Ceann and Samaire in turn assured their countryman that Cutha Atheldane had been a sorcerer of considerable skills.

After a time Cormac began to realize what they were assuming, and deliberately he mentioned the ship, and their need of gaining new crew for her. The booty they'd taken away from this ancient keep would see to that.

Samaire looked stricken. She and her brother made clear that they assumed Cormac would return with them to Eirrin, there to aid them in wresting the throne away from the man already surnamed "the Dark": *an-Dubh.* Cormac mac Art shook his head.

"I fled under sentence of death," he said, "and dare not return." He gave his dark head a jerk. "Besides, Eirrin is no longer my land."

Samaire and Ceann stared at him. It was she, at last, who spoke.

"There are no *former* sons of Eirrin, Cormac of Connacht! It's a spell there is on the fens and the bogs, and the cairn-topped hills of green Eirrin called Inisfail, and it envelops us all at birth like a cloak about the mind. We are forever under it — even those who so long and long ago moved across Magh Rian to Dalriada in Alba. Eirrin-born is Eirrin-bound, as if by stout cords and golden chains."

With his belly sloshing, Wulfhere sat silent. He stared at the fine cloth covering the floor between bloodstained leggings, and mayhap he thought of the land of the Danes.

"I have not felt such chains, and me twelve years gone," Cormac said quietly. "I am an exile, a man without a homeland, a *Scoti*; a raider."

The moment Ceann began to speak, Cormac remembered that the prince, third in line to his father's throne and no plotter he, had oft amused himself and others in the minstrel's way.

"He is the raven that has no home,
The boat flung from wave to wave;
He is the ship that's lost its rudder,
He be the apple that's left on the tree:
This the Exile, a man alone, unfree.
And it's dark grief and sorrow
Are e'er his boon companions."

Though he was sagging and nigh asleep, Wulfhere wagged his great shaggy head. "Aye," he said morosely, and began the difficult task of getting his alesack again to his lips.

"I want no homeland," Cormac said without grace, "and it's time for bed."

He rose, catching up a cloak and half a bale of cloth. "Wulfhere will never leave this room until he next awakens. The next chamber is as well appointed for sleeping; as for me, I shall go out under the sky as I have thousands of times."

"Cormac—" Samaire began.

But he left them.

Behind him he heard Ceann, gently singing:

"Seagirt it lies, where giants dwelt of old;
This Eirrin Isle sacred to all our fathers . . . "

Grinding his teeth, Cormac hurried along the corridor and down the steps. Outside, he relieved his ale-filled bladder in the moonlight. A little way from the palace, and shielded from view of the entry from the sea on the very off chance that men might come, he spread his bedding and lay down.

The stars gazed down, and twinkled, and they seemed green like Eirrin. With a snarl, Cormac turned onto his side.

But in the morning Ceann found his sister gone, and was much fearful until she came in from outside, with Cormac, and they announced that it was to Eirrin Cormac mac Art would be going.

Wulfhere added nothing to the discussion as the others talked of Eirrin, and their returning; the Dane suffered from the presence inside his head of Thor and his hammer of thunder.

This was the year of the great triennial gathering, Cormac was told, the Feis of Tara at Samain. High summer smiled on Eirrin now, and Samain — the New Year of the old faith: November first — was not long off. Once every three years to Tara hill in Meath came all the kings. Came too the historians and poets and judges, the druids — and bishops, now — and doctors of law, for the reading of the old laws, and discussion of the state of the land, and hearing and redress of wrongs, and the great ceremony that was the meeting of all the kings of Eirrin with the *Ard-righ* or High-king.

"There," Samaire said, her eyes fixed on Cormac's, "Ceann and I can gain safety, and make our accusation and claim!"

Cormac only nodded. He said it not, but knew they had no claim: Feredach an-Dubh was *older*. The throne was legally his. *So long*, Cormac thought automatically, *as he lives*.

They spent much time amid the booty crowding one room and strewing the throne-hall as well. With some judicious cutting and pins and brooches, the making of new clothing to replace ruined was little difficulty, though Cormac thoughtfully counseled against the finest fabrics. They chose to carry off not only the most valuable of the Viking-stolen goods that was now theirs by the ancient right of conquest, but the lightest and most easily concealed, as well. Into Wulfhere's sword-scabbard went the pearls he had coveted. Both Ceann and Samaire armed themselves well. Cormac found a buckler he pronounced better than his old one, and more handsome besides. A jewel-set belt he buckled on under his clothing. Huge enveloping cloaks they created from this bolt of fabric and that, and Samaire cleverly sewed squares of fabric inside, open at the top, for the secreting of valuable treasures.

A torc of solid gold Cormac presented with ceremony to his sword-companion. Wulfhere dutifully thanked him and then brought laughter on them all by showing that the twisted circlet would barely encompass his wrist, much less his bull neck. With a gentleness and gallantry that made Cormac's eyes pop — before he turned away to hide his smile — the Dane presented the gift to Samaire.

Cormac bade her wrap it in leather cut from a Norse boot ere she wore it around her neck, for they must not look too rich.

Finding a pair of strange high boots of soft doeskin, Samaire coveted them for her own. She contrived to equip their tops with holes, through which she threaded strips of hide. These she fastened in turn to her belt, which was broad as her waist and fastened with a buckle nigh as big as her hand. The buckle they hoped all would assume was brass, for who would believe it for what it was: many coins' weight of solid gold! The boots came halfway up her thighs, to where her scarlet tunic fell.

One trek they made from palace to the Viking ship, which waited safe and dry on the beach where they'd hidden it. All were laden with food and ale, for they'd found no fresh water. And back they went, and returned to the ship again, groaning and staggering under the weight of booty: gold and silver and gems and fine leather. A third journey through that narrow defile from shore to palace brought forth more booty, and many weapons — and Ceann's prize, a small harp. He strummed it, and pronounced it a fine instrument.

"Never," Wulfhere rumbled, "have I had thought of sailing the sea with a prince as minstrel!"

"Nor ever have I had thought of sailing the ship playing the lute for a Dane as big as a tree!" Ceann retorted, and the two men laughed together.

Chapter Seven: "The sea is angry!"

> *Their ocean-god was Mannanan Mac Lir,*
> *Whose angry lips,*
> *In their white foam, full often would inter*
> *Whole fleets of ships . . .*

—D'Arcy McGee: *The Celts*

Built in the clinker way of the Scandinavians, the ship was small and light, no more than sixty feet long. Her crew of four left her light in the water, despite their having heavy-laden her with food and ale and the Vikings' booty.

The quartet would be able to handle her well enough, with her one sail, and with Cormac's and Wulfhere's experience. They'd need it, as well as their strength, if heavy winds rose. True, they needed near-perfect sailing conditions; there'd be little the four of them could do with fourteen sets of oars.

South of Britain as they were, they could not sail directly to Eirrin. A direct northeasterly bearing would carry them into the realm of the Wind Among the Isles that had hurled them here — and the whirlpool off the island called Ire of Manannan. They must head westward before bringing about on a northerly bearing, and then at last swing northeast to seagirt Eirrin.

With a nice little breeze rippling the sea and blowing their hair, they raised and braced the mast and made ready to hoist sail. Cormac already thought of this island as Serpent's Lair, since it was that deep-laired reptile that had nigh got him his death. But he said nothing when, as they prepared to depart, Wulfhere called it otherwise.

"Farewell, Samaire-heim," he said and received a smile and a thanks for the inspiration for that Irish-Danish name.

Away and out from Samaire-heim they slid, and with ease. Skirting the rocks and bearing away from the islands, Cormac and the Dane did their best to impart to their Leinsterish companions the mysterious lore of seamanship. Soon they were clear, and stood forth to open sea. With smooth sailing, Ceann began testing his new smallharp, plucking and strumming. After a time he raised his excellent tenor in song.

"I sing of rescue, and a giant from the land of the Danes," the slender redhead said, and Wulfhere blinked and strove not to swell his chest.

> *"His beard is a bush of flame,*
> *His ax a stout tree of steel;*
> *His legs the sturdiest of oaks,*
> *His wrath like a forest afire.*
>
> *He splits the Norsemen's shields*
> *On the edge of his great red ax;*
> *He vents the armour of them all,*
> *He breaks the bones of the Vikings!"*

Grinning broadly, Wulfhere struck a pose at the prow, his chest like a great iron bound barrel and his fiery beard jutting. Fighting a smile, Cormac turned away.

"How fares Eirrin?" he asked, of her who had persuaded him to return.

It was Ceann made reply:

"Summery Eirrin! Delightful time!
How beautiful the colour;
The blackbirds trill the full day;
The cuckoos sing in constant strains.
Now welcome is the twice-noble
Brilliance of the sun's seasons!

On the marge of the branchy woods
Summer swallows skim the streams,
The swift horses seek the pool.
The heather spreads her long hair;
High grows the fair bog-down —
Flowers cover the earth of Eirrin!"

Smiling, Cormac continued to look on Samaire's face.

"How fares Eirrin? Fair and beautiful, son of Art. Flax and corn crowding the very foothills of Mount Leinster. Silver and gold still pushing up out of the ground without digging of it, and singing peasants wear carbuncles while stout branches break from the weight of their fruit."

"Another poet!" Wulfhere cried grinning, while Cormac bellied up a short laugh.

"How fares Eirrin?" he repeated.

"Leinstermen still resist the Boru Tribute," Samaire said. "But he is a good High-king, is Erca Tireach. The land basks in his wisdom and his peace, and the sons and daughters of Eirrin see to the business of Eirrin whilst the rest of the world wars like rival ants."

"His *peace!*" Cormac burst out. "The business of Eirrin . . . " He shook his head. "Gaels of Eirrin

83

should be carving out fine haunch and tenderloin of Britain as from a roast at fair-time! It's these eighty years since Alaric and his Goths carried the sword into the streets of Rome, and the legions and administrators torn out of Britain after five centuries and more, like the legs from an old table. Now it's Saxons and Jutes and Angles are creating what they call kingdoms of Britain. *Kingdoms!* Kings without the price of fivescore sheep, and with three hundred subjects — even less! Britain's ripe for the taking, and it's being taken! Where be the sons of Niall when there lies a land next door, like a jewel-coffer with the lid open?''

"Tamed," Ceann said.

Cormac stared at him. "Tamed! *Eirrin? Gaels?* Why man it was in Gaul over the wide seas that Niall got his death, and him chasing the Romans all the way from Londinium in Britain! Can the descendants of such a warrior be *tamed?*''

"Not all," Samaire said quietly, gazing upon the son of Art. She had clamped her teeth at the mention of the death of Niall of the Nine Hostages. For it was a king's son of her Leinster had slain the great conqueror-king whose descendants still reigned, and that skulking from ambush.

Ceann only shook his head. "That," he said, "was before Padraigh came to Eirrin."

"Padraigh!" The name tore from Cormac's lips like a curse. "And him mealymouthing about peace and love your neighbour! Why, by neighbour that maniac meant *Vikings*, and Jutes and Picts, and those that have yet to crawl from beneath their slime-bottomed rocks! Would that Padraigh were alive that I might aid him along in his blitheful journey to the afterworld of his weakling's god! Tell me — is't true what I heard tell in Britain, that his strange faith has stolen even our New Year's and the Vigil of it?''

Samaire sighed. "Aye, and the mistletoe of the

84

Druids as well, and the Behlfire of Midsummer's. As to the ancient New Year — aye, the Christians have . . . *borrowed* it. Samain they claim is dedicated to all the souls of Christendom, and its vigil they call the Hallowed Eve of All Saints. As to the festival-time of winter, that has been such for Celts these thousands of years — it's then Bishop Patricius — Padraigh — says the son of the Christian god was born, and that *we* celebrated it in honour of this Eastern man-god."

"Why, he was born but a few centuries ago," Wulfhere rumbled from the prow. "Compared with our Odin and your Crom, Iosa is a mewling child!"

Samaire shrugged. "It's said we *anticipated* the coming of Iosa Chriost," she said. "And all our festivals were merely warnings and anticipations of his arrival to rule the world, through bishops rather than Druids, through the Son rather than the Sun."

After staring in horror and anger at her for a time, trying to digest that this one man, this Patrick, had begun the taming of his people, Cormac swung his head alee. There he showed his love of Patricius/Padraigh/Patrick and his selfish and thieving religion: he spat.

"And . . . Leinster?" he asked at last.

"Like all Eirrin, Leinster is home now to many Christians, Cormac mac Art."

"And . . . her royal house?"

"You know that King Enda drove off the cross-worshipers, but that his son Crimthann gave them a church-plot, a 'see' as they term it, over in Aghade. As for our father, it's lip service he gave them, because it was politick. But . . . no, Cormac, we are none of us of the new faith."

"Good," Cormac nodded. "I'd hate to be throwing ye into the sea, dairlin girl, and after delivering ye of the Vikings and their sorcerous Druid."

She looked at him whimsically, eyebrows up. He read a challenge there, and thought again that this

85

woman he called girl was of stout stuff indeed. She'd issue challenge to the Dark Ones themselves — and there'd likely be wagers on both sides at that!

"Behlfires yet burn on all the hills of Eirrin," Ceann said. He plucked idly, but did not sing.

The ship scudded along with taut sail and silent crew. They were thinking of the new faith, and what it might bode for Eirrin in future. It was not a tolerant cult, and already there were stories of murder and awful death visited on non-adherents in lands where it was strong. Though the man Iosa was a Jew, Christians were now treating Jews as filth, supposedly for having brought about his death — when they knew he had been executed by some Roman governor for speaking sedition and rousing the people. Too, surely it was a spear from a Christian hand that had slain the Emperor Julian, he who tried to curb the growing power of the new faith and restore some of the old. A soldier, Julian had most likely been a devotee of Mithras. That old soldier's god had been born in a cave or stable under a bright star, attended only by animals and some wise men who came from afar to pay their respects.

As he had hurled down Crom Cruach's statue on Magh Slecht in a symbolic slaying of the old god of Eirrin, so had Patrick set in motion the forces to destroy Crom in truth, with the others of the old pantheon. As for mewling Brigit, who gave away all hers and her father's holdings so that none would accept her even as a servant in the household . . . surely quite mad was that follower of Padraigh and his Eastern god!

"Remember our need of fresh water," Wulfhere at last rumbled, "and turn those moping eyes seaward. Be those trees I'm seeing?"

They looked. Samaire smiled. It was indeed trees the Dane saw, and the sun was but a little past its zenith when they were easing into a lovely little

86

arbour. Trees rose above from the high stony banks, and birds sang their joy. Crystal water came tumbling down from steep rocks to add to the ocean's gallonage. Splashily, they made fast their long, long canoe.

Wulfhere groaned when good ale must be poured out to empty leathern bags for sweet water. Warning that such a lovely isle surely would not be unpeopled, Cormac kept a keen watch while the others cleansed themselves. It was much in love with cleanliness his people were. He took his turn in the water after, while Wulfhere scanned inland. No one else came.

Bathed and with water taken on, they put to sea again without incident.

The wind was good. The ship cut her way through the water with a long white trail of foam seething in her wake. For a long while on the nearly flat plain that was the sea they were as alone as travelers can be, surrounded on five sides by water and roofed over with a summery sky that was almost the same colour.

The sun was low when Wulfhere spoke Cormac's name quietly.

The Gael joined the giant at the prow. They were coming up on an island off to starboard, a small chunk of cone-shaped rock like a Pictish granary of stone. A wispy tendril of smoke curled up from it.

"See you that piece of rock?"

"Of course," Cormac said.

"Of course, the man says, as though speaking to a child. Cormac — I know these waters, I've been here before, and I know *not* that isle of stone!"

Cormac squinted, staring at the bristly cone that rose above the deep blue of the sea, and he said, "Ummm."

"A fine comment from a man who's spent a halfscore years asea!" Wulfhere snapped in exasperation. "Look here — I swear by all the gods of the Danes and aye, those of your people too: that overgrown chimney was not here when last I sailed

87

these precincts!"

Cormac blinked. "But — we must be off-course or you remember awrong. Islands don't just . . appear."

Wulfhere snorted. He was certain of himself, but not of the new land. For many minutes, as they drew abreast and then passed the rough-hewn and totally forbidding cone, they were sore confused. It defied them, brooding sullenly and trailing its sinister smoke. It was Ceann, then, who provided the beginning of the answer.

"The water . . . it's *hot*."

"Be that a storm ahead?" his sister asked nervously.

On their course well ahead was indeed a great darkness on the sea, with no cerulean sky visible. And when Cormac leaned out and down, he discovered that Ceann was right; the sea was unnaturally warm. He and Wulfhere exchanged frowning glances.

Ahead, there was the sound of thunder. The sea raised waves, which grew and billowed. The sail commenced to flap.

"The heat, Cormac — that land we just passed is new-risen, and so recently it is still earth-heart hot!"

The Gael was wrestling with cordage and the tiller. "The sea is angry about it — and glad I am we came not upon that pile of stone when it was a-rising from the keep of Mannanan macLir!"

Then the sun vanished.

There was darkness in the hours of day. The sea ahead erupted in fire and black clouds and great billows of hissing steam. Their slim, one-sailed craft was rocked as waves came rolling to meet them. Abruptly they were all down and groaning, for with a loud crack of sail, the ship lurched to port.

The sea rolled high. Waves rushed and spray was flung high aloft by an angry wind with no mind as to which way it would blow.

Cursing and ready to admit fear, Cormac mac Art struggled over their cargo — well lashed down, thank all the gods — to the sail.

"The sail! We've got to get it down!" he yelled. Whistling wind flung his words heedlessly aside — and sent him rolling as well. The small ship swung half about and raced a hundred yards eastward before starting to swing again.

Then there was the ear-splitting crack and roar of a thousand thunders. From the very sea ahead a blazing hell erupted. Orange flame shot skyward to singe the clouds themselves. A mighty torch lit the sky, greater than all the Behl-fires of Eirrin put together. In its glow danced thousands of black dots and spinning, whirling, sky-flying chunks of rock the colour of flame. Dust and black cinders blotted the sky. In an instant night was upon them — lit by that groaning, billowing column of flame ahead. There was a counterpoint sound: a deep-voiced hissing, as molten stone from the sea's floor and the earth's entrails struck the water. Steam boiled up in mile-high columns of boiling billowing grey-white.

A great lava missile, surely equaling Wulfhere's weight, came end-over-ending from the very sky to strike the water with a splash and a hiss not twenty feet off the starboard side — no, the port side, for that swiftly the ship heeled and spun almost completely about.

The ocean and the air round above it were confused, so that waves came rushing and visibly *swerved*, while the wind howled and changed its direction more swiftly than a bad king's whims.

The brightness of flame danced on four faces in which the eyes were huge and staring. Never had any of them known the lord of thunder to be so angry, or the god of the sea to be at once so berserk. Now coarse black ash rained into the water in thousands of tiny plops, and Ceann batted away a spinning ball of fire

89

the size of an eyeball.

The flame lowered, while beneath it rasping, grumbling rumbles and deep coughs arose. The wind lessened —

"CORMAC!" Wulfhere bawled.

But Cormac was doing what he knew he must, and that horrorstruck cry of his friend did not deter him or his slicing sword. It fell in a rush driven by iron muscle. Sharp steel edge bit through rope and into the wood of the ship itself.

The sail dropped, its mainline sheared through.

"We're HELPLESS now!" Wulfhere shouted.

Ahead, the world grumbled and coughed sullenly, and black smoke poured, wildly rolling, through where the gouts of flame had erupted from the sea.

"We were helpless afore," Cormac snapped back, roughly grasping Samaire's arm. "Hang on, dairlin girl." And more loudly: "This way we preserve the sail. An we survive this horror, we'll need it later! Now — it menaces us more than it aids, for — "

Another tremendous and sky-shattering explosion interrupted him and swallowed his words in its mighty sound. Almost immediately a wave of palpable force came rushing from the new pillar of flame that leaped up from the ocean. Still clinging to Samaire's arm, Cormac was hurled back against the bulwark — and had he not sought to help the woman and retained his grip on her, he'd have gone over.

The sail flapped, tried to billow this way and that. But now it was no more than an oversized pennon, fluttering loosely from its mast.

The northwest horizon was a curtain of flame and dancing ash and cinders and wheeling, spinning lava missiles that plunged back into the sea from many feet in the air. Ever higher rose the heat. The four seafarers showed sweat on flame-lit faces. Steam hissed and billowed up to join rolling black clouds that fell over on another on their upward climb. There was the odour of rotten eggs in every nostril.

Volcanic eject splashed into the waters. Something pinged sharply off Cormac's helmet. Seeing it drop into the ship, he moved automatically. Only at the last instant did he remember himself, and use his left hand. Nevertheless he grunted in pain in the second he held that cinder in his wet, hissing hand; he shoveled up the cinder and hurled it into the sea all in one swift motion. Ceann cried out, slapping at his tunic, which smoked.

Then a new shock wave struck, and the mad waves came again. An enormous wave caught them, bore them with it as it raced from the emerging volcano.

The unnamed Viking boat swung and was driven so swiftly southward that all became a blur to its four helpless passengers. Streaks of golden fire in the night that had seized the sky before sunset, glowing chunks of lava arced. They rained down into the sea—where the ship had wallowed, but seconds before. Black ash blotted the sky and sullied the waves. Cinders were a thick swarm that constantly pocked the waters as if by a heavy thunderstorm. Behind them the sky glowed like a bloody orange sunrise; all about them was darkness.

On raced the frail boat, borne on a wave sent forth by the cataclysmic vomiting from the deeps. Four people clung with white knuckles to whatever purchase they'd found with scrabbling fingers, and all knew their faces were no less white. All knew, too, that in this gale and rushing wave that bore them along as if they were above the water's surface, the sail would have been torn in strips like ragged ribbons.

Instead, the sheet Cormac had slashed free streamed out behind them from its mast, a brave striped banner that belied the horror of the fleeing ship's riders.

91

Thunder, both a constant rumbling roar and a series of *poom*-ing explosions, assaulted their ears. They rushed on in a direction opposite their goal, riding a great wave that carried them smoothly as the finest of gaited horses. About them, they felt the air current changing wildly. East- and southward they were hurled, while behind them raged that fiery monster from the floor of the sea.

As if it had not been enough, staring eyes and numbed brains now reported the new menace before them: all beheld the white water about the emergence of some menacing monster of the deeps. Up it came, with water rushing off its back in the four places where that grey and green hide split the sea — and they were swept directly toward it.

"Sea monster!" Ceann muttered, and knew he'd never see Leinster again.

Forty feet separated the first hump from the second, and twenty or thirty from the third. A longship's length stretched between third and fourth . . . and Cormac realized of a sudden that it was no living creature he saw.

With cataclysmic convulsions, the ocean's floor was flinging up more new land!

Up surged those humps of grey rock slimed with green and clumped and shot through with brown and black — and directly toward the emerging island raced the ship. Without sail or workable rudder, it seemed mindlessly bent on smashing splintering destruction.

Closer and closer rushed the first great ridge of new land, and still higher it rose. The distance between it and the second closed swiftly. Frozen with horror as they sped toward doom and sea-graves, not one of the four victims of the sea's wrath so much as cried out.

But their ship seemed to possess instincts of self-preservation. The vessel shot between the first and second humps, riding high so that there was no rending grate beneath. Four heads swiveled on their necks to see the long new isle, now behind them.

Cormac slouched, his heart surely beating more rapidly than it ever had in battle, and that with the red berserker rage on him. Covered with sweat, he felt weak as a kitten just whelped. His eyes showed him that the others were the same. Even Wulfhere looked like a great doll dropped by some giant's careless offspring.

The wave that bore them lessened in its power, cut off behind them as emerging land connected the ridges. Now new waves rushed after them. Displaced by the sudden appearance of rocky land, angry foaming water sought new space for itself.

Ahead, they saw the skyglow of sunset, and this time it was the real sunset.

Discovery that their ship was leaking was far from horror; all emotions of that ilk were spent. It was almost jubilantly that they commenced bailing with their helmets, for here was a menace that could be met and fended off. Behind them lay power that challenged the gods themselves and made all men less than insects in a hurricane. Sea and wind had threatened and attacked them, and fire and brimstone as well, and then rocky land, so that it was a combined attack by all the elements had been launched against them. And whimsically, by some shrugging natural force or yawning god, they had been spared.

Spared . . . in a leaking ship . . . and many many miles off their course.

Chapter Eight: Black Pool of Horror

Monstrum horrendum, informe, ingens...

—Virgil, *Aeneid*

Northwest they must go; southward and eastward they had been sent, even after Cormac had struck sail. Now the ship moved on, though not so swiftly, and they bailed the long night away. It was just after dawn that they espied the line of islands ahead, so similar to those they had watched rise up behind them. They were all in a line, and closely set, so that they resembled the seven ridges of a great serpent.

Yesterday they'd have had no thought but of putting into one link of that chain for rest and repairs. So shaken had been their world and their minds, though, that the four travelers stared long at that little island group. It was a strange feeling and it chafed Cormac, this business of staring at islands to be certain that they did not move.

They did not, and the quartet fixed their sail. Bailing, they made for the largest of the seven. They were rocky, like so many of the tiny isles in this sea south of Britain, and only the hardiest of vegetation lifted scraggly heads above igneous stone. The weary four furled sail, brought their ship in, and spent an agonizing hour wrestling it up a beach hardly worthy of the name.

There were no woods here, not so much as a single tree that could be seen, so that they were forced, nervously lest it splinter, to use the mast itself to careen the ship.

The hole in her keel was not much, but — how to repair it?

"We trouble our heads over it later," the prince of Leinster said, asserting himself now that he had a solid and motionless surface beneath his feet. "For now, let us sit on that which moves not, and eat — and it's some of the ale, not pallid water, that I'd be washing it down with."

Wulfhere beamed at him. Stripping off their armour, they sat or squatted in the shade of the side-turned ship. Sea-watered rations were a feast, and the good ale they quaffed had in it none of the salt of the ocean. Wulfhere did not drink that much, he was exhausted: he slept. Ceann regarded him, and yawned. With a small smile, the young Leinsterman also lay back.

Cormac and Samaire looked at each other. They too were weary. But . . . there was no opportunity for embraces asea, with the four of them clustered in the boat. Rising without a word, they left the two sleeping men and walked inland, over ground that was hard and pocked: solidified lava and magma. He left armour and helmet, but took his weapons.

When they topped a rise and found themselves staring with both incredulity and delight at a small pool of water that was surely not of the sea, the man and woman seemed renewed in energy. They hurried down to the pond, which was merely a shallow bowl formed naturally in the cooling rock. It contained a few feet of rain-water.

Samaire turned to look at the man beside her, and he drew her against him to surround and cherish her lips with his. She pressed close and her hand

95

moved up so that her fingers slipped into the hair at his nape.

"An we reach Eirrin after all," he said huskily, "all will be different between us."

She met his eyes directly with her green gaze. "And why?"

"It will. You are the widow of a prince of Osraige and daughter of and sister to kings of Leinster."

"Not," she told him, "until someone recognizes me, and it's not straight into Leinster we'll be going, my over-thoughtful love." His mouth opened to speak, and she pressed a finger to his lips. "The others will not sleep forever, and we'll be needing our rest, too. Must I force myself upon you?"

It was not necessary, and after a time Cormac and Samaire fell asleep there beside the tiny pool of saltless water.

Upon awakening, Wulfhere made two discoveries: the couple by the little pond, asleep and their clothes disarrayed — and a broad stretch of black, near the shore. The substance was not hard. Using the helmet of a Viking who had no further need of it and shouldn't mind its debasement in good cause, Dane and Gael dipped the pitch. Repairing the ship then was a simple matter, and the two smeared most of the craft's keel with the smelly tarry stuff.

"Ho," Wulfhere called when he saw Cormac and Samaire approaching, nor did he miss the hands they so quickly disengaged. "And where have you been, whilst the work was done?"

"Slaying twenty Picts, three monsters," Cormac replied equably, "and a huge Dane who had in him neither civil tongue nor the restraint to avoid stupid questions."

Wulfhere shook his head. Then he glanced skyward. "The sun has completed over half its day's journey, and the pitch not dry. It's here we'll rest this night."

Samaire chuckled. "Good! Suppose we take a bit of food and a sack of something to wet the throat, then, and explore our new harbour."

"Explore!" Wulfhere snorted. "This giant's dinner-trencher of solid rock?" He gazed about at the small island that boasted neither animals nor insects and here and there but the fewest tender shoots of new grass from wind-borne seeds. "Cormac — note you the makeup of this land?"

Cormac nodded. "Risen from the deeps. And that recently, judging from the tiny bit of greenery."

Wulfhere stamped his foot as if testing the crust. "I hope it does not decide to return whence it came, and us upon it!"

Ceann's frown demanded why the Dane had felt constrained to voice such a thought.

"And it's such words," Samaire said snippily as she knelt beside their stores, "you may keep to yourself, splitter of shields and skulls."

Cormac was astonished; Wulfhere looked apologetic. The giant developed an abiding interest in scratching under his beard and in gazing out to sea. Ceann watched Cormac lift a gurgling sack while Samaire appropriated a discreetly small amount of food; seawater little harmed salt meat.

"Wulfhere and I," he said, "will remain to this hand of the island's center." He waved his right arm and received a sunny smile of gratitude from his sister.

"You remain the best of men and brothers, Ceann," she told him, and looked at Cormac.

Together, they walked away, rounded the rearing and jagged teeth of stone upward of the beach, and were out of sight.

Like lovers on a picnic and without care, they wandered, stopping to look fondly on lonely little sprigs of green that struggled up from the hardened lava here and there. The couple shot each other constant looks and secret smiles.

Though narrow, the island was long, and they walked far. Samaire fell once, and twisted her wrist in catching herself against harsh pumice: The man who squatted swiftly to draw her up was more solicitous than she had thought him capable. She looked almost wonderingly upon his scarred face.

They remained just where they were for a long while, holding each other, thinking their separate thoughts in silence. The land around them became less ugly.

A tall column of rough-hewn stone towered over their heads, like a stony sentinel watching over the island and brooding on its ugly barrenness. They walked past it, and found the strangeness of the skeletons of fish. Since they lay atop the stone and were not scorched or a part of it, Samaire pointed out, this island must have been formed first beneath the sea, and then risen already cool.

"It is pleasant to keep company with a brilliant person, and her a woman besides," Cormac said.

The statement was so formal and serious that she laughed aloud in delight. They walked on, laughing together.

The wide hole they came to was like a well, nigh filled with dark and brackish water that had the smell of the sea about it. There was no way of knowing the depth of the natural cistern, whose diameter was twice Cormac's height. On a whim Samaire suggested, then urged, that they sit and pass the ale-sack.

They sat at the edge of the pool. When Cormac bent and pushed his sword into the water, the blade palled almost to invisibility a few inches down.

"A pool of black water," Samaire said. "I cannot

think of anything less appetizing or romantic — but everything is pretty today, Cormac, and romantic as well."

He looked at her. Their arms moved as of one accord; they united their lips again. His heartbeat had quickened when she drew back and suggested a taste of ale.

"I like better what I was just drinking," he said, and slid a tugging hand onto her waist.

"And is it honeymooners ye think we are, or an iron man yourself? It's been but a little while — " She broke off, and her face clouded at his look. "No no, my dairlin boy, we've time, there's all the night. Nor will I ever be able to say no to you."

He smiled, raking her eyes with his gaze, and nodded abruptly: there, then. He opened the sack of leather. Starting to drink, he remembered, and passed it to her. It was long and long he had been out of the company of woman, and of gentlewomen even longer.

She drank, jerked the sack down, spluttering a little.

"Oh Cormac! Wulfhere would hurl you into the Black Pit here, and I'm a mind to, myself!"

Frowning, he took the sloshing sack from her. It was one of those they had filled with water. Cormac fell back, laughing. After a moment she was up on her knees and bending over him, her hands on his throat and pretending to squeeze, while he rolled his eyes and made the proper gagging noises.

It was thus he saw the waving eyeless serpent rise from out of the pit behind her, and swing blindly about until it found her.

Samaire screamed. At its first touch, the eyeless, mouthless snake, a cable the thickness of her wrist and with no end in sight, seemed to lengthen as if by magic. It whipped around her upper body, sliding naturally up toward her throat.

On his back, Cormac sent his two hands leaping

99

up to grasp and pull at the boneless arm that threatened both to strangle her and drag her into it wet black lair. He could not break its hold, and he saw her eyes start to widen as the fleshy cable tightened — and pulled. With one hand Samaire tugged desperately at the thing threatening her life; with the other she flailed until her fingers hooked blindly in Cormac's belt. With no thought of what she was doing, she clung.

Cormac grasped her wrist, pulled her fingers loose. Holding her wrist tightly, he rolled onto his side and dragged out his sword. He looked up, seeking the place to strike — without striking her.

Her green eyes were huge and her face had gone scarlet. "C-o-r-mmm . . . " But Samaire could not even get out the rest of his name.

She went over backward. Cormac, clinging almost in panic to her wrist, was pulled up to his knees. He saw what he must do, and that swiftly. Up swept the sword, to rush down in a flash of silver. In one chop Cormac cut all the way through the eyeless serpent, so that his blade struck sparks from the rock edge of that pool of horror. The severed portion whipped back into the pool as blood gouted up his arm. Released, Samaire fell forward. Cormac, still holding her arm, was pulled down with her.

Now he could force the coil from her neck. She gasped, sobbing and sucking air desperately. Cormac, meanwhile, stared in horror at the puckered red marks all about the loveliness of her throat. He looked at the rubbery thing in his hand. Its underside was equipped with *suckers!* What sort of impossible, eyeless and sucker-equipped snake had they come upon, that it could —

Three more of the fleshy, cold cables came whipping, raking the air, up over the edge of the pool. One found him, and he battered at it, but had to pull his blow lest he shear into his own leg. Another touched Samaire's leg, and she shrieked in horror when it whipped about it.

Samaire was once again in the cold clutch of a blindly seeking horror — that immediately slapped down with another serpent-like length, and began to pull and tug at her.

Fighting with the muscles of his leg against the powerful rope of muscle enwrapping it, Cormac struck and had to swerve his blade, desperately, as the woman was drawn a foot backward and he came near to swording her. He and the monster pulling at his leg were of a mind, and his movement to pit's edge was simple. There he aimed another chop. Pulled off-balance, he saw his sword slide harmlessly along the ropy, writhing *thing*. The blade pushed a little rumple of scaly skin along it as though he were carefully cleaning a fish.

Then, with a shriek of terror, Samaire was tugged over the lip of that natural well. A splash, and she vanished from sight beneath dark waters that Cormac was sure had gone even darker since the attack.

"SAMAIRE!"

His rushing sword cleared his leg and left another writhing piece of serpentine horror flopping. It wriggled, as if alive even while cleft in twain. Dropping his sword and drawing his dagger, Cormac took a great breath and dropped feet first into the pit. If there was anything at all for him to be glad of, it was that he wore no armour.

He sank like a stone, nevertheless.

Dark streamers swirled about him, and surely it was not water but some black ichor from the monsters that made their home in this hell-pit. The water—or that strange inky stuff—stung his eyes. He forced them to remain open. A serpentine length brushed him; he ran his dagger into it and jerked it out in the strange water-slowed motion he had experienced before. The stabbed serpent leaked its juices and

101

writhed in pain. The man's feet kicked desperately. He twisted about in the liquid murk. His flailing hand slipped through water, touched something cold and slippery—and came into contact with cloth.

Reflexively Cormac caught at it, felt the trembling warmth of Samaire's flesh beneath. His moving fingers touched the cold-blooded cable of living flesh that enwrapped the leg he gripped, and he set the edge of his dagger to it. As if slicing overdone bread, he sawed.

The woman was madly jerking as her captor sought to escape its torment. Blood darkened the water all around Cormac's wrist. Then the dagger had sawed through, and a flopping dead thing that refused to die jerked and twitched over his arm. Kicking water, he jerked back his blade. His eyes were huge; his hair streamed upward as he began to feel the pressure within his chest. He knew that Samaire's lungs were in even worse straits, and that she was brief seconds from the awful death of filling her lungs with salt water.

He could see only for a few inches in the horrid murk, deepened by the swirling ink and the blood of the monster. There could be no hacking and slicing, then; the danger was too great of daggering the woman. No, he had to find another of those serpentine ropes with his hand, then set the dagger to it . . .

Samaire's body brushed his, moving upward, and Cormac gave her a mighty shove. Up went the woman to the sweet air, and the man hoped it was not too late. The creatures of the dark pool had realized she was not the source of the sharp-edge attack, Cormac knew, and had released her.

Now they would concentrate on him, not a helpless piece of prey but a dangerous enemy.

Cormac slashed at a grasping cable of muscle. It snapped away, and he kicked hard. Straight up he shot, and he emptied his lungs even before his head

102

broke water. He gulped in another breath and expelled it, seeing that Samaire was alive, coughing and spluttering, her hair straggling and stained. But she was alive. He drew breath again—and was grasped and yanked violently beneath the surface.

Flailing now, for there was none in the dark waters of this monster-haunted pit but himself and the serpents, Cormac mac Art shot downward.

It was then he saw that it was not suction-bellied serpents he fought, but a creature with serpents for arms. Dark it was, and its body was a truncated oval, sprouting those waving arms—and the stubs of those he had slashed away. Through the inky swirls he saw its eyes like huge plates, fixed maliciously on him, and its mouth. More strangeness, for it was the beak of a bird of prey, and like no water creature he had ever seen!

Eight-arm, he thought as he stabbed and kicked and struck, for he had heard tales of those monsters of the deepest waters, though never had he seen one. Until now, and his dagger raked across one bright malignant eye.

The creature went wild in agony and fear. Stumps and tentacles waved and jerked like hawsers in a hurricane. Cormac was struck, dashed back against the rocky side of the cylindrical pool. He struck back. Again blood spurted from a sliced tentacle. Suddenly, from less than a foot's distance, he was staring straight into the horrible eye of the monster from a god's nightmare. He saw the dreadful beak open, as cold, sucker-equipped arms slithered over him.

The desperate Gael drove his dagger straight into the hideous eye until the hilt brought up against cold flesh. Then, grasping a tentacle near its root, he twisted his dagger.

The pool erupted into a maelstrom of convulsive movements. Again Cormac was slammed away. A cable-like arm snapped around his arm, gripped it, whipped away. Another lashed his belly like a thick whip. A third grasped his leg, and held. He was dragged down by the desperately writhing, flailing creature that was surely in the throes of death.

His chest ached and his eyes stung. But the desperate man doubled himself in the water, and seized on the tentacle that held him, and set the Saxon dagger to it. It whipped away before it was severed. Cormac lashed at the water with both arms and both powerfully muscled legs, and shot straight up like a bow-launched arrow.

Again his head splashed free of the water of death, and this time he remained unthreatened. Treading water, he tried to spring upward the few feet necessary to grasp the edge of the well-like hole, for there was no handhold on its smooth walls.

"Cormac! Oh *Cormac!*"

Good, he thought; *an she can cry out like that, it's all right the darling girl is!*

His hand encountered something cold and slippery, and with a curse he grasped that severed chunk of tentacle and hurled it up over the lip of the pool.

"Ho! What's this, greeting us first with a scream and now missiles, is it?"

That was Wulfhere's voice; he knew when to joke, when a man was alive and valorously fighting to remain so. Hardly so accustomed to horror and battle as to make such instant judgments, Ceann shouted his sister's name in a voice that was more than alarmed.

Then their two heads were between Cormac and the sky. Ceann and Wulfhere gazed down at him and Samaire.

"I fare well," Samaire said, before her brother could ask.

Obviously Cormac was too, and Wulfhere shook his head lugubriously. "When ye've a mind for a swim, old friend, why not make certain ye can come ashore again before you go plunging in?"

104

"Wulfhere, I am going to add your severed tongue to that monster's arm I threw forth—but it's slowly I'll be slicing it off ye!"

Wulfhere affected to look extremely shocked. "In that event I'd be a fool to aid ye!" he said, and pushed a huge hand down to Samaire.

She put up her own, which was swallowed in a paw with fingers like ropes of steel. With one hand, and that not with a jerk, the Dane drew her up and out of the pool.

"Why, it's an octopus ye've found," Wulfhere called down. "Oh Cormac—have ye any idea what marvelous eating they are, man? Here, if you be unharmed and unattacked, then ye've killed him—do you dive down and bring him up to us, there's a good Cormac!"

"Ceann—it's your hand I'd appreciate the loan of," Cormac said.

A minute later he was out of the monster's lair and on rocky land that felt very warm, and more than passing good to the soaked mac Art.

"It's possible we could make a meal off these," Wulfhere said conversationally, as though his friend was not spattered with gore and the creature's black ink of defense, and gasping as well. "But methinks they might be a bit muscular and stringy—"

"Wouldn't ye consent to go back for it, Cormac? How deep is this black pool of brack, anyhow?"

"Tell me," Cormac said, swinging both feet against Wulfhere's legs, "when you come up with our supper."

With a great splash, the Skull-splitter went flailing into the pool.

Ceann looked horrified, as indeed he had all along, despite the obvious safety of his sister and friend. It was Wulfhere's attitude had so dismayed this young king's son; he had participated in little violence and never known the jocular camaraderie of

105

those who've faced death together many times.

But Samaire laughed, and once Wulfhere came up spluttering and began launching a volley of highly imaginative curses at them, Ceann Ruadh, too, smiled.

Then Wulfhere dived. Nor did he emerge without the dead beast with its dragging tentacles and stubs. They soon discovered its great weight, once they tried to pull and push it out of buoyant water. With much grumbling, Cormac at last returned to the pool, wherein he and Wulfhere carved up the slain monster and passed up to the others what the Dane insisted on calling *steaks*.

The creature had been in its deep rocky lair, they decided, when this island had broken loose and been pushed to the surface. As they had surmised, the land on which they stood had not been long above the water. But how had it survived?

"Mayhap there were fish and the like in the, uh, well with it," Ceann offered, "and they came up along with the beast."

"Possibly a few," Wulfhere said, shaking his head. "But we all noted that while Cormac could remember having severed three of its tentacles, the creature had three remaining; two others were missing, and the wounds hardly fresh. My mother's cousin once had one of these many-arms, which her husband Ivarr brought her. Even though she fed it well—on shellfish, in the main—it ate off three of its own tentacles in less than a year."

"Poor beast," Samaire murmured, looking down at the hacked-off pieces of the monster that had sought to make a meal of her. "To exist, it ate of itself—and now we've blundered upon it and here it lies, all its efforts for nought."

"And that's your feeling, daughter of an addle-pated chicken, it's leaving ye I'll be doing next time, and not wetting myself in your rescue."

106

She looked at Cormac with a stricken expression, but he was smiling.

It was then that Ceann Ruadh remembered, and pointed out that they had no wood with which to make a fire for the creature's cooking.

And it was then that Cormac mac Art shoved Wulfhere Skullsplitter back into the pool.

Chapter Nine: The Emerald Isle

> *O land of my birth, what a pride, what a*
> *pleasure*
> *To plow the blue sea!*
> *The waves of the fountain of deluge to*
> *measure,*
> *Dear Eirrin, to thee.*
>
> —Ceann Ruadh, the "Minstrel-king"
> (from *Voyage of the Exiles*)

It had been many days since Samaire of Leinster
had been kidnapped off her own coast, and that in
riding togs. A strip of green ribbon from the Vikings'
spoils held her hair back and was laced among the
red-orange tresses. There had been no other makeup
available.

Both the men and the women of Eirrin wore their
hair long, and both wore jewelry. Brooches held the
clothing together; torcs of gold or silver decorated the
neck, seeming to writhe about it. Both sexes spent
much time on their hair, braiding, creating spiral
curls, in the case of the women, that dangled
profusely—or binding up the hair, to be held in place
and decorated by gold rings and pins. Women of more
leisure buffed their nails and frequently dyed them
crimson, while occasionally using dyes of this and that

vegetable base to tint their faces. Eyebrows were nearly always dyed black with berry juices, whether the woman was blond or redhead or brunette.

Though they had no octopus "steaks," Samaire did make use of the inky stuff the creature exuded in its alarm: she darkened her brows. And was advised by two of her companions that she gave off the odour of fish. (Wulfhere's unexpected and heretofore unknown galantry forbade him to make mention of the fact.)

With sea water, Samaire washed away the sea-creature's ink—and then scratched, again and again, at salt-encrusted brows . . .

With good winds their longboat skudded over the dark blue waters, ever north and westward. And Ceann played and muttered, and sang.

Days straggled past, and islands.

"That," Wulfhere said, "is the Sea of Eirrin—and that Britain." He pointed to a misty coastland to northward.

Ceann and Samaire looked that way with enthusiasm, and then strained their eyes to the left of that dim-seen land, in search of their own. But Devon and Cornwall hung well below Eirrin's southernmost coast, and their straining scan of the horizon was unrewarded.

Nor did Wulfhere bring the ship half about, to glide up the waterway that separated the islands of what the Romans called Brittania and Hibernia or Ivernia. Ceann asked, and they conferred.

"We are no force to be inviting a fight," Wulfhere said. "The Sea of Eirrin is seldom empty of renegades from both lands, as well as my own countrymen, and Norsemen on the Viking path . . . and Picts, and occasional Jutes and Saxons as well."

Gazing green-eyed at him, Samaire heard and felt that half the world must be conspiring to prevent their return to their own land.

"An we did sail on up, in hopes of avoiding all those and finding safe landing on the Coast of Meath," Cormac said, "It's your own dairlin' Leinster ye'd be passing, and her great port of Atha Cliath, which some call *Dubh-linn:* Dark Pool, Wulfhere. For us, it might as well prove to be the latter!"

Ceann sighed, glancing wistfully over his shoulder at the way they would not take. "Aye . . . and it's no friendly reception we'd be getting in our own land, now! But . . . where, then?"

"The coast of Munster, I'm thinking, near Cobh. Well above your Cat Island, but . . . a safe ninety or so miles below Carman of Leinster. Thence to Cashel, I'm thinking, and up into Meath between Leinster and Connacht—where I might well be welcome . . . and might not."

"Up the Shannon," Cormac told her, "but inland from its east bank, aye."

The woman heaved a great sigh. "All this time and now this terror-fraught long voyage . . . and then it's days and days overland we must make our way. I despair of seeing Tara . . ." Up came her sun-glinting hair and dimpled chin. "Amend that! I'll never despair, until the black of death closes over these eyes!" these eyes!"

"That's a dairlin girl," Ceann said, appropriating the words he'd heard Cormac apply to his sister so frequently these past few days.

"That's a woman of Eirrin!" Cormac amended. "And . . . Samaire . . . it's after these many years of exile I return, and another seven-day or so in overland travel seems but little."

She smiled. "Aye, and it's pointing out the beauty of Eirrin to ye I'll be, Cormac mac Art!"

Wulfhere said absolutely nothing, but gazed stonily ahead along their course. Several of those years Cormac had mentioned had been spent in the Dane's

110

company. Their relationship had been ever good, with many adventures of the sword and good times withal.

The ship slipped across the water. Toward sunset they saw the sight that actually brought tears to one pair of eyes: the far coast of Eirrin. Rather than begin the business of working against the wind at this hour, Wulfhere suggested they furl sail and remain asea until after dark.

"Unnecessary hours with nothing under these feet but the planks of Norse trees and all the water in the world?" Ceann groaned. "Methinks I might not be able to bear that, Wulfhere!"

"We'll not be long in fetching the coast after sunset," the Danish giant told him. "Consider how much better all three of ye'll be with a bit of rest and sleep."

"Sensible," Cormac said, nodding.

Both Ceann and his sister glanced at their fellow Gael, but neither said aught to the contrary. Despite their being royalty, and of Leinster, it was the son of Art of Connacht they considered leader and best head among them.

Rocking asea, they made their meal, with Ceann plucking tender, lingering notes and singing very quietly:

> "The warbling of the blackbird of Litir Lee,
>> The wave of Rughraidhe lashing the shore;
>> The bellowing of the ox of Magh-maoin,
>> And the lowing of the calf of Glenn-da-maoil.
>
> The tossing of the hulls of barks by the waves,
>> The yell of the hounds of fair Laighin,
>> The cry of Bran at Cnoc-an-air,

Or the cry of eagles about Mount
Leinster."

"Was there ever a place, above or below,"
Samaire murmured,
"Better than Eirrin,
'Tis there Samaire would go,
At the side of Art's son."

She did not notice that all three men gazed at her,
and that two of them looked at Cormac son of Art,
and back at her, and then hastily away.

They rested, but little sleep was got by any of the
four that afternoon.

"But—we have *assumed* . . . why Wulfhere, you
must join us!"

Twitching the rudder to angle the ship toward the
shore, Wulfhere shook his head. "I will miss your
minstreling, Prince of Minstrels," he said. "But no,
Eirrin and its business are none of mine. It's enough
danger there is for you three, fugitives all, without
your bringing ashore a son of Odin from the land you
call *Lochlinn* . . . my Dane-mark."

"But Wulfhere—" Samaire began, frowning
deep.

"I can handle this craft, and ye have no use for it.
Soon I'll find a crew, and return to . . . what I know
and do best."

"And love best," Cormac said, and Samaire
noted well the wistfulness in his voice.

"And love best!" Wulfhere agreed, with his back
to Cormac.

The little ship slipped shoreward beneath the
stars. A division of their spoils was no easy matter,
with them wanting to leave Wulfhere more and him
refusing, saying they'd need all to make their way
through "civilized" countryside—meaning among
people where goods or their equivalent, money, spoke
loudly.

112

They contrived to leave him more than he knew, nevertheless, with him busy at the rudder. Ceann and Samaire took little note of Cormac's staring ahead; they had not the experience to know that any shore was a hostile one, and particularly to those who came quietly by night.

The Dane took their battle-won ship in to a spit of sandy land that came right down to the water and ran up immediately into loamy soil sprouting a wealth of greenery. In the moonlight they looked at each other, and tears sparkled on more than one Gaelic cheek.

"Be there objection to this ship's being called *Minstrel Prince?*" Wulfhere asked, thickly as though he had swallowed something to lodge in his throat.

Ceann shook his head, tried three times, and at last got out his quiet, "None." After a moment he added, "And it's honour I'm done, at that."

Wulfhere's teeth flashed in a smile. Then he looked at Cormac.

"We two be veterans of many adventures and strong sword-reddening combats," he said. "Blood-brothers?"

Cormac nodded. "It's enough we've shed together! Blood-brothers, you ugly great bush-face."

"Mayhap we'll meet again, if I were of a mind to have do with a battle-hogging son of a Gaelic pig-farmer."

"I regret ever the day I told you my father had pigs on our land!"

"Get thee off my ship, ere one of us says the ridiculous!"

"Or weeps," Samaire murmured, watching the two men. The ship rocked, lapped by gentle tide-waves, bumping the sandy shore.

"All the gods be with you, Wulfhere Skull-splitter, and fair weather!"

"And you, Cormac an Cliuin, and may ye ever avoid Loki and the plots of men and gods." A moment

113

he stood there, back to the moon, a huge dark figure with a bristling beard. Then he said it again: "Get thee off my ship! I've places to sail to, and work to do!"

Without another word, Cormac turned and slipped over the side. Samaire was looking back at the Dane, about to say something; Cormac hissed her to silence and Ceann made as if to hand her down. Instead, she swung over the side as Cormac had done, with the splash of one foot. Ceann followed.

They stood there long, watching the moonlit retreat of the Viking craft from the shore, marveling that the one man handled her at all, much less as he did: well and competently. Cord and wood creaked; up went the striped sail. It puffed out in the breeze. The ship scudded northward, to ride as swiftly between Eirrin and Britain as her lone crew could push her.

Ceann sniffed a second before Samaire.

Then the three of them, Eirrin-born, slipped stealthily onto the soil of Eirrin . . . creeping like thieves in the night onto the sod of their own homeland.

Chapter Ten: Picts!

> *The ocean's caverns, where armies daren't go;*
> *The mighty cataract of the great Eas Ruadh;*
> *The rolling wave of a spring-tide's flow:*
> *Were the meet images of CORMAC's wrath.*

> —Ceann Ruadh

It was natural enough that the fisherman and his family were suspicious of a trio that appeared as if from nowhere, and that after dark, and not looking like the fisherfolk that abode along this coast. But Samaire talked persuasively, and Ceann rhymed and played for them. Soon Dond and his family — up late because the day's catch had been so good — put aside their suspicions. They extended hospitality to the trio; it was the Irish way.

Nevertheless Dond retained some nervousness. Samaire was offered the little shaggy-roofed house for the night. That was all the room there was within, the fisherman said as if reluctantly. The two men were welcome to spend the night in the shed . . . .

Cormac and Ceann accepted with alacrity, understanding Dond's reluctance to admit them into his home, and it night and them armed.

They watched Samaire enter with Lendabaer, Dond mac Forgall, and his very young but powerfully

115

built son Dondal, and their younger son and daughter, Laeg and Devorgill. The contrast was fantastic, and not just in their colour; Dond and family were of the old dark, black-haired race as was Cormac, while Samaire was red of hair and dusted with freckles. It was not just in her slenderness, either, while Lendabaer had swelled with her birthing five children — two they had lost — and had remained swelled, on a diet of much plentiful seafood and barley-bread and oatmeal and leeks and sallit.

There was the clothing as well, and the bearing Samaire could not disguise. Dond and his son wore the lightest of tunics, the boy's without sleeves, and lightweight flax-knit leggings or trews that were a thousand wrinkles. Bustling Lendabaer with her rich mass of black hair (bound back with no less than three ribbons, of three several colours) wore a long skirt of dull blue. It flowed from beneath a tunic of unbleached white, with a voluminous apron over that.

Though Samaire was not so tall as five and a half feet, she stood several inches above Lendabaer and was nearly the height of Dond — but hardly that of the early-developing boy of sixteen. Plaited into Samaire's flaming hair was the ribbon, and a leathern jerkin covered her white tunic. It was belted to drape over the leather leggings she'd worn at the time of her kidnap — and they vanished into the soft, striking boots that rose above her knees and that she had contrived to fasten to her belt with hide thongs.

"She has the look of a warrior about her," Cormac muttered.

"Every inch," Ceann said, nodding.

Then the two men saw the family and Samaire disappear into the little house, and they heard the lowering and bracing of the heavy bar across the door. Exchanging a small smile, Cormac and Ceann entered the shed and found places to stretch out.

"Whew," Ceann commented, and Cormac

116

chuckled.

"Aye, and now ye know, Ceann, why they noted no smell of the sea on us. I'd lay wager that the interior of the house smells no less fishy than this shed!"

Ceann stirred in the darkness. On Irish soil, the two men drifted easily into sleep, despite the hardness of their pallets and the stench of fish and the salt sea.

Cormac awoke. It was still dark. His had not been a life that allowed a man to sleep deeply, and he awoke both easily and swiftly. He sat up. And heard the sound again; a twitching thrashing, accompanied by the faintest of whimpers.

Frowning, he slipped sword noiselessly from sheath and stepped as quietly to the door of the shed. Just outside, he saw the source of the sounds that had roused him.

It was the dog Flaith, and he twitched and whimpered no longer. From his throat stood a slender wand of wood that had ceased to shudder with his movements. Staring at the arrow, Cormac mac Art needed not step forth to examine it; he knew it was a flint tip that had stolen the dog's life, and that in moonlit silence.

With the blackness of the shed's interior behind him, he looked out onto Dond's moon-splashed land. He saw squat burly figures ghosting silently. They were ringing the silent little house. With an equal lack of sound, Cormac returned into the fisherman's shed. He crouched beside the sleeping Ceann. He knew not yet what sort of man Ceann was, save that his life had not paralleled his own. Wulfhere said the redhaired prince fought like a warrior born, but — how did he waken?

He was woken this time by two iron hands: one

closed on his arm to shake him, the other pressed over his mouth.

The moment he moved, Cormac, bending close, whispered, "It's Cormac. Be silent. Wake and take up weapons — the house is about to be attacked."

Ceann tensed, then Cormac felt him nod. He withdrew both hands. Ceann rose quietly. He asked no questions, but bustled. The prince had permanently borrowed a scalemail corselet from one of the Vikings on Samaire-heim, as well as a good sword and two daggers, with belt sheaths. The round shield he had worn on his back, like Cormac. Both men, in order to seem less warlike and fearsome, had arrived here wearing tunics and cloaks over their body armour. Nor had they removed aught for sleeping but shields and weapon-belts, and Cormac his helm.

They had just buckled on the broad, sheath-pendent belts and taken up their bucklers when the night air was rent wide by a hellish wolf-yelling that rose from many throats.

"God of my ancestors! What — "

"Picts," Cormac snapped, brushing past him on his way doorward. "They shriek when they attack. It's supposed to strike terror to the hearts of their prey, and render them stone-still with fear."

Ceann saw the other man's broad shoulders and helmeted head, filling the doorway where it was lined in the moonlight. And amid the din of the banshee-howling Picts arose another battle-yell, a ferocious bellow. The charging Cormac vanished. With a swift jerk of his head to clear it of the awful sounds, Ceann charged after him.

These Picts of the far coast were short and squatty men, powerfully built, with shocks of black hair they often bound with silver fillets. Few wore armour and indeed most had little clothing besides. They were normally armed with flint or bronze; when they bore steel, it had been stolen. They attacked in wild-beast frenzy, savages that struck and hewed without interest in prisoners or heed for cries for quarter.

Ceann reached the shed door to see them in a dark ring they'd made about the fisherman's hut, their number surely a dozen. They whirled from their encirclement to meet the man who ran upon them like a flying shadow. His Viking-won shield was up and ready to tip this way or that, and his sword was carried well out to his right side, streaking through the night like a flying ribbon of cloth-of-silver.

The next Pictish cry Ceann Ruadh heard, as he went running after the other man, was not one of those challenges; a shriek of bloody death rose as Cormac's sword ripped the warrior open. An arrow rang off his helmet and another thudded against his chest just inward from his sword arm. Turned by his good chaincoat, it dropped away — and the nearest of the yelling charging savages fell silently with a death wound under his heart.

Ceann hadn't time for niceties. The man starting to lunge at Cormac's back happened to have his own back turned to the prince of Leinster — but that was his fault. Ceann did not slow down. He slammed his shield into the man's back and arm and flailed over it to cut the Pict's other shoulder nearly off his torso. The short dark man went falling in a spray of blood from a wound that would empty him in minutes; it was too huge for coagulation.

The terrible cries continued to rend the air. There was added now the grunt and gurgle and gasp and cry of fighting men, accompanied by the ring and skirl of steel on steel — and its chunking sound as it found flesh, or brittle cracks when it bit to bone-depth. Cormac had gained the door of the house, and in his wake lay three bloody Picts.

With a bloodcurdling shriek a short, ape-built man sprang high into the air, having run in from the side. He landed directly in Ceann's path. Up went the

119

barbed Pictish blade for a death-stroke — and Ceann lengthened the man's navel, splitting him with the full force of his own charge after Cormac.

The Pict was carried back several feet, and his slayer had to pause and back a step himself, to free his blade. An Eirrin-made sword struck hard on his shield with a frightful clang and a force that staggered him. Narrowly avoiding a thigh-full dagger, Ceann kicked with all his might straight into the dark warrior's crotch. Only a loincloth of well-tanned hide protected the Pict, who was hurt so sorely that he could not even make an outcry. He dropped puking to his knees and soon was curled up there, twitching, holding himself.

Ceann had no time to end that foeman's life; two Picts came at him at once. He took a hardswung blow on his shield and another far down his sword, close to the guard so that the weapon was nearly carried from his hand. Blindly, he swung both buckler and sword inward toward each other, arms extended before his body. The shield sent one man staggering back with a grunt of pain, while the sword cut the empty air. That Pict had crouched under it. Despite his desperate swiftness in hurling himself aside, Ceann felt the cold kiss of steel on the skin of his leg and knew his leathern trews had been opened like linen.

His whistling blade came back around even as the Pict yanked his own sword back. For a moment the dark, burly man stood there holding it as if unhurt, though a great crimson stripe crossed his belly from flank to flank. Then, staring down at the eruption of his own entrails, he dropped to his knees. Ceann saw no more of him — he was rushing past toward Cormac.

Cormac stood with his back to the door of the hut, while his sword flashed and whirred in the air, round and round, keeping at bay the five squat dark men who strove to get at him like yapping dogs with a cornered wolf.

120

A Pict sprang at Ceann with high-lifted dagger, and lost teeth to the violently-driven edge of the Gael's shield. Then a sword struck Ceann's left shin with such force that he toppled, though no blood spurted.

Flat on his back he looked up to see his death coming, from a high-raised sword that would chop through two such corselets as he wore.

"HE-E-EEEEEEEYYAAA-A-A-AAAAAAAA!"

It was a ghastly, inhuman shriek, and a new one that shivered on the air from behind the Pict standing over Ceann. The fallen Leinsterman saw the squat body jerk, bowing — and then the point of a fish-spear appeared in a bloody spray from the man's muscular belly. He fell.

Ceann rolled away from the dying Pict, and gained his feet to find that he had been saved by Dondal, son of Dond the fisherman.

Having launched himself from one of the house's two shuttered windows, the strapping boy of sixteen had seemingly gone berserker on the instant. Now he had to use his foot against his victim's back to free the spear's barbed tip.

"Leave it, and with thanks," Ceann called. "Can ye use this?" He extended the Pict's sword — which was of good Irish steel stolen from some fresh corpse. It seemed more than fitting that it return into Gaelic hands the same way.

"Aye!" Dondal said — or rather shouted. He snatched the sword. With a blood-rage dancing in his eyes, the boy swung about.

He was just in time to find himself staring at a charging Pict who held his sword before him like a foreshortened lance. A heavy swing of Dondal's arm lashed the sword away with a heavy clang, and on the backswing he took the Pict's arm off.

"Dondal!" Ceann called, heading again for the house and Cormac, for though the Pict was down and down to stay, Dondal stood over him and hacked and hacked as if he were at the business of making kindling.

Dondal looked up, and Ceann had never seen such eyes. "Araughhh!" Dondal the fisherman's son snarled, and pounced forward, unarmoured and without shield, ready to face a world of steel.

Bodies strewed the ground before the cottage, and still Cormac was against the door, with four men lunging and feinting and hacking at him. The din was loud, chaotic; awful. There was the smell of gore on the air.

Abruptly the door jerked open behind him and an astonished Pict died two seconds later with a fishing spear in the throat.

"Nicely done," Cormac grunted. "Stay back now, Dond — it's no armour ye have!"

"The family stays back," Dond mac Forgall answered as he jerked back his blooded spear. "Step aside, that we may face them together!"

The man emerged, naked but for a breechclout like the Picts. Behind him his woman slammed and barred the door. Cormac hewed away the arm of the Pict that sought to take off Dond's leg at the knee; Dond sent another skipping back with a lunge of his spear.

Dondal had found himself an armoured man who knew somewhat of the play of sword and buckler. Though he defended himself from the boy's lunges and swings, both backhand and fore, so vicious and swift were they that the steadily backing Pict had no opportunity to leave the defensive. A similarly seasoned warrior Ceann had found, and they were trying each for the other, blow for blow.

Sword rang off shield and sparks flew, and then the launcher of that foiled stroke had to interpose his own shield to stave off a return hack. Around and around the two circled, Ceann with his red hair loose and swirling in the moonlight and his foe a man

122

wearing a necklace of bear-teeth and a ridiculous loincloth of bright yellow.

Lendabaer and her younger son and daughter remained within and were safe — but another was with them, and she was not content to remain sheltered inside. Amid the high-voiced sounds of Lendabaer's expostulations, the door was again yanked open.

"HA-A-A-A-A-A-AAHHHHHH!"

With that Samaire lunged through the doorway, right knee and hand extended. In that fisted hand was the great old sword of Dond's grandfather. Sliced but not killed, the Pict who had been attacking a man, and who had now been blooded by a woman, went reeling back. His eyes were huge as he stared at her.

She boiled forth like a fury, between Cormac and Dond, the big bronze sword in one hand and a kitchen-knife in the other.

"Heee-yahhhhh!" Samaire screamed again. She made a vicious swipe with the sword, and allowed that ducked attack to swing her completely about — whereupon she kicked the astounded Pict in the shin so hard that he fell.

"Ooohh!" she said, with impressed enthusiasm, for she saw how Cormac, without interrupting his parry of sword with sword, went to one knee and slammed his shield-edge down. So great was the force of that blow that it smashed the chest of the man she had downed. The stab she made into his hard flat belly with her ancient weapon of dull-gleaming bronze was unnecessary; already dark blood was bubbling from the man's mouth like a horrid spring.

Beside her, Don's sideswung spear sent a squat dark man a-rolling, and the fellow regained his feet on the run. He vanished around the house, racing toward the shore.

"No! Dond, NO!" Cormac bawled, but the fisherman paid him no mind; he charged after the

123

fleeing foe.

"Damn! You vicious son of a she-wolf—you've bloodied me!" Ceann cried, with a note of incredulity in his voice.

The prince had fought like a man, but now the berserker rage came upon him. It was a vicious animal launched a whistling tree-cutting stroke of his sword that clove his attacker half in two at the waist. Almost instantly, the prince was looking about, blinking as if coming awake. He was in time to see Dondal's foe break and run — and Dondal run in a different direction!

Past Ceann flashed the boy, and he dropped his sword. At the run he jerked free his fishing spear, and circled the house. Both father and son were gone, chasing the last two survivors of what should have been a Pictish massacre and had become instead a massacre of Picts.

"They've gone mad!" Cormac bawled.

With Samaire on their heels, he and Ceann raced around the house and along the path that led to Dond's diminutive wharf. The three warriors brought up short, for Dond and son were unscathed. They stood staring at each other with the much impressed look of fellow warriors.

One Pict lay half in the water and half ashore; the other was in his longboat. Both had been bloodily transpierced by hurled fish-spears.

Thirteen savages had attacked an easy prey, and had come upon a den of ferocious wolves, and the numbers of Pictdom were reduced by thirteen.

Chapter Eleven: A Warrior Born

> *After immortal battles abroad,*
> *In countries many and far distant;*
> *There fought he like the lion,*
> *Then slept the balmy sleep.*
>
> —Ceann Ruadh, the "Minstrel-king"
> (from *Cormac the Gael*)

The sun of Munster edged up above the horizon like a forming pearl. Its rays fingered down to pick out the yard of a humble fisherman.

It was a scene of horror and red carnage.

Samaire and Dond were unscathed. Ceann had been scratched and no more, though it was to the blood. He bore too a few fresh bruises, and limped from that whack across the shin. It had left a swelling and a purpling welt, the bone having been bruised. Dondal had sustained a cut on his left leg, above the knee, and another on his right arm. He had noticed neither, nor had he heard much since Cormac's laying a hand on his shoulder.

"Ye be a warrior born," he had told the lad.

Mac Art knew such when he saw him, himself having been just as ferocious a youth, albeit better at arms for his training. With his eyes bright and glowing, Dondal sat motionless, gazing into his dreams while his mother treated his wounds. Neither was deep.

Not only had Cormac mac Art gained several new bruises and scratches, he had taken a slice across two fingers of his left hand that would be troublesome. The Pictish dagger had caught his knuckles. A point had slipped betwixt the links of his mail and sunk into his side above the hip, but the steel ring had held so that the stab-wound was not deep. Samaire was careful to squeeze blood from it before she treated it with the hot water and Lendabaer's herb remedies. He'd another cut on his sword arm and on the back of that hand.

"It's the hero-light I was seeing about your head, Cormac," Dond gushed. "Not since Cuchulain of old has a man so valiantly and awesomely smit his enemies!"

The name Cormac had given these people was a combination of his own and of his old alias: Cormac mac Othna. He and his companions claimed to be of western Munster, far from here. For though its land was not the best and sparsely settled, Munster's territory was great; it took in fully a third of Eirrin, including the mouth of the River Shannon. Ceann was "Celthair mac Ros," and Samaire had chosen the simple old name Ess.

"No hero light I saw or felt," Cormac said smiling, for he was determined not to wince at the burning stuff Lendabaer kept on hand for the treating of wounds. "We did bring a massacre on them though, didn't we!"

"Indeed!" Lendabaer said. "And what's a woman to do, with her menfolk become warriors and the lawn all blood and bodies?"

"Rejoice," Dond said, looking at her, and there was an end to that.

"There's a gain," Ceann/Celthair said. "Dond mac Forgall, that excellent Pictish boat and their property — including weapons enow to arm a town

126

and sufficent arrows to take one! They be yours, by conquest."

"It's no towns we'll be taking," Dond said, glancing nervously at the rigid, entranced Dondal. "But — the other things — it was you three saved us all, and we've no doubt about it! Those trinkets — the fine belts they'd got off murdered men, the two who wore armour . . ."

Ceann was shaking his head. "None of ours. Dond, we've hardly told ye all the truth. We— "

"I've known that, nor need we hear more," Lendabaer said. At her cooking, she too glanced nervously at her older son.

Ceann waved a hand. "We have hid about us, even as Cormac and I disguised our armour lest it afright gentler folk, the loot we took from a Viking band. In a raid similar to this Pictish one on yourselves, the Vikings slew and burned, and made prisoners of Samaire Ess and myself. It was Cormac came to our rescue."

"I've no doubt on it!" Dond said, and he looked again on Cormac as though he were a god or at the very least the reincarnation of the legendary Cuchulain of Muirthemne.

"Well — it's much Viking-stolen booty we have secreted about ourselves," Ceann went on.

"There's more," Cormac said, regarding Dond very seriously. "We were better not dressed as we are. Admittedly we've some rents and filth on the clothing we wear, but — "

"Anything in my house that fits any of ye," the overplump woman at the stove said, "is yours, for it's our whole family ye saved."

"We'll insist on trading a bit of Viking gold, understand," Cormac said. When he saw that both Dond and his wife were about to argue, he added, "That the conditions of goods-trade may be fulfilled, and none of us in debt to the other."

"Oh, Mother!" the boy Laeg cried excitedly. *"Gold!"*

"'Twere danger-fraught for peasants such as we to turn up at market in Rorybaile with such as gold or jewels," Dond said. "And arousing of suspicion, as well."

Cormac stretched out a leg and smiled. He was seated in a chair made by Dond himself, and that with high competence.

"Not for you, Dond mac Forgall! Think you those who know ye, aye, and those who do not, will not soon know of what happened here? Why, total strangers even in Rorybaile will know of it, and think not this attack and its outcome will not be spoke of even in Cobh!"

The Rorybaile Cormac spoke of as if it were a metropolis was a little town a few miles distant, where agents came and bartered and took the fish caught hereabout inland. Cobh, with its excellent harbour, was a growing town on the two arms of the River Liagh.

The family stared at him — all save Dondal, who continued staring at that which only he could see.

"Cobh!" Lendabaer whispered.

Samaire hugged her big soft shoulders. "As for a bit of gold from the Viking thieves," she said, "why, you got it from the Picts, same as the arms and arrows ye'll be able to sell, didn't ye?"

Lendabaer looked at her, blinking. Then Dond laughed aloud.

"I've business elsewhere," he said, and departed them suddenly. He returned anon, beaming, swaggering a little, and carrying two earthen jars, well closed. His wife glanced on them and sighed.

It was ale, and there was celebration rather than work at the tiny keep of Dond mac Forgall of Munster that day.

Those neighbors who came were glad to sip of the

128

man's good ale and hear the story of the great war that had taken place here. It was not averse they were, either, to lending aid in the planting of Pictish corpses well away from the house of their now more-than-good friend Dond. The day wore on and the story was told again and again. Nor did it fail to gain and grow in telling. It was little enough there was to talk about on this oceanic border of quiet Munster, and the tale of Cormac son of Cuchulain — for so he had become — and mighty Celthair of the Flaming Head and Ess the Sun-tressed, along with Dond and Dondal and what they'd done with their humble fish-spears, would live and be told for years.

First Ceann and then Cormac became afflicted with the disease of drunkenness, and they were soon joined by Dond — and his son, despite his mother's efforts to keep the boy away from the ale. But he was now a countryside hero, and it was not only his father's ale he drank but that brought by this neighbour and that. Smiling, they plied the boy with it. In return they learned how Cormac and Ceann had saved them all — and how Dondal mac Dond had saved each man of them as well, meanwhile slaying seven fierce Picts. His head swelled and swelled, and so did his story, and it was not only the result of ale-fumes.

All were delighted that the trio spent another night there, save Samaire. There was little she could do about it, though. For Ceann and Cormac, like Dondal and Dond and no less than five others, fishermen from up and down the coast hereabouts were quite asleep before the fall of night.

On the morning of the morrow, Lendabaer had reason to wail. And wail she did. It was her son Dondal she saw, and him in Pictish armour too small for him, and wearing a helmet, and with sword and dagger on him. He stood grinning in the doorway.

The boy announced that he would guide the trio

129

of visitors to Cashel, the capital, and there seek service himself as a weapon-man of the king,

"Oh grief on me!" Lendabaer cried, flinging up her hands before her ruddy face.

Dond insisted that he needed the boy here. Lendabaer wept. And Dondal, a changed person and that overnight, remained adamant. The boy even sneered at such a weapons-handler and Pict-slayer as he wielding net and oar and fish-spear for the rest of his life, and the king mayhap in need of such a man for the good of crown and land!

Samaire gave Cormac a look, and his face and demeanor grew worse than sheepish.

"It was you, bloodthirsty hulk," Samaire muttered, "who just *had* to say 'Ye be a warrior born' to that poor peasant's son. Oh, Cormac! He'll be getting himself killed within the month for it!"

Quietly, walking along the shoreline just before dawn, Cormac mac Art told Dond mac Forgall a few facts. Around and about them birds twittered and called, and the sound of the sea was in their ears.

"I have pride in me, Dond, and — "

"Aye, and with good cause!"

"Hush a moment, friend, and list to this prideful man," Cormac said quietly. He shot a glance in the direction of the hut. "That pride will not let me continue to lie, and have a good man as yourself, Eirrin-born and of heroic bent in the protection of his family . . . what was I saying?"

Dond suppressed his smile. "I suffer from the same iron ball rolling about within my skull, son of Othna," he said. "Ye were — "

"I know now, for you have said it. I have no father named Othna, nor have I ever. I am Connacht-born, Dond, and it's Art my father was, and a name hard to wear he gave me."

Dond stopped stock-still, and he stared. "My lord!"

Cormac squeezed his shoulder. "Do not insult me by ceasing to call me 'friend Cormac,' friend. At any rate — it was long ago I was forced to flee Connacht, for the High-king then was fearful of a man bearing the name I do."

"Sure, and it be a name even greater than Cuchulain, Cormac mac Art. The High-king ye speak of was Laegair Niall's son?"

"The same. With, I think, the aid of Leinster's king, he did treachery on me, and I fled, years and years ago. Now it's on my way to Tara I am, and the High-king and assembly I hope to see, for a man Eirrin-born does not forget his land. But none must know this until I have made my way there, and had my reception, whatever form it takes."

"You mean to confront them all at the Feis of Tara, my lor — friend Cormac?"

"I do."

"Then until well after that time, it is Cormac mac Othna and his friends I have known and loved — but by Yuletide next, all will know that it was Cormac mac Art of Connacht who slept and slew here." Abruptly Dond chuckled. "And shared a headache with me!"

"Be careful, Dond. My name may be even less then than now, for many have forgot, in twelve years."

"Twel — why, ye were a mere boy!"

"Aye. And that be something else I'd talk with ye about. So is Dondal a mere boy, Dond, and not so proficient as was I with arms then, for I have been trained by fighting men, and Druid-taught. I make you this promise, friend: I'll not depart Cashel before I've sent the boy home to you."

Dond went pale, and actually stumbled. Cormac had seen men weak with joy before, and affected not to notice.

"Tell his mother and still her cries and her mind. But know this, Dond, and seek to set yourself and that good woman Lendabaer at peace on it: your son

131

Dondal is a warrior born. It's made to wield a sword of good steel he was, not a fleching-knife or net or barbed spear, and sure one day all the land will have the name of Dondal mac Dond in their mouths!"

"Ye . . . think so."

"Ye know me for a weapon-man, Dond, and one who has reddened his arms many times, though only once in Eirrin. Oh — twice, now . . . "

"Picts don't count!" Dond said in a boyish rush.

"At any rate — I know a warrior born, yes."

Dond nodded, and no more was said of the matter.

Even though he trusted the man implicitly as friend and one he had both saved and reddened arms with, Cormac said no word about the identities of "Celthair" and "Ess." True, their business was now his. But the telling of it, in Cormac's personal code, was not. Later he knew that Dond had already shared with his wife news that Cormac would see to their son's return, for she gave him a great hug and a cheek-kiss as they prepared to take leave.

Nowhere approaching so fine as he thought he looked, Dondal was their guide, in his Pictish armour and girt with their weapons. Samaire had retained the tall boots she loved, though now a tunic of homespun covered them past her knees. Ceann and Cormac, too, wore clothing loomed and sewn by a fisherman's wife. All three of them retained their broad long cloaks, into which Samaire had sewn secret pouches.

With the birds singing all about and the sun smiling as if happy with the thirteen savage bodies now nurturing its soil, the little quartet set out inland. Behind them danced and jabbered the two younger children of Dond and Lendabaer, until their brother paused to bid them return. With great respect, they showed him crestfallen faces but made no complaint. Back they went, with tears staining their cheeks. Dondal walked tall and Cormac was forced to slow the

132

boy's long stride.

Stiff-lipped, Samaire pointed out that they had enough wealth off the Vikings to buy horses sufficient to seat all Munster.

"This is peasant country, dairlin girl. It were best as we've agreed to make no bold display of our wealth. Horse or chariot would be the boldest. We continue afoot to Cashel."

"I swear by the gods the great tribes of Leinster swore by before Padraigh," Samaire/Ess muttered, "this walking will be the death of me, a good and strong woman who's fought the good fight even as a man!"

"No one told you to wear boots that fit you but ill," Cormac reminded her, and received a black look from beneath new-stained lashes.

Later in the day, when occasion arose, Dondal asked Cormac quietly — and nervously, with stammers and a licking of the lips that ill became a companion-at-arms, whether Ess Sun-tress was his woman.

Cormac thought a moment. Why, the boy actually — he dared — hmm! *Well*, Cormac told himself, *he's old enough, for all that!* Best not give him opportunity to undertake some ridiculous wooing of the handsomest woman he'd ever seen, then.

"Aye," Cormac said.

"Oh," Dondal said, downcast, and then, "I thought so," even more morosely. Then, after a few steps, he added hurriedly, "And it's a fine handsome woman ye've made your own, Cormac mac Othna, and her a fighting companion too!"

Cormac nodded, walking blindly now, heedless of the dusty road, the pretty blue and yellow summer-flowers, the trees that became more and more numerous, the bilberry and heath that paralleled their path, beneath a bright smiling July sun.

My woman, he mused, nor was he any the

133

happier about it than the tallish youth walking proudly beside him. *Samaire, daughter of a king, sister of a king, widow of a prince. No, Cormac, exile and riever of the coasts, it's not your woman that royal beauty is, and she'll never be. Have a care, landless exile, for ye be too old to be so foolish as this poor silly youth, with his head all swollen full of himself!*

An ye want this woman, he told himself, *it were better ye laid hands on her now, and backward ran with all your might, to put to sea with her in that Pictish boat. For chances of keeping her, and happily were better in that wise than this. If I clear myself, and aid them to confront their dark brother and mayhap gain for Ceann the crown of Leinster . . . well, it might well be as general of Leinster's armies I wear my sword. But not as the husband of a princess, no matter how fine a friend her royal brother is!*

In silence they walked, each in communion with the interior of his own head and their separate and common future. Afoot in southern Munster of Eirrin, a strange procession indeed: The fisherman's son Dondal in his Pictish armour, and the exiled winner of a hundred battles with his scarred face and his narrow eyes, and the royal heirs of Leinster's high throne!

Chapter Twelve: The Prince of Munster

> Crom was their day-god,
> and their thunderer,
>   Made morning and eclipse;
> Brigit was their queen of song,
> and unto her
>   They prayed with fire-touched lips.

—D'Arcy McGee: *The Celts*

Munster was rolling country, and the four pilgrims had well known it to this day. To their west had reared Galti Mor, pushing upward three thousand feet. Eastward was the lesser Comeragh range of hogbacks, while the travelers had made their way between, along the foothills of the Knockmealdown Mountains. They had seen few other travelers; this was a hard-working season for farmers, with both birds and bugs as anxious for their crops as they.

Little Kilsheed of Munster boasted perhaps a hundred houses that had grown out of four or five raths in times gone by. The village lay, sleepy in the sun, on the banks of the Suir. Northward of Kilsheed on this same river rose Cashel, the first destination on their journey north and then east to Tara.

In addition to its multicoloured homes and sprawling markets both open and closed and the tiniest of military garrisons, Kilsheed held precisely one inn. It was into its smoky, grease-walled interior the four repaired, under the broken sign of the Moondisk. A family of locals, doubtless celebrating something or other, left as they entered, and Cormac led the way to the vacated table. They gained attention: they were travelers. People smiled when they looked upon Ceann with his smallharp, and his dark red hair; men looked well and long at Samaire, with her exotic boots. They vanished enticingly up under an overlarge tunic that still did not disguise her slender and entirely womanly figure.

There were no smiles for Cormac — save that of a slatternly wench with overpainted face and nails like drops of blood tipping her long snowy fingers. The smiles occasioned by Dondal were of an entirely different sort. People nudged each other, and muttered. The young did not notice. Cormac felt that even if Dondal had, he'd have thought the people awed and commenting on his handsome build and martial appearance.

They were served fair ale, excellent bread, and greasy pork, ambushed in more grease lumpy with leeks striving to smother the meat. A happy-faced man, fat and ruddy, came bustling from the kitchen to welcome them. He advised that it was his own tender daughter serving them and he responsible for her and them, and to tell them he had fine accommodations for their over-nighting.

Beneath smoke- and grease-darkened rafters, Cormac looked about himself.

The fellow alone in the corner was a priest of the new faith, and though he nodded and almost smiled, Cormac vouchsafed him none but a sour look, and that quickly passing. Against the wall a dour man sat, the hood of his cloak drawn up to forbid interruption while he brooded over his ale. A smallharp stood against the wall beside him, but he made no move to

136

pick it up and play, nor did he more than glance their way; he was manifestly interested in nothing and no one, including his fellow minstrel just arrived. Nearby three soldiers lounged, swaggering and noisy. The leg of one was ˑstretched arrogantly out so that the landlord's daughter must be aware of it with each of her journeys to the kitchen and back.

There were no other patrons. And the biggest of the three soldiers, a man perhaps just at the age of thirty, kept his pale eyes fixed rudely on Samaire. Cormac looked at her, to see what the fellow was staring at.

A woman with the highness of pride in eyes and bearing, Cormac told himself. And those eyes blue as any flower of Eirrin's fair summer. Lips, he thought in the poetic manner of his ancestors, red as the berries of the rowan-tree, and her hair like a king's cloak of new gold or the sun just before it sets. And a face and form to cause a man's body to twitch.

The soldier's body, Cormac mac Art decided, was atwitch. He continued staring. Samaire had noticed. Obviously uncomfortable, she was keeping her eyes on her food. Ale-jack in hand, Cormac twisted half about to return the soldier's stare. It was many long seconds before the man noticed or deigned swerve his gaze from Samaire to the dark-haired man with the scarred face and eyes invisible in their slits.

For a time the two men traded looks, the soldier's insolent and Cormac's dark and warning. Then, without swerving his gaze, the man spoke to his companions. As he did, he nodded their way — or rather Samaire's. The other soldiers laughed.

Nodding, one said, "And scratch like a cat in heat once she's on her back too, I'd be saying!" The others laughed and nodded. When they fell silent, it was Cormac who spoke, from a distance of eight or so feet.

"But it's nothing ye'd be best advised to be saying,

137

little man. Cats abound; find one and get scratched."

All three weapon-men blinked. The dark speaker had not raised his voice, and his tone was matter-of-fact. His ale was still held carelessly in his big hand, which bore a small poultice to draw or ward off some infection endangering him.

With the merest hint of the ghost of a smile's shadow, Cormac turned back to his companions. He lifted his alejack. Ceann looked at him; Samaire at her trencher; Dondal past Cormac, at the trio of king's men. They were muttering, but Cormac recognized the way of men who intend to be overheard.

" — and none among the three of them man enough for her!"

"I know three more who'd rise to the occasion!" Laughter.

"Cormac — " Dondal began quietly, looking very nervous indeed.

"Eat, Dondal. Drink. They launch words to provoke. I've heard crows before — and the braying of asses." Cormac's voice was loud as the soldiers'.

Behind him silence, then a long, sucked in "Eeeeeeeeh," followed by a pause and an aspirated "Ha-awwwwwwwwn!" A passing good imitation of the animal mentioned.

Samaire anxiously lifted her eyes, keeping her head down, to Cormac's face. He smiled. She returned to pushing her food around, desperately keeping her attention thereon.

"I suggest either a walk or that we repair to whatever rooms he has for us," Cormac said quietly. "We needn't stay here, and I'm not anxious to fall afoul of a weapon-man of Munster's king!" He turned in his little chair, away from the insolent trio. The innkeeper's daughter was standing near the kitchen, watching, and she started his way before Cormac could speak.

Against the wall, the hooded minstrel brought

138

forth several soft, lingering notes.

"We'd be leaving ye now," Cormac said, "with thanks. And would you ask your father to — ah." The father was coming out of the kitchen that quickly, with anxious glances in the direction of the soldiers.

The girl's head jerked up and her eyes widened; a sneering voice spoke from Cormac's other side, and just behind him.

"Surely one who has lived here nigh onto a year, and a military man besides who's capable of protecting you, would be a better companion in the night outside, prettygirl."

Cormac transferred his alejack from his right to his left hand. Samaire continued to lavish her attention on the remains of her dinner awhile, then looked up. Her face was open, her eyes clear and the brows above them innocently arched; her tone was infinitely equable.

"I had not noted that it had grown dark," she said. "Nor have I need of protection, surely, with such fine soldiers about."

Silence followed. Under the table, Cormac very slowly moved his feet, bracing for a sideward lunge. He did not smile, but silently saluted "his woman"; her words might well cook the fellow's arrogance and ardour and return him like a chastised sheepdog to this table.

"And a good thing it is," the soldier at last said, "and you in the company of this moon-dark scarface and that hound-eared boy in his funny clothes!"

"Fish-mouthed ass!" Dondal snapped, more picturesquely than with attention to likelihood. He stood with dramatic suddenness that toppled his chair behind him — and raised one edge of his trencher high enough to spill grease and a gnawed bone onto the table.

"Dondal!"

It was Cormac's voice rapped out, but the boy in

139

his undersize armour was already around the table, moving with more speed than grace for the soldier. Backing his chair around, for the daughter of his host was in the way, Cormac looked up in time to see the briefest of encounters.

Almost negligently, the corner of his upper lip lifted in a despising sneer, the big soldier swept a hand out. Dondal was shoved, and staggered, and first his feet and then a table got in his way. He fell over it with a crash and a bang, his head struck the floor good and hard, and he lay still. Cormac gave him only a glance to note that the boy's eyes were closed, not open; he was alive then, and unconscious. Then Cormac was on his feet.

"You are a loudmouthed braying jackass who disgraces womanhood and the service of your king," he advised quietly. "And," he added smoothly as the man flushed and reached for his sword, "so unconcerned with the property of this good man our host as to fight here and endanger his property. Now it's outside I go. You are welcome to seek my company."

Cormac turned his back on the man, whose sword was half out of its handsomely enameled sheath. Cormac walked to the inn's door, and went out onto a twilit street darkened at intervals by the shadows of houses.

He turned to find the king's weapon-man rushing from the doorway with long sword in hand. It was too late for Cormac to meet him with his own blade.

Hand to hilt, Cormac awaited that charge, and at the last moment moved with hurricane swiftness. Sideward he stepped, listening to the whistle of the blade meant for his head, and he left his foot behind. The charging soldier tripped and stretched his great hulk on the ground with a crash. He grunted loudly, was still a moment while he gathered his wits, and then rolled swiftly to avoid an attack. None was in

140

progress. He stared up at the other man, who stood gazing coolly at him, sword in sheath.

"Unless his head be broke, in which case yours shall be, we are at quits," Cormac said. "You had no trouble measuring the boy's length; I had no more with yours." That should have been enough, but Cormac was not the pacifist he was trying so hard to be. He could not help adding, "It's boys and women you're more suited for troubling — though the words of the woman inside would have sent slinking a man who knew his father well enough to have been properly reared."

For a number of dragging seconds the fallen man stared at him in astonishment. His face changed as his anger rose. Then he was narrowing his eyes, gaining a firmer grip on his sword, and rising.

"I have been called Cuchulain this very day," Cormac told him, "and ye've not the appearance of a man to cross swords with such."

"There'll be no crossing of swords, arrogant pig from a peasant's muddy wallow! Mine wants only a sheathing — in your insolent belly!" And the weapon-man charged again.

The blade of mac Art scraped from its sheath and rushed in the air. It caught the other's sword on it, and pushed, so that steel scraped on steel rather than slammed down upon it; Cormac had had swords broken in his hand afore. Shieldless as was his antagonist, he lunged then to strike the bigger man in the chest with a shoulder. The soldier was staggered both mentally and physically. It was backward his uncertain steps carried him, and it was behind his ankle Cormac's foot sped.

The big man crashed to earth a second time.

Instantly Cormac glanced back at the inn; where were this man's companions, that they came not to his aid? Ceann and Samaire were boiling forth — and damnation on the luck, men were running down the

141

street, and with a most martial clanking!

It's trouble I've purchased with this sour coin, Cormac mac Art thought — but his regret was only that he had no shield, for he had cavalierly left it within the inn.

Back came his opponent, at the rush. With a sigh and a gritting of his teeth Cormac decided that if more foes were coming, it were better for him to lessen the odds now. The soldier struck a blow that should have sheared through corselet and flesh to the bone — had not its target dropped into a squat and stabbed him through the thigh.

The Munsterman fell for the third time. Nor did he rise, but remained prostrate, writhing in pain.

Cormac turned to face the naked swords of five helmeted, shield-bearing soldiers of the king. They were now no more than fifteen feet away, and running.

"HO-O-OLLLLLLD!" a voice bawled from the inn.

They held, Cormac and the king's men, and all looked at the inn door. There, flanked by Ceann and Samaire and with the other two soldiers behind him, stood the hooded minstrel. With a swift gesture he put back that hood, to reveal himself a slim young man, dark-haired, wearing a mustache and a slender silver fillet about his head at mid-forehead.

"Let those who do not recognize me, ask."

The body of soldiers who had been charging Cormac did obeisance to the long-cloaked man, while Cormac frowned. The leader of the military contingent soon solved for him the problem of the minstrel's identity:

"We know you, lord Prince Senchann Eoghanachta mac Eogain!"

Senchann of Munster pointed at Cormac. "That man *is* a man, and worthy of my father's service. Him in the dust at his feet, where he best belongs, is not worthy of that service, or of Munster or indeed Eirrin.

142

Ye all know well it is my wont to wander hither and thither in disguise, to hear the words and will of the people of our land. This night I heard and saw how that arrogant and insolent man — with the backing of these two behind me, who want disciplining — insulted a woman in this inn, and her gentle, and deliberately sought war with her companions. It is god's will that he found a man better at arms than himself, and now wallows in the dust like the base pig that he is."

There was silence. Cormac withheld his smile, but let it warm him inwardly. The little company of weapon-men in the street stood stiffly, awaiting the pleasure of their king's son. The two behind him stood just as stiffly — and the inn's lights showed them to be pale and apprehensive.

"Your commander will remain here with me," Prince Senchann said. "You others will carry — or drag, it makes little difference — back to your barrack . . . *that*." He indicated the man writhing near Cormac with a jerk of his hand, which was without jewelry. "With you also go these two, as miscreants." He turned.

Ceann and Samaire stepped aside, and the cloaked minstrel-prince faced the two ashy-faced soldiers directly. "Your swords," he said, and he received them, one by one, hilt-first. Back he turned, in an attitude of waiting, and the soldiers who had been bearing down on Cormac came alive.

They only glanced at him as they picked up their comrade with the bloody thigh. The two men came sheepishly out of the inn to join them. The whole company moved silently off up the street, save for the man who had called out the Munsterish prince's name. Long silent seconds passed before Cormac realized that the fellow was waiting for him to precede, into the inn.

Sword in hand, Cormac walked those few paces.

143

At the base of the inn's three steps, he solemnly reversed his sword and offered it to Senchann, hilt foremost.

"A good hilt, well shaped and enhanced," Senchann observed. "And a good hand, bandage and all. And a good man as well. Sheathe your weapon, warrior, and tell me your name."

Cormac's sword scraped and settled into his scabbard with a final thunk. "I am Cormac mac Othna, on my way with my companions to Cashel and then Tara, lord Prince."

"Well warrior Cormac, Munster could do worse than to have yourself tarrying long and long in Cashel in our service! Come in." He looked past Cormac. "Fiacc mac Cumail, is it not?"

There was surprise in the soldier's voice. "Aye, my lord!"

"Well, be not surprised, Captain Fiacc. I know what's about in this kingdom, and I assure you that my father does, as well."

Samaire and Ceann moved aside and Senchann re-entered the inn of the Moon-disk. Cormac followed, also passing between his companions; after him came Captain Fiacc.

"Lord Prince — " the innkeeper began.

Senchann waved a hand, his long brown cloak rippling. "It is a good house ye keep, Master Tuachel. We'll have ale."

"Lord Prince, had I but known . . . lord, I have — "

"Ale."

"Yes, lord Prince. At once. Boann!" The landlord whirled, and his wide-eyed daughter came much alive at his call. Soon ale was on its way, and good mugs. Senchann, meanwhile, had bent over Dondal.

"He lives, as we all knew, and is coming awake. Who is this poor strangely-dressed youth with the

144

heart of a lion, mac Othna?"

Cormac told him, briefly, and Senchann looked up at him with lifted brows.

"*Thirteen* Picts?"

"Aye, King's son."

The large brown eyes and lifted brows turned to Samaire. "And even yourself took toll among them?"

She nodded.

Chuckling, Senchann of Munster shook his head. "What a band of invaders I have met this night! Why, that insolent pig of a soldier was but a yapping puppy harrying a pack of wolves, wásn't he! A wonder he was not stretched in the dust by you . . . " He was looking at Samaire, and he let his voice trail off, on a rising note.

"S — Ess, lord Prince. And my brother Celthair."

"Cormac, and Celthair, and Ess, and Dondal son of a fisherman! Ah — he blinks and wonders where he is now. Be still a time, Dondal mac Dond, for it's your head you struck, and your honour avenged, and your prince at your side."

"M — my . . . prince?"

"Aye. And a brave young man I've seen ye to be. Cormac mac Othna has told me ye be a warrior born, and were on your way to my father, to offer him your sword. Is't true?"

Dondal's eyes shone. "Aye, lord prince!"

Cormac had already spoken to Senchann on that score. The prince looked up; Cormac gave his head a slow shake. Smiling, Senchann looked down at the fallen boy.

"Know ye now that there's a matter of being ever ready, and of training for proficiency, and that had he chosen to draw weapon the man ye so valiantly attacked would have robbed your father of his firstborn?"

Dondal flushed, and his eyes closed. His voice

was barely audible: "Aye, lord Prince." After a
moment he added, "And it's great shame I wear."

"Well," Senchann said, "I've worn the same,
Dondal, and more than once. I prefer a cloak! But
put it from your mind. Be assured that the man you
hoped to serve would say the same to you: return to the
house and service of your father, and ease the water of
the fine seafood we cherish even in Cashel. Meanwhile
practice, and be ever prepared to defend family and
life and country. But — be not anxious to wear sword
and be at the reddening of it, Dondal mac Dond."

Dondal whispered sadly, "Aye, lord Prince."

"Understand that I am not anxious to wear
Munster's crown either, Dondal mac Dond, for that
would mean that my father is stretched in the earth.
But — if ever that day comes, you are to come to me in
Cashel, and hand me this."

From within his cloak the prince brought forth a
slender torc twisted of three strands of silver, each no
thicker than ten strands of hair. He slipped it about
the neck of the fisherman's son. Dondal was
speechless, though his mouth was open.

Senchann rose. "Now get up, mac Dond, and join
us at ale." He looked at the silent soldier. "Captain
Fiacc, a lesson learned. First that your men need be
told what manners and honour are, and that being in
the service of Munster is for peace, not war in taverns
and insults made to women, known or unknown. And
another: that things are not always as they appear,
and questions must be asked, an you serve well and
properly. I speak of the five men ye led — had I not
called out, the just man in that encounter would have
been set upon, and slain, is it not?"

Fiacc was chewing his lip; Senchann caught
Cormac's thin smile. The prince, too, smiled.
"Well, an *attempt* would have been made to slay
Cormac, who but defended woman and self and
honour, and more blood would have been spilled. All

because the man he wounded is less than a man. Remember, Captain Fiacc."

"Aye, lord Prince."

Senchann heaved a sigh. "Well, now I seem all unwontedly to have struck dumb both Dondal and Fiacc, let us sit down and sip, and see if we be capable of holding speech together."

Chapter Thirteen: The Capital of Munster

The oak spreads mighty beneath the sun
   In a wonderful dazzle of moonlight
   green—
Oh, would I might hasten from tasks
undone,
   And journey where no grief hath been!

—Edna Carberry: *I-Breasil*
(the afterworld)

"And *practice,*" said Cormac mac Art.

Dondal nodded dolorously. Crestfallen, somehow not quite so large as he'd been yet just as hulking, the boy wore his Pictish armour—in a roll across his shoulders. Stillborn was his brilliant military career, at least for the present. The fisherman's son turned and set off along the homeward road, like a hound who'd been out overnight and now returned, weary and empty of belly.

Cormac turned to Prince Senchann. The two men exchanged a smile that was not without empathy for Dondal's feelings. Senchann's mustache writhed and his oversized front teeth gleamed in the morning sunlight. His great hooded cloak, with his smallharp, formed a pack behind his saddle, and today the slender noble wore a soldier's tunic and sandals.

148

Nothing else; the summer day was warm and leggings unnecessary—and Senchann had good well-muscled calves to show off.

He twisted in the saddle to look around at the little company. The innkeeper Tuachel, standing behind his belly in the door of his inn, beamed, thinking the prince had turned to bid him good fortune. He was wrong, but kind Senchann mac Eogain nodded at the man anyhow. Then he looked from face to face of his companions.

With two soldiers from the Kilsheed garrison, Samaire, Ceann and Cormac were well-mounted. The two from Leinster hardly looked like prince and princess, but then neither did Senchann Eoghanacht. Samaire had spent much time with her hair, which was circled and woven with three bands of gold and silver—hair-jewelry formerly hidden within her peasantish clothing.

Senchann squared in his saddle. At his nod, the soldier who would lead the little group twitched his reins. The six horses set off along the road to Cashel.

Cormac rode beside the prince, with Ceann and Samaire just behind. The other solider rode last. As they walked, then trotted and cantered and then again walked their horses, Cormac gained information. He was careful, his questions seeming no more than normal curiosity.

There was no bad blood, he learned, betwixt Munster and its neighbours, Connacht and Leinster. Between those western and eastern kingdoms a small portion of Meath's southern land bordered Munster, forming a corridor between the Shannon—with Connacht on its other bank—and Leinster. All was well, too, with Meath. Munster was at peace; Eirrin was, as Samaire had said, at peace.

As careful with his answers as Cormac was with his queries, Senchann allowed that the Munstermen heard that Feredach an-Dubh was no good king.

149

"There might be . . . a certain . . . nervousness in some quarters among us," the prince said, "that Feredach might, ah, see the need to . . . *mollify* his people and make them forget their . . . dissatisfaction with him, if such exists."

Cormac watched the flower-tasting of a bright yellow butterfly. *He's learned to talk like a king. It's "if" and "maybe" and "perhaps" and "might be" and "some quarters among us," and even those not without further modification.* He said, "Oh . . . by seeking an enemy, you mean, to give the Leinstermen some common purpose, someone to rage against?"

"You understand considerable, Cormac mac Othna."

To that Cormac made no reply. Aye, he knew the way of kings. There was nothing new about a king, finding himself in trouble at home, looking about for some excuse to make war and thus unite his people—and appease them with sword-won booty.

"Lord Feredach, then," Cormac said, "is not the man his father was."

"Ah no! That man was well-known and well-liked by the crowned head of Munster. For the matter of that, it's good His Majesty Eogan felt about Feredach's older brother Liadh's being on the Leinsterish throne."

"Is't true King Feredach had his brother Liadh slain, lord Prince? Or is that not a question to ask of a king's son?"

"It is not a question to ask of a king's son," Senchann said tightly. "But I will tell you this—who knows?"

"I've heard naught of Feredach's younger brother and sister, since his ascension."

Senchann mac Eogain shrugged. "People in other lands hear little of me either, I suppose, or my brothers and sisters!"

Cormac chuckled. "They'll be hearing of you,

lord Prince—a king's son who goes about in a plain brown robe, and hooded, with a smallharp and no horse!"

"It is a way to learn . . . things," Senchann said, with a little smile. "Ah—now this section of road I well remember as a good one. Rossa!" he called to the soldier ahead. "Let's let them run, until we come to Brown Dog Hill!"

The soldier turned back a grinning face, and booted his mount. So too did Senchann, and then Cormac. The latter rode with his teeth clenched and an expression of some pain on his face. He tried very hard to relax and roll with the horse's gait as one did on a ship asea. He'd spent very little time atop a horse, and much preferred the unsteady planking of a ship beneath his feet than hard leather saddle under his hams and a horse's broad frame tugging at his thighs. The hill, named long and long ago for a reason no one remembered, came near not soon enough for Cormac mac Art.

They slowed, paced their restless mounts up the long incline. As they began the easier descent, Cormac started to speak, but then they broke into a trot.

Again he clenched his teeth to keep them from clacking and against his grunts; this trotting was worse by far than the gallop, which was relatively smooth—by comparison. Men yet wondered and strove to learn whether it was true all four of a horse's feet left the ground when he galloped; there was no way to be certain, but wagers and arguments were still made. As to the trot—to Cormac that gait felt as if the beast he rode was dancing on one foot. He gripped tightly with his thighs, and was happy when they reached the base of the hill, where the road both leveled and grew as full of curves as a cow's pathway.

The prince's words had assured Cormac that it were safe for Ceann and Samaire to make known their identity to King Eogan. Cormac felt it politic to

151

advise the prince in advance of their identities, rather than letting him learn in his father's keep. He waited until they stopped, just after crossing a stream, and made a midday meal of bread and cold meat. Then, quietly, he asked Senchann to find duties elsewhere for the two weapon-men. With a look, Senchann did.

"There is nether bad blood nor high friendship between the kings of Munster and Leinster," Cormac said, looking at Ceann and Samaire. "King Eogan held regard for both King Liadh and his father."

Ceann nodded. "Then we might tell the prince and his father the reason for our journey northward."

With narrowed eyes, Senchann looked from one of them to the other, then opened his mouth to speak—or demand, morelike.

"Lord Prince, as we are wary of all men, we three have been less than honest with you," Cormac said, gazing into Senchann's eyes. "Lord Prince Senchann of Munster, I present the Lord and Lady Ceann and Samaire, prince and princess of Leinster."

"We hope you understand the reason for our deception, my lord," Samaire said, while Senchann sought to grasp again the loosed reins of his mind.

After a time he said, "My Lady . . . I do not."

So they told him, and Senchann's jaw tightened. In coming to the end of their tale of dark treachery and captivity and then bloody rescue, Ceann and Samaire identified Cormac only as "Cormac mac Othna, and him of far Ulahd."

At last there was silence but for insect-buzz and bird-song and the nearby gurgle and ripple of the little stream they had just crossed. After a time of thought, Senchann heaved a great sigh.

"It is an ugly tale. A man does treachery on his brother to gain a throne not rightfully his—and then on his younger siblings as well, to keep the throne he sits . . . less than regally."

"Less than competently!" Ceann snapped.

152

"I thank you for your confidence," Senchann mac Eogain said, "and suggest that it be yourselves and not I who tell this ugly story to my royal father."

Of course; they had assumed nothing other.

"Then if we've finished here," Senchann said, "let us tear the horses away from their grazing, to be certain we raise fair Cashel before dark."

They did, but only just. The rearing little mountain called the Rock of Cashel hove into sight well before the city itself, and the sun was already dying. It was reddening the land with dusk when they reached the gates of the city at the base of the skeletal hill. Atop it, they saw that the adherents of the new faith had been allowed to raise a chapel. Before it, huge and out of cut stone, stood the symbol of their faith.

Cormac was not happy to enter a city watched over by a Roman execution device; that mighty cross was to him a somber and most ugly sentinel. Many men the Romans had bound to such horrors, to die of thirst and hunger and exposure. Nor had there been many such as that first Caesar, nearly six centuries ago. He had gained a reputation for mercy by ordering his men to slay with swift swords and spears the slowly dying men they had crucified. (Most likely, Cormac thought, because their groans went not well with Julius's dinner!)

Now the long-exiled Gael felt foreboding. He frowned and his lips were tight.

His Celtic bloodline ran back thousands of years, even to Atlantis, whose cross had been open at the bottom: a symbol of life, not death. He had rather they arrived at some time other than when a dying sun sent that granite cross's long sullen shadow over Cashel. It reminded him of betrayal and death, and he brooded nervously over their decision to reveal all to Senchann and Eogan his father.

Chapter Fourteen: The King of Munster

> *The berried quicken-branches lament in
> lonely sighs,*
> *Through open doorways of the dun a
> lonely wet wind cries;*
> *And lonely in the hall he sits, with feasting
> warriors round,*
> *The harp that lauds his fame in fights
> hath a lonely sound.*

—Edna Carberry: *Art the Lonely*

Once in his riever days Cormac had taken a
bone-deep swordcut in the back of the right thigh. It
was both agony and danger to his life, and his men
sadly took him to a little island above Alba, there to
heal or die. There he lay, for a long month. With the
aid, whether medical or arcane he never knew, of an
Alban Druid, Luchu and the strange voiceless girl
Seimsolas—Light of Beauty—mac Art had recovered.

Sure, he mused the morning after their arrival in
Cashel, *and it's that wound I'd rather have again than
these saddle-born kinks in legs and backside!*

At least he had rested well last night. Tired,
dusty, saddle-weary, they had assured Senchann they
wanted nothing so much as a night's sleep. The prince
had practically smuggled them into the Hall of

Guests. In that many-chambered building next the royal house, they had eaten well. After a brief talk, they retired. Out of the conversation had come agreement that Cormac's true name would continue secret.

Now, in mid-morning of the following day, they followed Prince Senchann into the royal house.

Two spearmen with ornate sword scabbards, gold-worked hilts and tall, lozenge-shaped shields presided over the double-doored entry. Both men wore tunics of white and were well-girt with fine gleaming armour of red leather, studded with faceted bosses of steel. A long plume of white hair fell down each man's back from his helm; dyed or bleached ox tails, the three pilgrims supposed.

Between those men and the tall doors passed the four, and into that long broad room.

Massive, squared beams of oak roofed the Hall of Kings in Cashel of Munster. Others, even thicker, supported the beams from a floor of cut, set stone; these uprights were stained a deep red-brown and banded about with ruddy bronze. The area they framed could have accommodated easily the milling of a hundred people. Over a hundred more could sit simultaneously at the tables that ran along the sideward walls. Cormac mac Art wondered if so many supped here nightly, and he thought not.

There were no other weapon men; indeed the hall was entirely deserted. Not even the king was in his great hall this day, and the three foreigners wondered.

Well-attired and long-cloaked, the trio exchanged bemused looks as they followed Prince Senchann. Up the center of the broad long hall he strode, and with each step the purple-worked hem of his voluminous and swirly cloak draped over his rising heel. The yellow of primrose was the cloak's colour; pure shining silk was its cloth.

Cormac walked with no more comfort than he

sat. A day in that unaccustomed place—the saddle—had left him with buttocks tender to the bone. They were muscle-sore when he walked, as were his inner thighs. He bore it, and concealed his discomfort, as he followed the son of the king to audience with the king.

But where was the king?

They soon learned: behind an unmarked door with no handle or sidework, disguised as one of ten black-stained panels at the head of the hall. Beyond was an over-warm little parlour hung all about with thick, heavy draperies of deep carmine. The flooring between them was covered from corner to corner with a rich carpet of an even deeper red.

A man sat in a chair on a raised area at the far wall. He was the room's only occupant.

The room was the colour of blood; its single denizen was not.

Indeed he appeared to have in his veins no more than a pint of the red juice of life, for all his fat. Shadeflower white was this man with the double circlet of twisted gold about his head, resting on thin locks of auburn and grey. The outsize red mustache that bushed beneath his nose and covered his upper lip and part of his cheeks only emphasized his pallor, as did the deep, deep blue of his robe. A great carcanet of gold covered his upper body from neck past the pectorals, where his belly began. The huge necklace winked with garnets and pearls and blue agates.

His visitors entered and stood, for the Eirrin-born did not bend knee even to crowned head.

In addition to the armchair from which presided the king, there were five other seats in the room: backless chairs of wood, like those of the Romans.

His Majesty Eogan Eoghannact, Cormac mused, sped the words and departure of his visitors and petitioners by seating them as uncomfortably as possible! They were bade to sit, and did.

"Majesty," Senchann said, "I met these three in

an inn of Kilsheed two nights agone. A rude weapon man—and him in our white and scarlet—made several remarks about the lady. At last he was so insolent as to approach her and solicit her company even before her brother and her guardian. It was our soldier provoked the fight, and deliberately; it was this man who ended it, and without difficulty. Eogan King of Munster, I bring to you Cormac mac Othna of Uladh, and will let these twain make known themselves to you."

Eogan regarded Cormac from brown eyes that blinked often and obviously strained to see. "Have you aught to add to what the prince has said, Cormac mac Othna?"

"None, lord King."

"A man of arms and few words, then. Seek you the service of a king, weapon man?"

"With your indulgence, lord King: I do not."

The king received that with an extra blink, and was silent for a few moments. Then, "And were I guardian to this lovely lady, nor would I seek service under others, be they gods or homely kings! My son has said you will introduce yourselves. Please do, for the prince's petition for audience was urgent, and I detect mystery here."

"My sister, Sire, was named Samaire at birth, and I Ceann, by our royal father Ulad King of Leinster."

Eogan received his second surprise with aplomb and little hint of his shock. He assured them that they were thrice welcome. Then he inquired as to the reason for such a visit, without heraldry or retainers. Cormac and Senchann sat silent then, while the others held royal converse and the king's Leinsterish guests told their story.

Hearing them out, Eogan let them see that he was both astonished and disturbed. He sat back and thought a space, beringed white hand toying with the end of his leftward mustachio—and joggling his jowls.

"It is your brother's head wears the crown, no matter how got," he ventured, but lapsed again into silence. Then he sighed, looked into Ceann's eyes, and told them that which assured Cormac this was a thoughtful head under its crown, and a pragmatic one withal. Keeping his face as composed and serious as Eogan's, Cormac listened, with care to remembering.

"I can and will do no less than offer ye, all three, the hospitality of this house, for so long as you would visit. Nor shall I be less than honest." He regarded them somberly, blinking, leaning a little forward. Cormac wondered whether the king saw more than blurs and hazy features at distances past the length of his arm—or perhaps his nose.

"It's troubled ye cause my mind to be, royal guests, and it's danger your presence here represents, to my land. I must beseech ye both to keep your counsel as to your identity. For it's bad blood could result between Munster and Leinster were it known to my lord Feredach that I harbour his sibling exiles—and know their woesome story of evil as well."

Ceann spoke with asperity. "It's long we've journeyed since those honourless men of Norge captured us on the fen, Lord King of Munster. Nor do we intend to end that journey here. We thank you for your hospitable offer, and assure you we will depart in short order for Tara and the ear and protection of the High-king."

"Nor," Samaire said, for she was no cowed woman to sit silent while men talked, "shall we stop there either. We have a home, Eogan Eoghannact, and it is not Munster or Meath, Cashel or Tara!"

"I liked your upspoken words to the king this morning," Cormac told Samaire.

"Overly straightforward words," Ceann said. "Note well that the uncrowned heads of Leinster were

158

not invited to sup at the king's table!"

The trio sat in the two-room suite they'd been given within the royal house itself. Before them was the meal brought by two servants in red and white. The suite was handsome, sumptuous; the dinner well suited for visiting royalty. Yet there was the pervasive feeling, almost a scent, of their being so treated only out of duty, and them hardly welcome.

"Eating with others would have been difficult," Cormac pointed out, "for people are curious. Nor could we have been seated high up, remember, for we are all three with names in hooded cloaks."

"It's more than that, and we all know it," Samaire said.

"A Roman gallows stands in granite atop Cashel Rock," Cormac said, "and broods over Eogan's capital, and Eogan fears its shadow!"

"And his own!" Samaire snapped. Bringing her tooled goblet of good silver close to her face, she studied its ornate tracery.

His own rich cup newly filled with ale, Cormac leaned back and crossed his ankles. His saddle-sore backside objected; he tensed its halves along with his resolve to show nothing and bear all. He'd soon be back on a horse again, and was angered that his well-toned body was at odds with him, and it not wounded.

"He is not the first king to be so cautious," he said, "nor will he be the last. A king does, after all, have many people to consider. We know too little of Eogan of The Eoghannachta to judge whether he thinks only of himself. Like Lagaire of the ua-Neill!" He was tight-lipped as he added that last. "But . . . I have been thinking . . . "

"When you've thought upon you, Cormac mac Art, we be ready to listen," Ceann said, with the air of a king.

Cormac did not move but remained in his relaxed

159

position, while eyes like ice a hundred fathoms deep made cool at the other man. "Play not the king with me, Ceann Ruadh! Guardian I seem in truth to be—in your service I am not!"

There was silence among them, with Samaire looking passing nervous. Then Ceann smiled, though thinly.

"Very well, Cormac the Wolf. If I did sound as prince to subject, I'd correct tone and words."

Cormac smiled and nodded. He recognized a royally-disguised apology, and was delighted not so much to receive it as with Ceann. "By the blood of the gods, Ceann Ruadh, but it's a king you'd be making, and this I'd swear!"

"Fealty?" Samaire asked, with great ingenuous innocence, but her brother lashed her with a stare of approbation.

"I remember distinctly there were words I had to share," Cormac mac Art said, and prince and princess looked chastened—mildly. Both sat attentively gazing at him.

"Consider. Suppose that Eogan is thinking, as he may well be, thus: *I am Eogan and king, and whatever else he may be, so too, is Feredach a king.* Matters are looked at differently, between kings. *Now right well might bond be struck between us—I, Eogan, and Feredach—were I to return Feredach a message.*"

Without taking his eyes off Cormac, Ceann reached for his goblet. Samaire sat forward, staring with lowering brows.

"The message would advise Leinster's king that I, Eogan, have in my household those . . . *troublesome relatives* he sought to dispose of, oversea." Cormac's hand swept out in a smoothing gesture. "And Feredach is in Eogan's debt, and Eogan has less to worry about—and you more!"

"Surely," Samaire began, "no man would—"

160

"Not a man, but a king," her brother interrupted. "It may well be as ye say, Cormac. By the gods of my people, there may be serpents in Eirrin after all, and them walking about on two legs."

"Waddling," Samaire corrected, but no one smiled.

"Yet he was obviously not anxious for us to tarry here," Ceann said thoughtfully, seeming to study the wall opposite.

Suddenly Cormac smiled, and his feet came uncrossed and thumped the floor. "Aye, and that before he had time to think or counsel with his poet. And you assured him that we were anxious to be off! Therein our clue lies! We shall know Eogan has taken counsel and decided as I have said—if he undergoes a change of heart and tries to persuade us to tarry here."

Next day Eogan sent for them. Kindly he pointed out that the Great Feis of Tara was not long off, and that he would be traveling up to Tara Hill with royal retinue. Surely the three of them would abide here with him until then, as honoured and welcome guests, so as to travel with proper accompaniment . . . .

Having given Eogan no hint of their suspicion at his half-expected words to persuade them to tarry here—presumably whilst his messenger betook himself into Leinster—the trio got themselves well out of the king's house and into the town that afternoon. There, walking and talking in quiet tones, they took counsel as to what must be done.

"We cannot be certain," Ceann said with a frown. "*His* offer"—for they would speak no names on the streets of Cashel—"is, after all, a natural one, and logical as well. Brigands do exist along the roads and in the forests."

"And in large houses in certain towns of

Munster," Cormac said, affecting not to look at a pair of men lolling against a wall; both wore white tunics and steel-bossed armour of red leather.

"Then we face the dilemma," Samaire said unhappily. "The dangers of the road, alone, or . . . the other we have talked about. Either may exist—and both may not!"

Cormac chafed under the self-imposed responsibility for the two of them. If it were he alone, he'd be on the northward road from this town already, and without leavetaking or care for dangers ahead: danger was to be kept in mind, and met when it reared.

They turned down a noisy street that formed an open market. There they made pause to examine a great array of juniper berries set colourfully side by side with piles of crinkly sloke, or sea-spinach. A foot thumped Cormac's, and not by accident. He looked around to find beside him an old man, bent, leaning heavily on a staff. A white beard scraggled forth from the face-shadowing hood of his tattered orange cloak.

The staff swung to gesture, and the old fellow hobbled off. Cormac stood staring at the bent, orange-covered back until the hood swung back his way, surely to see if he followed. With a hand on each arm, he bent between Samaire and Ceann.

"We are beckoned. Come with me, but as if aimlessly."

The old fellow made good time, for all his bowed back and leaning on his staff, and the trio pushed their way through buyers and sellers halfway along the street. Their hooded leader swerved into an alley made dark by a great awning of deep green sailcloth. Cormac entered after him, with his hand wrapped around his dagger hilt.

In the gloom, the old fellow partially straightened and with both hands pushed back his hood. His face was revealed for but an instant, but it was long enough for recognition of the mustached young man's face

162

and overlarge front teeth. It was disguise-loving Senchann mac Eogain!

"This day a messenger leaves Cashel," he muttered, and Ceann and Samaire crowded close. "He rides to the house of Feredach in Leinster. That king will be advised that it's safe and watched ye three are here, and that it's safe here ye'll be *held*."

Ceann's breath hissed in between his teeth; the other prince continued talking in that low, hurried voice.

"Too, the messenger will suggest that mayhap a *tryst* might be made, twixt the kings of these two lands, as they fare forth to the Feis-mor in Tara of Meath—and an agreement struck as to your . . . *futures*."

"We'd have none," Ceann said in a whisper that was close to a guttural growl, "in Feredach's red hands!"

"Then listen, and with your mouths closed, for I bear no enmity to any of ye, but dislike a betraying of my own father as much!"

And they listened, while Senchann muttered rapidly.

It was a little later in the afternoon when the minstrel, plucking and singing softly, unhurriedly left Cashel by way of her northern gate. He wore a tattered old orange cloak with its hood up, and the watchful weapon men in white and red paid him only the slightest heed.

At another time a little later, a crippled woman hobbled through that same gate, a blowzy wench whose muttering voice proclaimed her to be well past her prime. Her hair was close-covered in the Old Manner to show she was married, and she did not miss one guard's sneering to another that she must have been within Cashel's walls to earn her husband's keep on her back.

163

At about that same time, a well-mounted man departed Cashel from the Connachta gate to the northeast. Bent he was, and scarred of face, and a filthy tunic and cloak on him. There was nothing remarkable about him, save that the two beasts he led looked remarkably good horseflesh to be pack-animals.

One of the white-and-reds at the gate watched after him, but the dirty scarface did not straighten once he was out on the road, nor did he increase the pace of his roan horse. Then there was a group of merchants approaching the gate, and them to be watched, and the scarface was forgot.

The scarface rounded a turn in the road, saw that a hill now stood between him and any view of Cashel's gate. Straightening, he tugged sharply at the long rein of the packhorses. At the same time he nudged his mount in the flank with his heel. It was ill-advised, for the man bounced as only a bad rider does, when the horse broke into a fast trot. In the wake of the man and the three horses trailed his curses and grunts.

There were none to see when he swerved off onto the skimpy trail that connected the northern road with that to Connacht. Still he cursed, all the way. As he approached the wide ribbon of the other road, he heard the hallooo from within the trees. He drew rein, and turned in among the cool stand of yew and hazelnut. Two people appeared to meet him.

In short order the blowzy woman and the orange-cloaked minstrel were mounted, and despite the cursing of the other man, all three of them set off northward at the gallop. Thus did a prince, a princess and an exiled warrior gain departure from Cashel of Munster, and without so much as a thankyou or farewell for the king who had extended them the hospitality of his own house.

Chapter Fifteen: The Highwaymen

> *Red were their swords and dark each heart*
> *Black Carbri's men of Brosna Wood;*
> *All four they met Cormac mac Art,*
> *And soon each leaf was dark with blood!*

—Diarmuid of Tulla Mor (?)

That night the trio of pilgrims, now reduced to the status of fugitives, knew only that they were somewhere east of the Shannon. At dusk they turned off the road and into a heavy stand of timber.

The trees were black, eerie menacing forms rising all about them as they made their way into the forest, without light. They were soon forced to dismount and lead their horses. Cormac winced at the pain his muscles shot up through him as they walked, but he said nothing. The others, more used to riding, had not considered that he might be suffering, and he would not let them know.

Coming to a small clearing, they tethered the horses so that they could avail themselves of what little grazing there was to hand; the animals had drunk at a ford only a short time ago. In darkness and near silence, Ceann, Samaire and Cormac broke out the meat and cheese Cormac had bought in the market at Cashel.

They spent the night there, taking turns at watch. Ceann drew that chore first, and awoke Cormac for his turn. While mac Art sat there fighting to keep awake, there was a rustling and Samaire joined him. She bent, and it was her lips came to him first. With their mouths united, she sank down onto the saddle blanket he'd spread over a great patch of moss. He felt it; her body vibrated against his like the tightly coiled spring of a siege engine.

He spoke very quietly. "Sleep, Samaire, for I'll not spare ye your turn at watch. We all need what sleep we can gain."

Sulkily, she settled down beside him, pressed against the body he held under control. He did not touch her. Soon her breathing deepened, and he felt more radiant warmth from her curled body. She slept. Cormac sat, giving his leg and arm vicious pinches from time to time to insure wakefulness.

At last he woke her, and when he was sure she had her wits about her, he slept. Years of the life of a warrior and seafaring coastal riever had given him the necessary ability to be asleep within seconds after he'd decided.

She woke him at dawn, and Ceann roused at their voices. The triple watch had been unnecessary; there had been nothing but normal night-sounds of the forest. They ate, wished there were a stream for bathing, and put that out of their minds.

Suddenly Samaire looked around with wide eyes. Her voice was close to panic. "I — we know not which way the road lies!"

Cormac mac Art smiled at her. "We do, unless there's been a visitor in the night, and he so silent we heard him not. Follow."

Leading the horses, they followed. Their direction was marked by the bush Cormac had deliberately broken. A few feet farther on, he paused to pluck forth a gleaming brooch, which was pinned to the

166

bark of a linden.

Samaire began, "How — "

Ceann answered with a chuckle: "Our clever Cormac stuck that there last night, to mark our way back! You and I'd have been lost for certain, sister."

On they went, and Cormac retrieved the slender chain of gold that dangled from the rough bark of an oak. A little farther another brooch twinkled in the thin rays of sunlight that fought their way through the thick leafy boughs; the brooch was pinned to a tree, above the level of Cormac's head. It was unnecessary. Past it they saw a thinning of the trees, and bright sunlight.

Cormac's arm swept straight up and he twisted his head about at the two following him. "Not a sound! Be still! Listen!"

Holding the horses in tight check, the three stood motionless. In seconds, hearing what had caused Cormac to warn them was no problem. Many equine feet rapped the road and so rapidly were they moving that their galloping hoof-falls formed a steady drumming. Those fast-moving horses came closer and closer, and then through the thinning trees the three fugitives saw them.

They went by at the gallop: a troop of eleven men, all well mounted. Red leather armour gleamed over their white tunics. They were past within the space of two breaths — though the trio of watchers in the forest was unconsciously holding air in motionless chests.

A cloud of dust eddied in the rattling drumming wake of the soldiers of Eogan of Munster. The sound of the galloping hooves receded rapidly.

"My grief!" Ceann muttered. "Those be men sent to . . . *escort* us — "

"Aye," Cormac said. "Our escort. *Back* to Cashel that is, and close-watched '*hospitality!*' "

Samaire's voice held despair. "Vexation upon us!"

167

Cormac turned back to them. Though his eyes were narrowed into invisibility, he was smiling. "Not at all. We wait but for the stir of the shadow across that branch yonder, and . . . we *follow* those north-bent soldiery!"

Prince Ceann Ruadh grinned.

They trusted to Cormac; it was he waited until the dust settled and there was surely no sign of their being seen by the men riding so speedily ahead. Also, though he had not bothered mentioning it to his companions, he satisfied himself that there was not another troop riding behind the first. There was not; neither Eogan nor the commander of the little battalion had thought that their quarry — their prey? — might come onto the road behind them.

The three did. They rode without stopping for a mile after plodding, saddle-creaking mile — and, in Cormac's case, they were butt-breaking miles as well. Now and again when they topped a hill or came upon a long level stretch of the narrow road, they saw dust well ahead, and knew their seekers remained unsuspicious and in great haste.

"What do we do if they stop to break bread and catch sight of us," Samaire asked, "or if they leave the road as we did and we overtake them?"

"An excellent question. Ceann! Heard you Samaire?"

Ceann nodded, and his hand went across his flat belly to touch the pommel of his sword, for weapons and armour had been in the packs Cormac had brought from Cashel and its well-stocked market.

Cormac shook his head. "No, we'll not fight them unless we absolutely must. They were not bow-armed, which indicates they want us alive, as we might expect. It also means that they could not bring us down on the run even should they try. Next, they have been riding longer than we, and at the gallop. No, an it should out that we overtake them or are seen, we clap heels and

168

ide!"

Ceann wagged his head. "It's kings that are going a-begging for good counsel without you at their sides, Cormac mac Art!"

"Mac Cuchulain," Samaire murmured, gazing at the big scarred man, her green eyes full of regard.

They rode, beneath a sky that was a great vacant tent of azure and white, set with the blinding jewel of the sun. Twice they passed farm-wagons, and once a family in a field of flax. All waved merrily, as they did when they met a cart-riding family, and another time two men on foot. Cormac was sorry that they all had to eat dust, but there was no help for it.

The sun was well into the west when a line of trees marked a waterway. Without a word Cormac swung his mount from the road.

Soon the blowing beasts had been watered. They were given a short while to munch grass while their riders wet themselves in a lazy, rocky-bottomed stream that was broad but far from deep. Refreshed and remounted, they rode splashingly up that creek for the distance of a couple of what the Romans called after their fighting men's pace: *miles*. At a ford they left the water and rode along the opposite bank for another mile.

Night was starting to fall when they came upon the peasant lad. Ten or so years of age, he was just leaving the creek's bank with five nice trout on his line. He stared at them, without apparent fear.

"A good catch!" Cormac said in greeting.

The boy beamed and hefted his fish, but said, "Three days gone I caught seven in the same space!"

"There are good days and bad," Cormac said, "and it's glad I am you are fisherman enow to make them all good! We have come far . . . tell me where we now find ourselves."

The boy stared. "Why, near the rath of my father Mogh mac Findtain!"

Samaire chuckled; Cormac nodded without smiling. "Ah, and it's a good man he must be to have a son who's such a fisherman. This may sound strange to ye, mac Mogh, but — we've come over from Leinster, and have lost track of distance. Are we — "

The boy smiled. "Why, ye be in Meath, pilgrims, 'twixt Shannon and Slieve Sidhe — could ye not tell how greener the land was?"

Ceann laughed at the boy's chauvinism. His companions smiled; they had succeeded in escaping Munster, and avoiding both its soldiery and the land of Leinster, and were well across the border into Meath. Without incident, they had gained ground well to the northeast and in a land where surely none wished them harm. Meath — and up ahead: ancient Rath Tara, and the court of the High-king.

They were not averse to accompanying the boy, Lugh, to his home. It was a lovely little house of good planking, built so that it backed up into a hillside which formed its rear wall.

Short, unshaven Mogh mac Findtain and his wife and other son were told that the pilgrims were Ceann, a poet and minstrel, and his wife Samaire who also played, and that Cormac, traveling with them by chance, hoped to take service with the Ard-high in Tara.

The farm family was happy to be entertained and forget awhile flax and cows and the vagaries of weather that ruled their lives, bringing them both joy and sadness. Their shared food was increased by the last of the bread and cheese and meat the travelers had with them, and there was foaming milk for all.

Without doubt Mogh's family was both surprised and well pleased on the morning of the morrow, too, when they discovered what their guests had left behind. There were gifts of gold and silver worth a year's crop, and the note that Ceann had picked out in Ogham, in hopes someone among the family could read:

"Say you did uncover these at your plowing, friends."

The prince had chosen to sign the note with the old Ogham characters surely recognized by anyone: Anu, and Grannus, and Cu Roi mac Dairi. Ancient gods of Eirrin those were, the last a habitual traveler who carried the sword in martial conquest all over the ridge of the world, but who had never reddened his blade in Eirrin.

And the three had birthed a new legend.

"Now we've gained escape from Eogan's hospitality," Cormac told his companions as they proceeded at a sedate walk. "And good relations have been preserved with Cashel and his good son Senchann in whose debt we all are. For we bought all we took, and left behind as much, and shed no blood in Munster or on Munstermen."

"It were well done, Cormac, and it's good to know we have a friend in Munster."

Aye, Cormac mused, for already he was considering the future, and its possibilities. *And a good friend Senchann will be when he one day sits Munster's throne . . . and once we've set you, Ceann Ruadh, on the throne of Leinster!*

But as to that he kept his counsel. There was much to risk and still to be feared, ahead. The prospect of toppling Feredach was surely far in the future. First there was the matter of the High-king, and the Great Council, and . . . the reception given the exile, mac Art, and the decision he risked as to his very personal future. If the High-king and Council did nought about Samaire and Ceann — as Cormac expected, since Feredach was king by order of birth — they were still a prince and princess. In exile they'd be, aye. But safe, and well-treated on account of their births. They need not fear Feredach in Tara!

As to Cormac of Connacht, though . . . he risked his life, and well he knew it. He might be slain out of

171

hand on the old charge. Or there might be a stay, while the Council and perhaps the Druids considered and decided — and *then* had him put to death for breaking the King's Peace, twelve years agone.

He said nothing of any of this, as they rode through Meath.

This road, they learned, led not to Tara. To their right lay a forest. Beyond it, a broad road would lead them to the capital!

Thanking the peasant for his information and guiding their horses carefully around his laden cart, they entered the woods by a lane wide enough for but two to ride abreast. These, without discussion or decision, were Cormac and Samaire; Ceann's horse paced contentedly along in their wake.

The horses plodded sedately along the shade-darkened road. Trees rose rustling all about, thickly crowding the narrow lane through the forest. Within the foliage, birds trilled, whistled and cheeped, while insects maintained a steady accompaniment of hum and buzz. The shade grew deeper and deeper, for the broad forest completely obscured the lowering disk of the sun. The three travelers cared not. They were in Meath, and ahead lay the broad road to and past TullaMor to Tara.

The sun was low and the lane darker than twilight when the highwaymen accosted them.

The first two bandits appeared simultaneously, one on either side of the lane. They stepped from the bushes at the edge of the trees, and each had arrow nocked to drawn bow.

"Hold!" called the man with the bushy black beard, staring into Cormac's eyes. "Hold and keep your hands where they are."

From just behind the halted horses of Cormac and Samaire, two more men appeared. Each held drawn dagger. One grinned, gazing hungrily at Samaire.

172

Cormac's trained eyes took stock and reported quickly to his trained warrior's mind. All four thieves wore leggings and leather jerkins. That was their only armour; though one of the vests was embossed with steel, none wore mail. Helmets covered the two dagger-men to the brows. A sword was sheathed at the hip of each. One of the dagger-wielders also bore a shield, small and round.

The trio of pilgrims sat unequivocally still. Samaire's horse shifted nervously; she held a tight rein-hand. Cormac did not so much as glance back at Ceann.

"What will ye have of us, countrymen?"

The blackbeard smiled. "Why, three handsome horses, and whatever else ye'd care to contribute to four poor, worthy countrymen!"

"Nothing!" Ceann's voice lashed out, from behind Cormac.

"Why then we'll just have to take what we fancy from your *corpses*, minstrel. Whirl your mount and flee if ye dare — but when ye hear the twang of two bowstrings, ye'll know your abandoned companions are dead!"

Both arrows were aimed at Cormac's chest and one of the two dagger-wielders stood three feet from his left side. The other began edging back, toward Ceann. At this distance, Cormac thought, his concealed armour was not likely to turn those arrowheads of iron or steel.

"Naturally," the bowman with the broken nose and bushy brown mustache said, "we'll have to see what . . . trinkets, *milady* has hid in her clothes!"

His comrades laughed.

Cormac looked down at the dagger-man to his left. "Stay back," he said, "I'm dismounting."

Before any could consider or demur, he drew his right leg up and over. He slid down, wincing and twisting his face when his feet struck the ground and his inner thighs objected vehemently.

The man with the dagger grinned broadly. "Thisun's *crippled*," he called, and stepped forward with new confidence.

Cormac's left arm swung out to attract eye and dagger — and for balance. It was his right foot did the damage; it drove directly up into the fork of the smiling fellow's leggings.

The smile became a look of horror and pain, and the beginning sweep of the dagger terminated in mid-stab. Rather than draw steel, Cormac clutched the man's right wrist with one clamping hand and his throat with the other. Crouching, for the man was shorter than he, Cormac swung him rightward, toward the bowmen.

Two bowstrings twanged, almost in unison. Cormac heard one of the archers cry out in dismay, knowing he'd loosed shaft too fast. At the same time, there were two *thunk* sounds and the man he held jerked. His dark eyes went wide, terribly wide, and his mouth gaped in a silent scream. The highwayman went limp, with both his comrades' arrows in his back.

At the same time, Samaire was clapping heels sharply inward. Her horse lunged forward while Cormac held his limp human shield before him.

The blackbearded man was too swift in his archery for his own good. In a clever attempt to down the human-shielded man who dared resist, he loosed a second arrow. It hissed between the knees of his late companion, but only snipped Cormac's leggings as it rushed on behind him on its downward course. If more slowly drawn and nocked, that goosefeathered shaft might well have stopped Samaire's forward rush.

Instead, her bounding horse covered the ten feet between it and the bow-armed highwayman in little more than two blinks of an eye.

With arrow to string but not full-drawn, the mustached man saw the sorrel bearing down on him.

He yelled. In desperation he tried to dodge aside. Only partway he ducked. Then he was struck by the galloping horse and sent flying. Into the bushes he went, his arrow arcing a few feet to drop harmlessly. His bow cracked loudly against a tree. And already Samaire was hauling her mount leftward.

Behind him, Cormac heard a shout, a scraping clink, and a cry of pain, followed by the pound of hooves. But his attention was fixed on the blackbeard, who now forewent attacking him. The man swung his drawn bow and third arrow toward the nearer danger: the woman whose horse had downed his confederate.

Cormac mac Art bellowed with all his throat and slung the shielding corpse from him. His shield hung on his saddle; he had known he'd be feathered if he tried to loose and lift it. He rushed forward. His arms formed a streaking X across his belly and his hands filled themselves with sword and dagger. Fury, the danger to Samaire, and a flood of adrenalin drove away all thought of discomfort in the muscles of his thighs and buttocks.

All he thought of now was the wetting of his steel.

The black-bearded man had jerked at the ferocious yell behind him, as Cormac hoped. Nevertheless his bow twanged. The arrow rushed only a few feet — and struck between Samaire's breasts. With a cry, she was rocked back and aside, and fell from her horse.

"SAMAIRE!"

Past Cormac galloped Prince Ceann Ruadh. From his gaping mouth tore a shout of horror and rage; the redness of anger was on his brain. The magnificent muscles of his white-stockinged mount bunched and rippled to hurl it forward like a juggernaut. His rider clutched the beast's barrel sides with both legs; above his head his sword hissed in a flashing arc of silvery steel.

175

All happened at once. The archer started to turn and shrieked as he saw grim death rushing down upon him; Ceann's sword began its downward sweep; the horse plunged past the highwayman; the sword cut down through the air with a moan. When it struck, the sound was as of the splitting of a dropped melon.

On past plunged Ceann, reeling in the saddle from the ferocity of his prodigious chop, desperately gripping with both legs. His reddened sword dripped. Cormac stared at the highwayman. Driven to his knees by the force of the sword-blow, blackbeard remained there, with his face divided into scarlet halves from crown to lips. Then he toppled forward, and his legs jerked in spasms.

Blood of the gods, Cormac thought, *the man fights like a fiend from the Norsemen's Hel!*

Cormac turned to look back. He wanted to rush to Samaire, but there was the other dagger-man; until Cormac mac Art had himself seen a man fall and lie still but for the blood-kicks, he considered him enemy still.

The fellow was no longer an enemy. Ceann had chopped off his dagger hand, and his horse seemed to have bowled the man over and then stepped with a hind hoof directly on his face. His head was a flattened mass of gore.

Cormac ran to Samaire. Just as he reached her, Ceann's horse dug in its forehooves and the prince's feet thudded to the ground beside the other man. Both of them cried Samaire's name.

"Uch," she said, remaining flat on her back. "It's a month I'll be bruised, and surely this pain when I draw breath will be with me for days and days!"

The two men stared down at her. The arrow lay atop her tunic, which it had pierced in the center of her chest. There was no blood, but within the rent in the fabric there was a ruddy glint.

Lifting a hand to her neck, she tugged at the slender chain of gold there; from within her outer tunic she lifted a disk of the same metal. It was some two inches in diameter — and its center was concave, bent inward.

"He ruined my medallion, too!"

Shock and awful fear abruptly broken as they realized the medallion had not only saved her life but kept her unscratched, Ceann and Cormac burst into loud laughter that threatened to go out of control.

"You idiots wouldn't bray so an *your* chests hurt with every breath!" Samaire railed, and her lower lip ran out.

Chapter Sixteen: To the Fair!

> *These in fullness were there,*
> *The clans of Rudraighe*
> *without lasting grief —*
> *To be under the protection of the Fair,*
> *Every third year, without prohibition.*

—"The Great Fair"; tr. O'Curry

Three highwaymen were dead. The fourth was unconscious, scratched and bruised, and his wrist sprained. Nevertheless he walked at the end of a rope after the three he'd sought to rob. And it was company he had behind their horses, for they dragged the bodies of his dead comrades.

"We've eased Meath of four forest-thieves," Cormac pointed out. "It's welcome we'll be, with the proof stirring the dust behind our mounts!"

It was thus the three travelers reached Tullamor, and it was within the house of its lord they partook of a sampling of that town's food and drink.

The thieves' bodies hung for all to see at the town gate — all four bodies. They were only too well known; Carbri Black-beard and his band had been at their dark work in the Wood of Brosna for over a year, and it was many travelers they'd robbed. Too, the ruthless quartet had six counts of rape and seven deaths to their debit.

"Carry this with ye to Tara," Tullamor's lo[rd] Milcho told them, "and show it to the High-king, fo[r] even he knows of Carbri Black-beard and hi[s] murderers." He handed the sealed message, to Cormac, who passed it to Ceann. "But tarry here, friends and heroes three, at least until we've brought forth the loot they'd hid!"

The fourth highwayman had been in a great hurry to tell precisely where he and his companions in thievery had cached their booty — once his eyeballs were threatened. He had been rewarded for that loosing of his thief's tongue. It was the swift end of hanging he received, rather than the uglier and much slower forms of death the citizens of Tullamor had clamored for. Drawn mercifully up with rope about his neck, he'd messed his leggings and danced in air. Only the breeze moved his companions at the ends of their ropes, and soon they were joined by the victim of Samaire's plunging horse, and now swift justice; he danced not long.

"Their booty belongs to its original owners," Ceann said. "And what remains unclaimed is for Tullamor. We're for Tara and the Fair, Lord Milcho, and despite your kindness we'd be on the road at break of day."

"Kindness!" Milcho exploded. "Why your name will be on Meathish tongues for years to come, Celthair, and your valiant sister Ess — and yours, Cormac, who slew first!"

Samaire smiled rather wistfully. "In Munster where we slew Picts, we be called the offspring of Cuchulain," she said. "In the home of Mogh mac Findtain of lower Meath, it's Anu and Grannus and Curoi we are. Now it's back to Celthair and Ess for me and thee, brother."

Milcho was frowning. "I have not . . . your true names then, heroes of Eirrin?"

179

"Lord Milcho," Cormac said, "ye have not. It's ...mac mac Art of Connacht I am. As for my ...mpanions . . . they be lord and lady. An you'll wait ...l we're after reaching Tara Hill, a messenger will ...oon bring ye word of their true names."

Frowning, Milcho looked from one of his guests to the next. "Lord and lady?"

"Cormac," Ceann said, "has for once said too much. But aye Lord Milcho. We travel with our names in hooded cloaks, and I believe ye'll soon know the reason, once we have held converse with the Ard-righ."

A while longer Milcho mac Roigh gazed in frowning puzzlement on his guests. Then he heaved a sigh and touched the table near Ceann's arm. "Well, my lord and lady, I shall rephrase my words to the High-king then, and say no more; no man need tell all his business lest the crows fly off with it. Too, when ye've done what ye three have, why — " Milcho broke off. He pointed triumphantly.

"Prince Senchann!"

His three visitors laughed, then apologized. Nay, they were not of the Eoghannacta of Munster, and surely even disguise-loving Senchann mac Eogain came not so far north in his minstrelish role.

Again Milcho sighed. "There are stories," he said, but he did not trouble to add more of Senchann, who was already becoming legend. Milcho beamed upon the trio, pausing to regain composure.

"Well, my goblet has gone empty, and it's filled I like it best! My lord, my lady . . . mac Art?"

Samaire shook her head; careful Ceann peered into his cup. But Cormac extended his with alacrity, without a glance within.

"Aye, Lord Milcho, my throat would welcome a wetting with more dairlin drops of the dew of Tullamor!"

The three, their finery now undisguised, set off

once more on the morning of the morrow. Now there were many on the broad road, the Slighe Dala, one of five great highways that led to Tara of the Kings. It was the last day of July but one, and brightly clad pilgrims from every walk of life thronged to the capital for the great Fair. It preceded the less festive but more important — to some — gathering of Feis Mor.

The air was silent by the shrill voices of pipes and flutes and gaily chattering people.

The three heroes of Brosna Wood were unable to trot their restless mounts amid that teeming pilgrimage, much less gallop to reach their goal the faster. Other horses plodded along, some gaily decorated draft-animals, others richly caparisoned, prancing pacers. The latter were sat by lords and ladies in fine fabrics and jewels that flashed and twinkled from settings of gold and silver. One-horse carts there were too, and some drawn by teams of two big-hoofed horses or stolid oxen with decorated yokes. The carts were laden with produce or the handiwork of many a long winter's even, and mayhap after the fair more than one of the proud nobles would ride home wearing some sample of the superb workmanship that now burdened peasantish carts.

People of festive mind called out gaily to each other. Smiles, like precious metals and gems and brightly-coloured clothing, challenged the sun for brilliance. Men and women alike, aye and children and beasts of burden, stood tall and proud. Hair was fresh-trimmed and well washed, bedizened with ribands and pearls, bands of silver or fine-coloured leather set with stones, and sometimes gold. Precious or no, the stones were bright and twinkly and varicoloured, and proudly worn.

It was Fair time, and there were no Munstermen in the throng, or Connachtish or Meathish fairgoers yet either, no Ulstermen or Leinsterish travelers to Tara this day. All were Eirish. The Irish gathered

181

together in peace, and with high happiness.

Insofar as it were possible, there were no peasants or merchants, no creditors or debtors; and a lowborn son or daughter of the soil was as one with the high-chinned scions of well-known old houses and their richly draped and dazzlingly bejeweled ladies.

All were of Eirrin, and free, and proud of both.

No creditor held power over those in his debt, for such was the law of Fair-time; lenders had even to return, on request, the personal possessions pledged against debts. This so that all the sons and daughters of Eirrin might hold high their heads on this great occasion, be they descendants of Celts or Sidhe, of fishermen or warriors or poets, of the ua-Neill or from generations of raisers of flax or snorting swine. All were free at the Fair. And all were safe, for the King's Peace prevailed, on pain of death — as Cormac mac Art of Connacht well remembered.

As the day wore on, the trio that had been all but deified at Tulla Mor was recognized, and that noisily. The "fighting minstrel Celthair" was prevailed upon to strum and sing. Glad Ceann was that he had been at the composing in his head of a few lines concerning the encounter in the Wood of Brosna.

> *"They closed full fast on every side!*
> *No slackness was there found;*
> *And many a fierce highwayman*
> *Lay bleeding on the ground!"*

"Many?" Samaire murmured, smiling. Her brother, undaunted, sang too of the Fair:

> *"Trumpets, harps, wide-mouthed horns;*
> *Cruisechs, tympanists, without pause —*
> *Poets, balladeers and troupes of*
> *agile jugglers,*
> *Pipers, fiddlers, even outlaws!*

182

> *Bow-men and flute players,*
> *The host of chattering flyers like elves,*
> *Shouts and loud bellowers*
> *At the Fair do all these exalt themselves!"*

Laughter and cheers rose roundabout from throats highborn and low-, and snow-haired oldsters skipped with the young and very young. Bright garments whirled and fluttered. Someone called out happily, and Cormac turned away, for a man did not forget a Connactish accent, not even after twelve years and more.

THE GREAT FAIR

—from O'Curry's translation of the old Gaelic, with
amendments

Listen, O Eire-sons of the monuments!
    Ye truth-upholding hosts!
    Until you have from me,
    from every source,
    The history of famed Teamar called Tar

Tara, the hill of a splendid fair,
    With a widespread unobstructed green.
    The hosts who came to celebrate it
    —On it they contested their noble races.

The renowned field
is the high ground of kings,
    The dearly loved of noble clans;
    There are many meeting mounds
    For their ever-loved ancestral hosts.

To mourn for queens and for kings,
    To denounce aggression and tyranny,
    Often were the fair hosts in summer
    Upon the smooth brow of noble old Tara.

Heaven, earth, sun, moon and sea;
    Fruits, fire, and riches;
    Mouths, ears, alluring eyes,
    Feet, hands, noses and teeth —

The people of the Gaedhil did celebrate
   In·Tara, to be highly boasted of,
   A fair without broken law or crime,
   Without a deed of violence,
   without dishonour.

On the first day of August without fail,
   They repaired thither every third year;
   There aloud with boldness
   they proclaimed
   The rights of every law, and the restraints:

Not to sue, levy, or controvert debts—
   To abuse the steeds in their career
   Is not allowed to contending racers;
   Elopements, arrests, distraints . . .

That no man goes into the woman's
Airecht,
   That no women go into the Airecht of
   fair clean men;
   That no abduction is heard of,
Nor repudiation of husbands or of wives.

Whoever transgresses the law of the
assembly
   (Which of old was indelibly writ)
   Cannot be spared for family connection,
   But must die for his transgression.

There are its many privileges—
   Trumpets, cruits, wide-mouthed horns,
   Cuisigs and tympanists without
   weariness,
   Poets and lesser rhymesters.

Fenian tales of the Finn, an untiring
entertainment—
Destruction, cattle-preys, Courtships,
Inscribed tablets, and books of trees,
Satires, and sharp-edged Runes . . .

Proverbs, maxims, royal precepts
And the truthful instructions of Fithal,
Occult poetry, topographical
etymologies,
The precepts of Cairbre and King
Cormac;

The Feasts, with the great Feast of Tara;
Fairs, with the fair of Emania.
Annals are there verified:
Every division into which Eirrin was
divided.

The history of the household of Tara—not
insignificant!
The knowledge of every territory of
Eirrin,
The history of the women of illustrious
families:
Of courts, Prohibitions, Conquests;

The noble Testament of Cathair the Great
To his descendants, to direct steps of
royal rule;
Each one sits in his lawful place
So that all attend to them and
listen, listen.

Pipers, fiddlers, chain-men,
  Bow-men, and tube-players;
  A crowd of babbling painted masks,
  Roarers and bellowers loud!

These all exert their utmost powers
  For the magnanimous king of the
  Barrow;
  Until the noble king in proper measure
  bestows
  Upon each art its rightful meed.

Elopements, slaughters, musical
choruses,
  The accurate synchronisms of noble
  races,
  The succession of the sovereign kings of
  Meath—
  Their battles, and their stern valour.

Such is the arrangement of the Fair,
  By the lively ever happy host;
  May they receive from the gods
  A land with choicest fruits!

Chapter Seventeen: Champion of Rath Cumal

> *Steeds, swords, beautiful chariots,*
> *Spears, shields, human faces,*
> *Dew, fruits, blossoms and foliage,*
> *Day and night, a heavy flooded shore!*

—"The Great Fair"; tr. O'Curry

Long ago the Milesian settlers of Eirrin cam
from Spain, and it was after a Spanish woman tha
Tara was named. The first Milesian High-king
Eremon, had as wife Tea, the daughter of Spain'
king. After she died and was laid to rest here, th
sprawling eminence came to be called "Tea-Mur": th
burying-place of Tea. In other forms the word wa
Teamhair, and Teamair, and Temair and Tamara—
and so eventually Tara.

Called "Tara Hill," it was more: a grea
sprawling high place covering full twenty acres
Smaller *duns* or hills rose on it, and each had becom
the natural site for a *rath* or walled enclosure. Seve
such raths rose on Tara. Each was like a small towr
with imposing buildings that housed the nobles, a
well as lesser ones for their relatives, and the necessar
outbuildings. Round about pressed close the thatche
roofs of the houses of the common folk, whic
crowded too the plain around the foot of the broa

high-land. Every structure was of wood. Some were decorated and strengthened with bronze; a few were actually faced with the ruddy metal.

It was Ollam Fodla in the misty past had given Tara her pre-eminence over the emerald land, by calling together the kings in the first triennial council or parliament: the Great Feis. The Feis-mor had now been held on Tara Hill each third year for a half-score of centuries.

The greatest of the rath-duns was that of the High-king or *Ard-righ*. Within were one house for each Irish king who came to the Feis, and a *grianan* or sun-house for their women-folk and attendants. This structure High-king Cormac had raised two hundred years agone, as he had the Stronghold of Hostages and the House of a Thousand Soldiers, and the Star of Bards. In the latter met the filays and seanachies, the brehons and ollams: poets, historians/storytellers, judges and learned doctors of law and letters.

Most magnificent of all—aye, more so than the residence of the Ard-righ himself—was the banqueting hall and meeting-place, the Mi-Chuarta.

Ceann and Samaire of Leinster and Cormac mac Art would have their time in that mighty structure, but now it was Fair-time in Tara of the Kings.

Everywhere were pennons and brightly coloured tents and striped awnings, and what was not bartered for and sold was not worth the having. Horsebacked arrivals could hardly move amid all the colourful—and noisy—press. Cormac was just beginning to wonder where he and his companions would take their nightly rest when a contralto voice called out Samaire's name, loudly and with much surprise.

Cormac could not be certain who had so shouted, for more than one stared at the mounted trio. Nor would he have expected the hail to have emanated from the young woman in whose ornately-coiffed topaz hair glittered and sparkled a seeming thousand

189

pearls and small blue stones. Tall she was, and willowy in a long heliotrope robe and silken cloak of deep mauve sewn all with silver crescents and moons.

Samaire picked that woman from out the throng at once, for she recognized her—and cautioned her to silence with finger to lips.

It was thus Cormac mac Art met Samaire's cousin Aine, wife of the noble prince Cumal Uais of the ancient Boar sept, and he of the ua-Neill. Thus too did Cormac and his companions come into one of the noble houses on high Tara, where they were well-housed and fed and treated with honour as royal relatives.

A man of rising forty was Cumal Uais, who had lost much hair above and replaced it with much belly below. He was warm enough to his wife's cousins and their "protector." It was he who handled the exchanging of their personal property: the balance of the Viking loot that had seen them all across Eirrin. Ruddy-faced Cumal and milk-skinned Aine would keep secret the trio's identity for the few more days they wanted. The High-king was more than passing busy with the Fair.

There was a gifting on both sides, with the guests receiving far more than their hosts; Aine, naturally, was horrified by Samaire's story but delighted by the unexpected visit.

Cormac met burly Tigernach, who'd be representing the house of Cumal the Noble in the martial games that would be the major Fair event two days hence. Cormac and Tigernach agreed to Cumal's urging, and met under "arms": shields and swords of hardened wood, blunt of both point and edge. With nothing to gain by putting defeat on his host's champion, Cormac allowed himself to be put down, narrowly, in three several skirmishes.

Himself no weapon man, Cumal only beamed and nodded, without knowing that Tigernach's opponent had not striven his best.

But Tigernach knew. "It's holding back ye've been, Cormac mac Othna," he said quietly. "Ye could have defeated me at any time, not so?"

Cormac looked at the man wearing the Boar-and-the-Red of Cumal Uais.

"What is a man to do, who won't lie?" he asked piously—and falsely, for he was no *amadan* or fool, and had lied many times. He stood before Tigernach a liar even now, both in name and deeds: the one was invented, the other hardly his best.

"Enter the arms-striving contests yourself," the thicker man said, "and show all what prowess is! It's twice now I have claimed the second honours, with first going to Bress of the Long Hand, mac Keth of Leinster. Now I know he respects my ability, and we will see what comes out this year. But it's yourself could drive the sneer from off his supercilious face."

"Bress mac Keth . . . with sorrel-horse hair and feet on him like loch-boats?"

Tigernach chuckled. "O'course! All know Bress of the Long Hand—and feet!—champion at every Fair these nine years have seen Leinster hog all the honours."

Aye, Cormac mused, *I know him. But not in that way, the mocking sneering young wolf sent to arrest or bring death on me these twelve years agone!* Bress had volunteered for that task that many wanted not, Cormac remembered, for Bress mac Keth was far from fond of mac Art of Connacht. Better at arms and far less arrogant and better liked, Cormac had received the Command of Fifty that Bress thought should have been his.

Twelve long years ago. And now Bress was champion of Eirrin.

"It's yourself must put him down, Tigernach mac Roigh,for I have no wish to enter the contests at arms."

Tigernach sighed. "Because ye be guest in my lord

191

Cumal's house and would not contest with his champion, whom ye know ye'd best!"

"For reasons of my own."

They were crossing the practice field to the bronze-girt house, into which the smiling Cumal and his belly had already disappeared. Tigernach said, "Cormac."

"Aye?"

"A gift to me, Cormac!"

Cormac sighed, and waited for Tigernach to ask his boon.

"Contest with me again, in private, and with might and main!"

"Tigernach . . . and if it's harm I bring to your hand or arm? Ye'd be no fit representative of your lord, and I'd be disgraced."

"We'll be wearing then full armour, and faulconer's gloves."

Tigernach pushed the more; Cormac agreed. Armoured, helmeted, gloved, in a privy place they met with buckler and wooden sword.

Five times was defeat put on Tigernach, though he strove his best. And he was naught but delighted. Yet Cormac shook off the man's urgings that he enter the "Rites of Srreng," after the champion of many centuries gone; 'twas Srreng who'd cut off the hand of the De Danaan king in the war for Eirrin.

At last Cormac went surly and worse, so that Tigernach left off urging and each went his own way.

He's not enough confidence on him, Cormac thought, *and it will be his defeat.* For a man without confidence was a lamb among foxes.

Caer, a busty girl who served Lady Aine, made heated eyes at Cormac mac Art that afternoon, and they dallied in the room provided him by Cumal. Nor did the passionate wench know that his mind was first much distracted by remembrances and dark thoughts on Bress mac Keth, and later that he thought only of

192

Samaire. Knowing not where his mind had been but only that his body had pleased and him a genuine weapon man with scars and iron muscles, Caer left happy and with stars dancing in her eyes.

Samaire's appearance at dinner that night did naught to aid Cormac's mental state. Gone was his companion on sea and half the length of Eirrin, the sword-girt warrior with her tall boots. The beautifully gowned and bejeweled woman at table, her orange hair elaborately ringleted and besprent with pearls and tiny red stones, was the Lady Samaire, daughter of Ulad and Princess of Leinster.

To the exiled son of Art it was as if an ocean had appeared between them, and him without bark or sail.

It's girls like Caer for you, exile and riever, he told himself, and the others wondered at his moroseness. He had turned his mind to thoughts of leaving both Tara and Eirrin, this time forever. Samaire watched, and knew there was an ache on him.

It was no happy son of Art went to his bed early that night. The fact that sleep refused to come on him made him the angrier. He was aware, past midnight, of a commotion elsewhere in the Rath of the Boar, but considered it no business of his.

Hearing the stealthy opening of his door, he wrapped his fingers around dagger hilt and waited, holding his breath. But Cormac soon smiled; the hooded visitor was seen to be small in the moonlight. *Caer,* he thought, *or another the silly girl blabbed to!*

He was wrong. The visitor who came so stealthily to him in the night was no servant, nor even of Meath, nor a girl either. She was a woman, whose orange-red hair had lately flashed with jewels and pearls. Now it was down, and flowing loose, for it was not as a princess nor yet even a noble that Samaire came to Cormac.

Next day he learned the cause of last night's commotion. An angry and shattered Cumal Uais announced that his champion was ill; indeed he feared the man had been poisoned. Now no less than two priests of the Jesus-god were with Tigernach. A Druid waited impatiently without, for he'd not set foot in the room occupied by Patrick's followers—nor would they remain, were he to enter.

Cormac visited Tigernach. The man was ill. Both head and lower bowel objected to their existence, he said, with weakness upon his voice and big warrior's hands. The two men talked, quietly and at length. Then Cormac walked, with his mind turned in, and after a long while he went to his room and fetched his sword.

Astonishment was on Lord Cumal when his guest approached him, grim of face, and sword-girt. "What means this, Cormac mac Othna?"

Cormac tugged forth the sword slowly, with his left hand. He transferred it to his right, but by the blade. Then he extended the hilt to the other man.

"It means I come to offer fealty and service to the House and person of Cumal Uais of the ua-Neill, and hope it will be accepted . . . until Fair's end."

Cumal blinked, frowning. "But . . . why man, ye be guest in this house!"

"Aye. And the man who—secretly from yourself and at Tigernach's hard urging—did put defeat on him five times on the day just passed. I claim right to be called champion of Rath Cumal—and to wear your colours on the morrow my lord, in the Rites of Srreng!"

Chapter Eighteen: The Championship of Eirrin

> *"There hath not come to the battle gory,*
> *Nor hath Eirrin nursed upon her breast,*
> *There hath not come off sea, or land,*
> *Of the sons of Kings, one of better fame.*
>
> *There hath not come to the body-cutting*
> *combat,*
> *There hath not been aroused by manly*
> *exertion,*
> *There hath not put up shield on the*
> *Field of swords,*
> *Thine equal, O mighty son of Art."*

—Ceann Ruadh, "The Minstrel-King"

The Boar faced the Stag in the Rites of Srreng, and the latter smiled with confidence. For who knew aught of this helmeted, bushy-mustached champion of Rath Cumal of Meath, with his slitted eyes and his long roan-hued braids?

All about them clustered the fairgoers, held back from the area of combat only by many broad flat-topped stakes driven into the ground, and braided cord stretching from one to the next and the next, all around.

Confidently the champion of Rath Fergus

195

advanced, and waited for the other man to attempt the first blow.

He did, and it was both first and last.

Up swept sword of wood hardened to the likeness of iron, and up rose the spiral-decorated cerulean shield of Fergus's champion. Then, moving so swiftly that even some of the vast crowd of onlookers missed the act, the boar-blazoned shield slammed mightily into the lifted one. The representative of Rath Fergus of Uladh groaned aloud and staggered back. The edge of an unsharpened sword struck his right shoulder with such force that his hand twitched and sprang open to drop his own brand.

The judges were not hard put to decree that the man from Uladh would have been minus an arm, had the sword been of good steel.

Cumal was practically dancing when his victorious champion walked back to him. His eyes at least did, and so did his belly as he laughed with delight.

"Magnificent!" he cried. "Never have I seen a man put down so swiftly! Surely ye have no peer, no peer!"

His champion's voice was low and snarly. "That was the twelfth man down here this day, my lord, and already two more contend. There be many shields and toy swords betwixt me and Br—the last combat."

"It is yours, yours," Cumal enthused, "It's ours! Why ye were not so much as—he struck not one blow, or even feinted."

"The next man will not be so disrespectful of me and thus so incautious, my lord. But my main concern is this ridiculous mustache."

Cumal glanced around. All eyes were directed on the next set of combatants. He bent his red face close and spoke quietly, under the noise of the crowd.

"It will stay, man. It's the getting off of it that need concern ye—but not till tonight! As to your fine

196

dark-red locks . . . ye've only to remember they be part of your helm, Cormac, and *keep it on!*"

"Your pardon my lord," the disguised man said with ill-contained anger, "but it's *Ceann mac Cor* I am. Use that other name in someone's hearing and it's gone your smiles and hopes will be, Cumal, for you will have one champion abed and the other disqualified."

Cormac swung away from him then, and Cumal and his wife exchanged a shocked look. But the green-eyed woman with the veil-obscured face bent out around Aine to speak to them both:

"Look not so pride-smitten, my lord and cousin. You called him by an inappropriate name and he but treated you the same. You endanger his life, husband of my cousin. Oh—and if ye knew him as do I, it's happy and proud ye'd be to be called your proper name by such a man!"

A trumpet sounded amid the crowd's sudden roar; a good blow had been struck. Another winner was proclaimed, and soon two new contenders circled each other with bucklers and swords of stony-hard wood.

Wearing the red tunic and boar-blazoned shield of Rath Cumal, Cormac watched every combat—and himself fought to keep his hand from checking his mustache. He noted well the big-footed, ham-handed man in the colours of Leinster's king.

So too was Cormac watched, for Cumal had two good men set as watchdogs and protectors of his new companion. After assuring himself that Tigernach could not contend and that a false mustache and the old helmet-wig well disguised the dark Cormac, Cumal had approached the judges. They had not been swift to accept the entry of a new champion, and at the eleventh hour, with him some "Ceann mac Cor" unknown to them. Eventually they had, and now Cumal wanted none to do treachery on the man on

197

whom he set such high hopes—and, quietly, stakes Cumal of the ua-Neill was a lover of the wager, as well as of good food in quantity.

At last all had contended, and after midday' meal the second round was begun. The number Three was drawn by "Ceann mac Cor of Meath" and also by a Munsterman, a wiry fiery-haired fellow with terrible dark teeth, Iliach mong Ruadh.

The swift smaller man wore a tunic of orange and bore a bronze-faced shield on which a horse's head was picked out in black and white enamel. It was he who struck first. His sword clattered off Cormac's quickly-interposed buckler, but Iliach was away before Cormac could strike with a blow of his own. They circled, watching only each other.

Iliach feinted; Cormac ignored the partial thrust for he'd noted Iliach's gaze directed elsewhere. The smooth-rounded tip of Cormac's wooden sword struck the other's shield directly, with a loud thud and clang while Iliach's "edge" slid across the mailed thigh of "Ceann mac Cor." A trumpet sounded, but no judge called out or dropped his white cloth. Even had the sword been of the best steel, the little slice would hardly have opened Cormac's armour.

"A gentle blow such as that," Cormac said, "would not slice a bedsheet, Munsterman!"

"I *thought* ye looked like a chatter-bird," Iliach said with a tight smile, and feinted with his shield.

It was meant to be only a little diversion; the other man turned it into war, and carried the battle into Munster.

His left arm whipped across his body and his buckler met Iliach's with a terrible grating clash. Back he jerked it, his arm straightening and his powerful legs already driving him forward. His foe's swiftness was of no use to him; Iliach was hurled violently back. Even so he chopped viciously at Cormac, who was following up with a direct charge.

Held aslant, Cormac's shield guided away the wooden brand, while Cormac's rang on the top edge of Iliach's buckler. Up bobbed the shield, automatically. Then an "O-o-oh" rose from the onlookers, for the arm of Cumal's champion moved so swiftly as to blur in the air like the form of a diving eagle. His sword's rounded tip pounded against Iliach's leg just above the knee, and with such force that the Munsterish weapon man staggered.

White cloths dropped and the trumpet blared.

"Wounded" and eliminated, Iliach returned to his backers with a slight limp.

Cormac only backed to the nearest ring-stake, for the next clash was between the personal champions of the kings of Connacht and of Leinster.

Thud and clangour arose, and Cormac nodded. Bress of Leinster was strong, and had a way of using his sword to catch the other's lunges and cuts. He'd then twist his big hand to turn his opponent's sword in his grip—or force his wrist to turn the wrong way. At the same time, Bress used buckler to push, following that with a ferocious flurry of stabs and feints and cuts.

Aye, Cormac mused, and he nodded.

Connacht lost, and for a moment the eyes of Cormac and Bress met. The man looked older of course, and even more sneerily supercilious than when Cormac had known him, twelve years past.

"Ye block my view, Boar," a voice said from behind Cormac.

He turned to see a merchant of some sort, holding by the hand a boy of no more than seven years. Cormac squatted before the man, and held his buckler upright beside him, shielding the child to the shoulders. Happily grinning, the boy watched the subsequent combats from behind the shield of a champion and winner of two bouts.

Pairs of men came and went; the clash of hardwood sword on buckler tore the air again and again. Cormac won again, and Bress as well, and then each again, and the afternoon wore on, and then but four contestants remained. Drawing for foe and position, Bress and "Ceann mac Cor" again exchanged the searching looks of good weapon men.

"One," Bress announced, regarding his marker.

"Two," said the truly excellent Ailechman to Cormac's left.

"Two," Cormac echoed, and Bress affected to look disappointed.

It was sham, for he faced a man who had been as much blessed with luck as skill this day, and all four of them knew it.

The fellow gave a good defense, at least. But he was actually knocked to the trampled sward by his foeman's mighty shield-drive.

"Striking with the shield, by the gods of my ancestors!" This from the man beside Cormac, for they two had not troubled to move apart after learning they were to be opponents. "Bress of Leinster fights like a farmer wielding a plow!"

This, Cormac thought in wonder, from a man bearing the name Oisin *Pictslayer*? He sounded as though weapons were toys to him, as though he'd never drawn steel in anger or in necessary defense.

"Is use of feet forbidden here?" Cormac asked, with high innocence.

"Feet!" Oisin Pictslayer of Ailech managed to sound both scandalized and scornful.

Cormac gave him a steady, deliberately doubtful look. "Your name says ye've slain a Pict or more, Oisin—surely you made use of arms and feet and even teeth, had opportunity arisen!"

"It was *three* Picts, and I be no animal to use aught but weapons, and it is *my lord* Oisin, weapon man."

"Oisin of Ailech, it is our time to contend, and were I a Pict, it's not alive but dead ye'd be leaving here

200

today," Cormac growled wolfishly at the other man, who now looked as offended as scandalized. And Cormac added, drawling, ". . . my noble lord."

He thought, *And it's a Pictish charge ye'll soon be facing, my noble lord of the false name.*

But while the perimeter of the combat area was large, it was not huge. The man bearing the boar-shield narrowed his eyes still more, seeking a means to mount a good running charge . . . .

The trumpet's notes cut the air and trembled there. Affecting to ignore his fawning admirers and wearing a supercilious smile, Bress of Leinster watched Cormac and Oisin Pictslayer advance onto the Sward of Srreng.

Astounded spectators saw Oisin strike, saw and heard his wooden blade bang off the shield of the red-tunicked man—and saw that man break and run! His deep auburn braids streamed out behind him as he dashed directly toward the encircling watchers, and the foremost among them became suddenly anxious to possess less status. A great cry arose, of mingled wailing and anger.

It was still in voice when Cormac, at the very edge of the circle of spectators, wheeled in a broad semicircle.

Around he swung, to race back at the staring Oisin. Then many jerked violently, Oisin among them, for a ferocious shrieking cry tore from the throat of this strange champion of Cumal of Tara. His antagonist was as shaken and dumbfounded by that awful ululating cry as the onlookers—and the judges themselves. There was naught in the rules forbidding any of this, but—a charge away and then back, and with the shriek of a blood-enraged eagle on the swoop?

Round his head whirled Cormac's sword of dark wood, and fell not where any suspected — again including Oisin Pictslayer of northeasterly Ailech!

For at the last possible moment in his maniac's

201

charge, Cormac half spun, and chopped mightily down on the other man's sword-arm. Oisin groaned and staggered, trying to cling to sword and regain control of a tingling, fire-assaulted arm that wanted to dangle and be cuddled. Even as the trumpet blared and while dropped signal-cloths still fluttered in air, Cormac's rounded edge rapped Oisin's upper shield-arm, and its "point" touched his mail over his ribs with enough force to wrest another groan from the haughty noble.

Cormac backed away. His penultimate combat, like the first, was over ere it had begun. A weapon man had found a way to make a berserker's charge in the arena of Tara-town, and voices talked on it now as they would for many a day.

Oisin of Ailech, Lord of Tir Connail, the judges decided, had lost one arm, the use of the other, and most probably his life with steel betwixt his ribs. Grasping his sword-arm the defeated nobleman left the field, not without casting venomous looks at his conqueror. Once again a victorious Cormac backed up against the braided ring that encircled the area of contention.

A passing pretty young woman with much golden hair tumbling past her diamond-shaped face, and her in a gown too thin for the mental equilibrium of many, laid fingers with painted nails on Cormac's mailed arm.

"Marvelous!" she gushed breathily, with obvious excitement; her breast was heaving and flaunting its peaks against the nigh-diaphanous gown. "And whence comes that fierce cry to curdle the very blood, warrior among warrior?"

"I learned it from the Picts," Cormac told her, without turning.

Others demanded to know what he'd said, and the words were passed back and around. Soon nearly all were laughing and shouting plaudits and "Oisin

202

Pictslain!"—for the Pictslayer had got his defeat at the hands of one who had himself imitated a Pictish savage!

The lips of the woman beside Cormac were close to his ear, and her hand clung to his steelclad arm. "You . . . have slain *Picts*?"

He nodded, still without looking at her. That knowledge was spread; he had slain Picts afore; the man of Rath Cumal ua-Neill was a Pictslayer! Wagers flew thick as arrows in a siege.

A bright-eyed girl in her late teens pushed around Cormac on the side opposite his other over-civilized admirer. Spacious were her white-draped hips, bold her eyes, broad and full the bosom that occupied every available inch of her chest and was so firm as to imitate helmets strapped to her.

"How *many* Picts, you beautiful hero of a warrior?" she asked, from the throat.

Cormac mac Art looked at her, and his face was stony. "In Eirrin, in the month just passed, four on the coast of Munster, with seven witnesses that live. In Alba and among the isles . . . I cannot say, girl. Many."

Those words were handed back by anxious listeners, and back, and around among the throng.

"Call me no *girl*," the shining-eyed girl said, pressing against his shield-arm. "It is Dectaira I am, and the High-king my uncle!"

"My apologies," Cormac said, and he twisted and drew forward, for both these hot-breathed women cloyed, and others pressed close behind. "My lady girl, then."

And he went round the circle, trying to ignore the shouts and reaching hands, for it was true battle and gushing red death he knew all too well, and not people so civilized as to fawn on heroes of combats fought with the swords of boys. He halted before the end of the nobles' platform where sat Cumal, and Ainc his wife, and the veiled Samaire, and Cumal's two sons and daughter. He who was to be champion or runner-up gazed into bud-green eyes above a grass-green veil.

"I meet the honoured weapon man of the King of Leinster now, for the championship of Eirrin, my lord and ladies. A token?"

"YE WEAR MY BOAR!" Cumal shouted, with boyish gladsomeness.

Aine's hand went to a brooch she wore purely for the beauty of it and no good cause, but she remembered to glance questioningly at her husband.

"Carry this against Bress of the Long Hand," Samaire said, "and would it were Dark Feredach himself, and your sword of good steel rather than mere oak!" And she bent forward to hand Cormac a linen glove. It was of blue, the primrose of her father's house — and of Feredach's.

"Were it in my power, I'd make thee lord of lands!" Cumal cried without restraint or dignity, as his "Ceann" held high Samaire's glove, to show all that he carried Leinster blue against Leinster itself.

"Mayhap it is within my power to make yourself lord of a champion," Cormac said.

"Mind ye keep your roving eyes on your opponent," Samaire snapped from behind her green veil, "and off those eager tid-bits I see crowding you, hulking barbarian!"

Cormac smiled, and looked about overhead. "Methinks I hear the Morrigu, and her gone all green of eye," he said. As he turned away he added, "But a dairlin girl, for all that."

The Lady Aine turned to give her veiled cousin a long look. Gazing after Cormac, Samaire either affected not to notice, or did not.

Bress basked and Cormac chafed in the adulation of their admirers and well-wishers, and shot each other occasional glances. The clowning pair of "weapon men" in the combat area was called back. A trumpet rose to lips and set a note atrembling on the air. The chief judge rose. Cheers greeted his announcing the name of Bress mac Keth of Carman in Leinster, champion of every fair and twice in Tara of the Kings.

Even on those loyal supporters Bress turned a smile that was open contempt, for he was a superior man and well knew it.

Then was called the name of Ceann mac Cor, of Tara in Meath, and others shouted and cheered. Earrings landed at his feet and about him, and a steward hurried to clear the ground of those possible obstacles, that might roll beneath the feet of contending men. Cormac looked not from the ruddy, not unhandsome face of his opponent in this final passage of arms.

It was time.

Bress walked away to the opposite side of the large circle, rather than to its center. He turned to stare at Cormac, and the Leinsterman held sword and round blue buckler contemptuously at rest.

Cormac walked forward three paces.

"MEATH ADVANCES ON LEINSTER!" That call rose above the many others, and there were grins — and dark frowns from the nobles on the platform. The shout was repeated by many.

As though ambling on a summer stroll, Bress moved forward three paces.

"LEINSTER COMES TO TARA!"

It's come to that then, Cormac mac Art thought. *First I was of Connacht, and then of Leinster, and then of Dalriada in Alba, and then I strove for none but myself. Now it's all Tara and Meath I stand for, and the ancient bad feelings over the Boru Tribute that Leinster hates.*

He watched Bress, who stood still, arms down.

So he does what I do, then, Cormac mused, *and raises not sword or shield — a fine sense of drama the man has!* He glanced back. *A little farther from the people, Bress dairlin, and then we'll see.*

Cormac paced forward two paces more, and halted, and mocking Bress moved the same.

Cormac pointed, and laughter arose at the one word he called forth.

"Stay!" he ordered, as though to a sheep-herding dog, and he turned and walked back toward the spectators.

A pace away from staring, wondering faces — a dark female eye winked — Cormac wheeled, again voiced that awful savage's shout, and charged at the run.

Bress, like Cormac, was a warrior. A professional studied others, and Bress had done. He'd seen this charging tactic worked on Oisin, and to good purpose. Naturally he was prepared — as Cormac knew he would be. The Leinsterman stood his ground as the other man bore down upon him. At the last moment he pounced aside and swung a mighty chop calculated to strike hard on the back of the Meathish champion as he raced past.

Unlike fighting with steel against strangers, this sort of staged combat, with opportunity for the combatants to study one another's ways, was like a war between great generals known each to the other. B knew L's ways, and assumed that L would in all likelihood think first of tactic N. For that, B could prepare. But L knew that B knew and expected, and so he considered other tactics. Still, this B would realize, and try to prepare for a surprise, except that L knew that B knew that L knew, and . . . .

Bress erred early in the sequence of second-guessing. He assumed that the man he knew as Ceann mac Cor was launching upon him the same attack employed so successfully against Oisin. Cormac did not; he did not consider Bress an idiot, but an expert. The passing back at which Bress struck was not there. Its owner had swerved quite differently, and turned, perhaps as much as a full second before the movement of the supercilious Leinsterman.

The sword of Bress of the Long Hand clove empty air; his shield was not at all in line; the other man's unpointed sword-end drove forward low to thud against a hard-muscled belly.

Bress looked at once much surprised and much in need of breath.

The crowd went still.

That quiet was shattered by the clarion note of the trumpet, as the air was disturbed by the white cloths dropped by judges. As surprised as Bress, they nevertheless agreed to a man that the Champion of Eirrin had just been stabbed in the entrails.

Withdrawing from that swift hard lunge, Cormac heard the long horn. His peripheral vision caught the white flutter of the judging-cloths. He straightened, triumphant — and Bress' wooden sword, hard swung in a sideward sweep, crashed into his side.

The crowd muttered and roared. The judges stared. One remembered to signal the trumpeter, who blasted forth another mighty note. By that time Cormac's grunt of pain had risen and he'd backstepped two full paces, gritting his teeth. His dark slits of eyes were fixed on the man who had struck after the combat was over.

Again Bress struck, his face twisted in rage. Command of his brain was lost to him.

Angered, Cormac knew he was expected to endure or flee until men of the High-king interfered. None had lost aught but Bress; gone was his hold on the championship; gone now too were honour and good name and high esteem. But Cormac mac Art was no civilized player at the game of swords, whether he held steel or bronze or wood. He too ignored the rules.

The second hard-swung swordcut of Bress he met with a sweep of his own hardwood brand, with all his strength. At the same time he struck with his shield — and drove his foot up like any sensible man of his time or any other, to whom fighting was no game to be played at, bounded about with limits and rules.

Bress was hard jolted, three ways at once. He was commencing to double over even as he fell back. When his elbow struck the ground, his sword flew from his grasp. A spectator cried out, struck in the leg.

Almost instantly, Cormac tossed away his own wooden brand, and with expressionless face he turned to the judges. Handsomely uniformed men were rushing onto the field; Cormac let them pass, and in his face and manner was such that none touched him.

They went instead to Bress, who had broken the King's Peace.

Then the great roar swelled up, for Eirrin had a new champion, and Leinster had suffered black defeat at the hands of a man wearing her king's own colours.

Chapter Nineteen: Cormac mac Art!

> *He is brave, O gods above us!*
> *He is a noble soldier above all;*
> *Until the wave of death sweep over him,*
> *Och! He is magnificent, and beloved.*

—from "Cormac the Gael" by Ceann Ruadh

Once the nervous man in the false mustache and helmet-attached braids was away from the beaming judges and the congratulations of Eirrin's High-king, he had to cope with the delighted, cheering, and oft-fawning crowd. There were womanly offers, both spoken and silently obvious, even pleas.

Then it was the great hog of an overjoyed Cumal Uais and his loud voice Cormac had to brace. Discretion forbade the more welcome embrace of Samaire.

At last they were away, escorted by handsomely accoutred weapon men of the High-king and of Cumal — the latter hard put to maintain expressions properly stern. To the rath of Cumal they adjourned. There Cormac mac Art told the others he must visit a friend, and him disabled.

Tigernach son of Rogh sprang up from his sickbed the moment the new champion entered. Grinning so that his face was like unto the sun of noonday, Tigernach embraced the other man.

Tigernach embraced the other man.

"Hail the Champion of all Eirrin!"

Taken much by surprise, Cormac accepted the warrior's embrace, returned it with but little pressure, and edged back. With his hands high on Tigernach's upper arms, Cormac looked into his dark eyes.

"Ye recover swiftly, Tigernach mac Roigh."

Tigernach's grin strove to stretch his smiling mouth even more. "Suspicion was never on ye, was it?"

"Suspicion?"

Tigernach took his hands from his fellow warrior and swung away, laughing. He turned back to say, "I've not been ill, Cormac mac Othna. Not at all. I merely saw to it that Bress was met by the *best* weapon-man in Eirrin, rather than the third, after him and yourself. For I knew what ye'd do to him."

Cormac stared at this most noble of men, and him no noble. For a passing long while his gaze rested on Tigernach, whilst he pondered with wonder what the man had done. At last he heaved a great sigh, and not without exasperation.

"In the name of the gods my father's people swore by, Tigernach! There be none other like yourself on all the ridge of the world!"

Tigernach sobered, though his eyes remained merry.

"Though," Cormac went on thoughtfully, "there is one other I love, and a war-man he, who has put on me this same feeling. Wulfhere the Dane he is, and Skull-splitter he be called, and it's both *his* legs I've oft felt like breaking, too!"

Tigernach spread his hands and bowed his head. "I'd not take up weapons, Champion of Eirrin. Better to have both legs broke than to defend myself against you and gain red death instead!"

Again there was silence between the two men. Cormac at last snapped, "Bastard!"

Tigernach chuckled. "Och! My secret's out!"

Then they both laughed, and laughing, they left Tigernach's sickroom. With their arms each over the other's shoulders, the two weapon men went to share drink with the boisterous Lord Cumal.

They found him calculating his wager gains.

• It was in glittering company and amid fine robes of costly fabrics Cormac supped that evening, and him with his braid-pendent helmet and mustache upon him.

All round about were lords and ladies, poets and judges and historians, aye and both Druids and priests of the new faith — well separated, those robed rivals. The new champion was in company of all those who stood the highest in Tara and thus, so they at least thought, in all Eirrin.

None had any notion that their honored guest would do what he did, not even he himself. It did not come upon him until late in the meal, when there was nought left but the quaffing of ale and wine. The High-king himself raised his voice and his jeweled goblet. All others fell silent and turned expectant gazes on Erca Tireach, King of Meath and High-king of Eirrin.

"Ceann mac Cor," the king over kings called, "CHAMPION OF EIRRIN!"

On the instant there was great noise of cheering. The stamping of feet and thumping of eating utensils and fine goblets on the thick tabletops thundered in the hall.

Cormac rose, and at that moment he decided.

Up went his hand to doff his helmet with the false braids of dark red, and that hand lowered only far enough to strip away the matching mustache. He hurled both to the inlaid floor. The helmet made a

211

great clatter, rolling and skittering.

Into the silence, gazing directly into the startled eyes of the High-king, the champion called out his revelation.

"No, lord king! Long enough have I worn this demeaning disguise! Long enough have I crept about my homeland with my name and that of my father in a hooded cloak!"

Only gasps disturbed the silence. Every eye fixed its gaze on the new hero of the Fair of Tara.

"It's Cormac I am, son of Art of Connacht, and it's the exile's life I've led, these twelve years!"

The magic name of the king two centuries in the ground went round and round the hall: "Cormac! Cormac mac Art!" His neighbors saw that Cumal Uais was no less surprised than they.

Once he'd recovered, even the High-king found it no swift or simple matter to quell the uproar in his banqueting hall. He prevailed at last, by standing and stretching out both robed arms, at right angles to his body.

Cormac had never taken his eyes from the Ard-righ, and he gazed upon him now: a king of kings who was the descendant of kings descended from kings and heroes of Eirrin.

A fine burly figure of a man was Erca Tireach, first among the Eirrin-born. Russet was his hair and scarlet his sleeved cloak of lustrous silk, and besprent with gold, as though it had been sown wet upon the garment by a farmer's hand. The front-and-back Irish cloak was girt low with a buckle of jewel-flashing gold, nor was there much belly to gird. Most of his chest, even his upper belly, were covered by his brooch — which was in truth a carcanet bright and atwinkle, fierily aflash with gems and lesser stones of several colours. Four rings circled the fingers of his left hand. On his right arm King Erca wore the plain leather bracer of a weapon man, his constant reminder to all that he was war commander and keeper of the peace, and ever prepared. Like his lady near, Ard-righ Erca mac Lugaid wore a tunic of white satin, broidered with thick gold thread.

The High-king's eyes, men had said, were like sapphires, though seldom of such hardness.

And now, with him standing tall and his wine-red sleeves hanging down from arms widespread for silence, all voices fell quiet and all eyes gave him their attention.

"Cormac mac Art. It is a name not unknown to me," Erca Tireach said.

Some laughed, thinking he was joking, referring to King Cormac of old. Others were grim; some showed excitement and perhaps apprehension. For many there were who remembered this king's father, wary of Art of Connacht and his daring though unwise naming of his son — and they remembered Art's fate, and his son's disappearance.

This scarred, rather sinister-visaged weapon man who had won the high championship . . . Cormac mac Art?!

Beside Erca then stood his chief poet and adviser, Cethern of the magnificent larynx and pharynx. He thundered so that other voices were as whispers. He bade them be silent, and looked about, and bowed to his king. Then, drawing up his poet's mantle, he resumed his seat.

Erca Tireach looked at Cormac mac Art.

Cormac spoke.

"I have worn other names, lord King. When I took service in Leinster after my father's . . . death," he said, his brief pause bringing a change of expression to many faces and nervous glances toward the king, "it was as Partha mac Othna. It was whilst bearing that name that I brought dishonour on myself, and upon Ulahd, for there I falsely claimed to be from — and upon Connacht, for there was I born

213

and I broke the King's Peace at Fair-time."

"And upon Leinster, whose king's colours you wore?" someone asked boldly, but Cormac saw not who it was, for he kept his dark gaze on the Ard-righ.

"Would you make reply?" King Erca asked.

"Lord King, I would reply thus: No. I brought no dishonour on Leinster, for that was done when a poor young fool was paid to provoke another — myself — into drawing steel . . . by the King of Leinster himself!"

There was a new outburst, girt with anger. The younger of those present bent their heads to hear hurried explanations from the older, who remembered.

When silence had been gained, it was Erca son of Lugaid who spoke, and his words brought new surprise.

"That too I have heard," he said, to them all, not just the unmasked champion. "Though this be a matter for deliberation by the kings assembled at the Great Feis, and that so soon to be, I will tell you this: There was, and there remains question about the death of this man's father, and too about the manner of mac Art's breaking the peace at Fair-time. It was I, Erca Tireach High-king of Eirrin, who set aside the old warrant, pending investigation and hearing. We are not barbarians, like the Saxons or Britons, to condemn a man without giving ear to his words! I assure you that Cormac mac Art . . . Partha mac Othna . . . Ceann mac Cor . . . has lived in exile *by his own decree*, not that of any king."

The voice that spoke up then Cormac recognized as the same he had heard before, challengingly demanding whether he had dishonoured Leinster. Now:

"He broke the High-king's Peace at Fair-Time! With a red sword, and thus it *was* barbarism, and the punishment *death!* No exile this — he fled justice!"

Erca's brows remained smooth. He stood blinking for a time, looking calm and yet stern, and the swell of voices soon ran out like the coastal tide at the time of the quarter-moon.

Erca said, "It were not seemly my lord, surely, that one of Leinster should raise a voice of accusation and prosecution!"

That was answered by gasps and murmurs, and Erca waved a hand impatiently.

"Cormac mac Art, this be no court and ye may answer or no. Did ye flee justice, twelve years past?"

"I answer you and your office, lord King, and no Leinsterish challenger. I fled, aye. As to *what* I fled — it was death, not justice. No justice was available then."

"SILENCE!" the king's poet thundered at the murmurers — and the louder voices.

"Methinks it may be available to me now," Cormac said, as though he had not noticed the interruption. "But I came not back to Eirrin as a supplicant — nor seeking death, for there's been no guilt upon me these twelve years."

"The High-king," Erca said into the new buzz, which diminished that its makers might hear him, "has no power over the laws, and I seek none. Of this, though, I assure ye all. Cormac mac Art may or may not deserve exile or death, and true it is that there was more to the matter then than met the eyes and ears of all of us. Mayhap he fled justice. Mayhap he fled death. And mayhap he departed his homeland to hope for a less . . . prejudiced hearing in some future time — as now. But — *it's he* who has returned, and revealed himself all willingly, and this be no coward's act. I repeat: I have no power over the law, and none do I seek. It is within my power to force custody or offer protection. This I now do, that Cormac Art's son may be heard and judged at the Great Feis."

In silence then, the High-king gazed upon the

215

returned exile.

"You who have borne more names than one but who were born and remain Cormac mac Art of Connacht, hear my command. You are to remain in the household of the lord Cumal of Tara, until we command your presence before kings and judges assembled, at Feis Mor."

Cormac inclined his head in a deep nod, and said nothing.

Considerably later that night, Erca mac Lugaid heard the story of Ceann and Samaire, and received the letter from the lord of Tullamor. The High-king listened. He nodded the while, and his face writhed darkly. In the end he granted them sanctuary and welcome in his household — and advised that Feredach their brother *was* older and thus heir, and that their problem, like Cormac's, was a matter for the Great Assembly.

"In private," he said quietly, "I am worse than horrified. It's welcome I make ye here, with sadness for you and your kingdom. Again in private, I assure ye and your friend Cormac that I do not share my father's . . . apprehension for the son of Connacht with the magic old name. I know, Cormac, that it's tricked and got rid of you are after being. Now I hope to see righted the wrongs against all three of ye. All, though, my lord and lady of Leinster and mac Art, must be up to the Assembly."

"And Leinster," Samaire murmured, "is part of it."

"And Feredach," her brother said, "is, at present, Leinster."

Chapter Twenty: Assembly of Kings

> *"Were all Alba mine*
> *From its centre to its border,*
> *I would rather have the site of a house*
> *In the middle of fair Derry."*

—Colm Cill, exile from Eirrin

Fourteen doors opened into the Mi Chuarta, and they were well separated.

Over seven hundred fifty feet in length sprawled that ancient banqueting hall, and just under fifty feet in width, while the beamed ceiling soared nearly the same distance above the floor. Twice and a half a hundred years this mighty structure had commanded Tara and awed all Eirrin, and still it stood.

Each third year came all the kings into the Mi Chuarta, in solemn gathering. And it was the third year, and the time was Samain or Hallowday, the Celtic new year known to some as first November. It was a day sacred to the Druids — and hurriedly adopted by the priests of the Jesus-faith, who adapted well and without embarrassment to what they were pleased to call pagan customs and feast-days.

A king named Cormac mac Art had builded the awesome hall. An exile named Cormac mac Art must seek his justice in it.

Within one of those fourteen doorways stood a trumpeter, tall and straight and splendidly arrayed.

Already he had blasted forth two long notes. The first summoned numerous shield-bearers into the massive hall. Directed by a marshal and his aides and presided over by the high genealogist, those colourfully-garbed men hurried about, carrying the flashing shields of their noble lords. No assemblage of butterflies had ever been more colourful. Soon it was as if gigantic butterflies of every hue had alit upon the walls, for they were festooned with the shields of families both ancient and relatively new. A poet had said it was as if the rainbow had come to Tara Hill, and taken up its abode in the colossal room.

The trumpeter's second blast had brought more men hurrying in. These bore the symbols of both Druids and the new priests, and more shields. The shields were of men who stood high in the favour and regard of kings, advising them, keeping their records, commanding their armies.

And now the hall was ablaze with shields newly painted and enameled, each behind a sturdy, well-carved chair, and the trumpeter sounded another long sweet note to tremble on the air.

In a rustle of robes and a blaze of jewels, the Kings of Eirrin entered the place of their triennial assembly, and the shields paled before their splendour.

In the vast room's center the High-king sat, with his face to westward. Munster's pale, fat lord took his place on his left hand, while the King of Ulahd sat to the Ard-righ's right. Behind Erca of Tara in Meath, Connacht's sword-thin king took his traditional place.

Across from them, facing the High-king, was the blue-and-silver bedecked monarch of Leinster, with his ever-rising forehead and his thin dark mustachios.

Some there were that had said both Leinster and

218

Meath insisted that they must be able to see the other, face and hands, at all times. Some had said that the High-king trusted none behind him but Connacht; others avowed that Connacht thus symbolically backed the High-kingship; still others had opined that Leinster felt comfortable and fully secure only when mighty Connacht was at such a distance, and the Ard-righ betwixt them.

Others still said that all was symbolism, and the true reasons forgot. It was pointed out that such an arrangement could be said to favour Leinster — but so too could Uladh's position at the right hand of Meath be considered to favour that northern land. All that was certain was that the arrangement did not repeat in miniature the geographical location of the kingdoms.

Munster and Uladh flanked Meath and the high throne, with Connacht behind, and Leinster faced them all.

Jewels glittered in green and blue and yellow and red. Chains of silver and of gold, both delicate and heavy of link, rustled and clinked. Fine brooches and ornate neck-encompassing torcs winked and flashed from many throats, for the room now filled with nobles and advisers, chiefs and priests, Brehons or judges and Seanachies or historians, ollams and sternly robed Druids. To the chairs backed by their colours they solemnly went.

All were aware that the last, the Druids, had failed in their attempts to keep out the priests and their god; all were aware that the priests would not rest until the Druids and all they represented had been ousted. The Celts were becoming Romanized.

"The Druids represent the snarling, dog-eat-dog Eirrin of the past and are a constant reminder of that which we should forget," some said of those who represented the son of God.

"The priests represent the transformation of Eirrin's hopes of Empire and her warhounds into

219

toothless old dogs with but memories of past glories," others said of the cross-wearing men who represented the son of God.

And mayhap both were right, and their god the same, and cared little for the petty way men acknowledged their creator. But history was upon them all.

The great triennial Feis began.

There were readings of genealogies and histories and laws, in voices sonorous, or crackling and breaking with age, and, in one case, nervously atremble with a genius's youth. There were agreements to reconsider and reaffirm, and petitions to be heard and deliberated upon by crowned heads; petitions to be granted in whole or in part, or denied, or held over, or remanded by common agreement to lower courts.

It was Munster's lord who bespoke an attack on his eastward coast by Picts. Heads nodded and frowns became smiles, amid some cheering, when he told how the barbarians had been slain to a man.

It was the High-king himself who directed the reading of a letter from the lord of Tullamor, of how Carbri Black-beard, thief and murderer, had been slain with his red-handed trio of men. Again there were gladsome faces and some cheers, and men called out that the slayers of that slayer should be brought before them . . . .

Erca Tireach waved a hand. On one finger gleamed a ring that was a gift from Viking spoils, brought to him by exiles, but none knew save he — and all knew him to be a man afflicted with conscience and blessed with a high sense of justice.

"The Assembly would greet the slayers of the murderous thief of Brosna Wood," he called, and most eyes turned to one of the fourteen doors.

It was not weapon men who passed in through that portal.

220

Into that awesome room bright with jewels and robes of many colours and more gold than the Romans had stolen out of Britain, came two of the three heroes. Leinster's lord Feredach an-Dubh was shaken, aye and visibly, by their appearance, though only a few noticed that he did not join the others in applause.

"And what would ye have of us, heroes?" called out the High-king himself.

"JUSTICE!" the regally-attired young man with the orange-red hair called back. "Justice for me, and my sister, and our land, and for our murdered brother — LIADH, KING OF LEINSTER!"

The uproar was not soon quieted.

Ceann and Samaire, well-favored of visage and well-attired of form, told their dark story. Their brother, who was prepared for the advent here of Cormac mac Art but not of these two, sat like a sullenly brooding stone.

Objections were raised. Feredach and his counsellors conferred again and again, in low voices and behind ring-bedizened hands. But the two finished their ugly narrative, and dark indeed went the face of Feredach the Dark — a sobriquet used not in public. Yet many including himself heard the whisper:

"Feredach the Dark, indeed!"

"Thus do we make accusation," Ceann Ruadh finished, gazing upon his older brother, "and now do we call for rectification of wrongs."

A scarred man in plain weapon-man's garb awaited just without one of those twice-seven doors, and he held his breath the better to hear.

Cormac heard that which he expected: that all this matter was one of the Leinsterish succession, an internal affair of that realm and not for this assembly that represented all Eirrin. Cormac's lips widened a bit in the hint of a smile nevertheless, for the chief judge and poet spoke with open disrespect for King Feredach, nor did any call him to task.

221

The decision was made: the assembly would not decide. Feredach's thin mustache seemed to writhe as his thin lips parted and drew back in a smile of triumph that few indeed took for justification.

"The will of the Feis-mor has been stated," the High-king said solemnly, "and it is written. I speak now only as King of Meath and as one with respect for the royal-born, as for all Eirrin-born of whatever realm: I Erca Tireach mac Lugaid make known to all men that Prince Ceann and Princess Samaire will remain in my personal household for so long as they choose, for they are Eirrin-born, and free." He paused, then added, "And under my protection."

The smile of Feredach faded like the mist of a sunny morning.

Hardly pleased, but with dignity, Ceann and Samaire departed the hall. They were welcome in Eirrin; they remained exiles from their home.

My lord the King of Uladh changed his position ever so slightly, so that without moving his chair he seemed somehow closer to Erca and farther from Feredach.

Again the Ard-righ spoke, turning his head about so that as many might hear as possible, even in the echoic vastness of that building that could have contained many, many houses.

"The leader of the tiny band that put defeat on the Pictish invaders of my lord of Munster's demesne, aided by Munsterish fisher-folk, is the same as he who laid low Oisin Pictslayer. The third member of the trio that put defeat on the land-pirates of Brosna Wood is the same as he who brought down Bress of the Long Hand. And all are the same man, a man who has borne several names, and birthed legends over half the length of Eirrin, and who is called even mac Cuchulain and Curoi mac Dairi.   ADMIT THE CHAMPION OF EIRRIN!"

The champion of Eirrin, attired as a weapon man

222

with empty sword-sheath, entered to applause — and some confusion, since he was no longer red-braided and mustached, but cleanshaven and crowned with a shaggy mane of black. Tall and rangy, he strode half the length of the hall.

He was asked to state his name.

Never, without shouting, had he spoken so loudly. "Cormac, son of Art, of the ua-Neill of Connacht."

Bedlam was reborn in the Mi Chuarta of Tara, and it was not soon brought under control. Art's son! The son of murdered Art! What a name this scarred man bore!

"You attacked the attacking Picts on the eastern coast of Munster one night within the year, alone?"

"Aye, lord High-king. Though I was soon joined by others, a fisherman named Dond and his son Dondal — and the Prince and Princess of Leinster, for whom I was acting as guard."

"You sustained wounds there, on behalf of your fellow Eirrin-born — though not men of your own land?"

"On behalf of women and children of Eirrin as well, lord High-king. But my wounds were only scratches."

"You experienced other . . . adventures in Munster, Cormac mac Art?"

"None to speak of, my lord High-king," Cormac spoke, and his eyes met the gaze of Eogan. That Munsterish ruler showed little, but gazed back impassively from those weak eyes set in his bloodless face. Cormac nodded, almost imperceptibly; neither he nor Eogan was disposed to speak of their . . . meeting. Good.

"You reached Brosna Wood without again reddening your sword?"

"No, High-king. In an inn in Kilsheed, a drunken weapon man . . . made advances, with

223

insults, on my lady Samaire of Leinster. I was forced to put defeat on him."

"He is alive?" Erca ignored the murmurs.

"He was when we departed the next day, High-king. His wound was in the thigh. I had no wish to slay him."

"There were witnesses?"

"Aye, my lord — and among them my lord Senchann, son of Munster's king."

Ignoring the new murmurs, Erca turned to Eogan. "My lord?"

"It is true, and as he said. The man was disciplined — is *being* disciplined."

"Methinks the champion of Eirrin saw to that!" someone called, and there was laughter.

Erca stared it down. "Has my lord of Munster aught else to add?"

"No, my lord High-king," Eogan said. "Only that I did not know this man's identity at the time. My son acts for me in . . . some matters."

Thus was no mention made of the visit to Eogan, or of his awareness of the identity of the two visitors. *Eogan must have succeeded in calling back his courier to Feredach*, Cormac thought. *Good!*

"And it was alone yourself and the prince and princess made your way up and into Brosna Wood?"

"Aye, my lord," Cormac said with a nod.

"And there you attacked Cairbre Black-beard and four men?"

"There, my lord High-king, Cairbre Black-beard and three men attacked us. Only a medallion saved my lady Samaire from an arrow in the chest. Prince Ceann slew one, and him in the saddle — the prince, I mean. The bandits themselves slew one of their number, for I held him betwixt myself and their arrows. Princess Samaire bowled over another, with her horse; he met justice and his end in Tullamor. It was Prince Ceann slew Cairbre, again from the saddle, and maintaining his seat the while. I did but little, in truth."

"It was you began the attack on them?" the Connachtish king asked.

"Aye, my lord, for they had spoke of slaying us and of molesting the lady."

"You have risked much for the royal couple of a realm you have no reason to love," Erca suggested.

"MY LORD!" That, in an accusing voice, from Feredach's chief adviser.

"A weapon man of Connacht does not argue with the High-king," Cormac said, and there was some laughter. Meanwhile, heads still bent and turned around the hall, as men exchanged memories and what knowledge they had of Art of Connacht, and his son, and the events of twelve years agone.

"It may surely be said with truth that you have saved the lives of the prince and princess of Leinster, and of at least one family of Munster, and of future travelers through Brosna. And too that you have saved more than the life of a lady — and finally that you maintained your control when the former champion of Eirrin lost his and attacked you in earnest."

"I could not gainsay aught of that, lord High-king," Cormac said.

"Yet all three of ye traveled this land with your names in hooded cloaks," Erca said, and many leaned forward. "Cormac mac Art: Why?"

"As for the prince and princess, they had been betrayed into the hands of men of Norge, and were captive, and all three of us feared for their safety until we reached Tara Hill."

The king of Uladh made obvious the fact that he was staring at Feredach the Dark.

"As for myself," Cormac went on, and he told them of his story.

He was questioned, and assured that he had not again reddened his steel in or on the coasts of Eirrin.

The affairs of the soldiers in Kilsheed and the bandits of Brosna Wood were matters for praise, not for the law.

Abruptly Feredach of Leinster rose with a rustle of primrose blue and much silver, which he favored over gold.

"As son of the royal lord in whose service this criminal was, I demand him for judgment and justice."

But there were scowls and worse; Feredach had been undermined already, despite his foreknowledge of Cormac's coming here. Recent events had transformed a boyish criminal into a heroic man.

"The previous petitioners," the King of Connacht observed, "owe their lives to this man. And they have accused my lord of Leinster. Handing over the champion of Eirrin into his hands seems . . . unwise."

There were sounds of agreement, and some laughter.

"And it is in your realm that the red-handed *champion of Eirrin* was *born*, and your realm from which he fled, *my lord!*" Feredach snapped, leaning toward Connacht's king.

"As such," that slender man said equably, and with a tiny smile, "I claim prior jurisdiction."

"I can see from my lord of Connacht's face that he would welcome not the head of Cormac mac Art, but his *arm* — and the sword it wields, rather than seek justice!" Feredach returned.

Into the royal squabble spoke its subject. "Were there *justice* in Leinster, its king's name would be LIAGH! And there'd be no crimson on my *lord* Feredach's hands . . . see it there!"

Cormac pointed, and his extended finger seemed to draw gazes, to make heads to turn and necks to crane. Feredach's face went rowanberry red. A staff thumped the floor and a man of many years growled "Unseemly!" Even Cormac agreed, though his little

226

trickery had worked.

"Leave to say that which is seemly," Cormac said, "with apology for that which was not." He received that leave. "I am of Connacht, and my father before me, and his. Were I to submit to territorial judgment, it would be to that king's." And he bowed to the lord of Connacht — and went on quickly. "But it was the Fair-time Peace I broke, my lords, the High-king's Peace. It be he had summoned me before this assembly, that all Eirrin may judge."

There was no warrant from the former king his father, Erca announced, nor from Meath at all, for Cormac mac Art — or Partha mac Othna. And there were cheers.

"An it were a matter for my deliberation," the king of Uladh said suddenly, "I'd not debate about it all the day. I would say that tricked or no, a young man made an error, and has paid for it — *slay* me, my lords, rather than send me from these duns and fens for twelve years! Mac Art has made expiation for his act of long ago, thrice over."

Amid the assenting shouts, Connacht nodded. And then Munster. And the High-king. And all looked at Feredach. He was indeed the Dark now, his face filled with the hot blood of anger and humiliation and frustration.

When there was at last silence, a silence heavy and thick with the awaiting of every eye for Feredach's nod, of every ear for his words, he made as if to stand. But another man rose up before him.

Feredach looked up, his eyes narrowing. The man on his feet, his poet's mantle falling gracefully away from his shoulders and arms, was Cethern, chief poet; adviser and judge in the court of the High-king — and thus of Eirrin.

"My lord, I beg leave," Cethern said:

Feredach made a jerky gesture and stared.

"When poets speak," Erca said, "crowned heads

227

listen."

Cethern of the balding head and golden tongue looked about, and raised his voice. "The kings have spoken. In his demesne my lord Feredach reigns supreme; here he is but one man of many."

The roar of assent and accolade had to be quelled by the rapping of more than one staff against the floor, and one of the staffs was that of Cethern himself. It had been said that he was more respected even than the High-king, for none denied that Erca Tireach respected Cethern the Poet.

"I would remind though that the precedent were dangerous," Cethern told them. "Let me pose a question. Had that Cormac mac Art of twelve years agone been put to death in accord with the Law, would we twelve years later speak of the possible apprehension of kings, even the High-king, and or royal chicanery, and consider it *injustice?* Ah — ye looked shocked that I dare. What for me that I dare speak words, then: death, or exile, for me who has not slain?"

A new silence fell, and men looked at one another.

"This man has slain, and fled our land. Now it's returned and as a hero he is, and we are ready to welcome him back. I state that for twelve years he has not been a son of Eirrin at all, and that before he again enjoys that most noble of estates, he learn what it means to be a weapon man of *Eirrin!*" Cethern shouted the last word, ringingly. It echoed round about the vast hall: *Eirrinnnnn, Eirrinnnnn, innnnn, nnnn* . . .

Cethern was gazing upon Cormac, the man of letters at the man of arms.

"A son of Eirrin could not object to such, nor debate the foremost poet of Eirrin," Cormac said. "Name the test."

"It would be a test harking back to a time not so

228

ong gone, but already a matter for poets and legend," Cethern said, to them all. He lifted both arms high. 'The Martial Tests for Him Who would be of the Fian!"

Erca's decision was swiftly reached. Weapon men and kings were necessary in all lands. In Eirrin, one stood ever above them, and had for centuries and would for centuries to come: the creator; the writer; the poet. High-king Erca nodded. And so did the other kings. And so did Cormac mac Art. He would submit to the martial portion of the tests of the followers of Finn, back when Eirrin had possessed a sort of national militia: the Fian.

And then a skeletal Druid arose from among the Leinsterish ranks. It was a robed arm he stretched forth with a rustle, and a bony finger that pointed at Cormac mac Art. Old that Druid was, but his voice had lost none of its power.

"CROM DEMANDS TRIAL IN THE MANNER BEHLTAINE!"

All men sat still and silent, shocked. Trial in the manner of Behltaine! A thousand years old, probably more, was that method of the old gods' deliberation, and never had there been appeal. Who dared deny judgment to Behl and Crom, the gods themselves?

A man tried. Direct from his see in Armagh, the fat Bishop of the new god arose. Scandalized he avowed to be, and he was noisy about it. Nor was he interrupted. Surely it was not Cormac he was interested in, but the power of the new priesthood against that of the old. That the life of the exile was involved surely did not concern this man with his crooked staff after the manner of Padraigh and Rome. But since Cormac's life *was* involved, all were happy to let this successor to Padraigh and Benin — Patricius and Benignus — try.

The old gods won, with the unexpected aid of an adherent.

229

Once the Bishop of Christ had finished his harangue, Cormac mac Art lifted his voice.

"As I am a son of Eirrin, I welcome the old Fenian trials. As I am a son of Crom, and no follower of the hanged god of this man, a follower of Behl of the sun over our heads, not the son buried in the ground somewhere over in the eastlands, I submit myself to the Holy Druids of my ancestors."

Many eyes stared at Cormac mac Art, and none with more surprise than the old Druid.

So it was written. First Cormac would endeavor to withstand the weapon man's trials undergone by the followers of Finn: the band of iron heroes wiped out in a civil war two centuries agone — a war between Breasil, King of Leinster, and King Cairbre mac Cormac.

And then Cormac mac Art would be submitted to the far more ancient test, amid the roaring fires of Behltain. Many and many were those who'd got their deaths thereby.

Chapter Twenty-one: The Tests For Him Who Would Be of The Fian

"In a trench the depth of his knees, the candidate shall, with shield and hazel stave alone, defend himself against nine weapon men who shall cast spears at him;

"In a thick wood, with the start of a single tree, he shall escape without scathe from fleet-footed pursuers;

"So skillful and agile must he be in this that in the flight no single braid of his hair shall be loosed by a tree-branch;

"So must his step be so light that underfoot he breaks no fallen or withered branch;

"In his course he shall leap branches the height of his forehead, while stooping under those the height of his knee, without undue delay—or leaving behind a branch atremble;

"He must, without pausing in his course, pick from his foot whatsoever thorn it takes up;

"Even though he faces the greatest of odds, his weapon shall not quiver in his hand;

"He shall stand to fight all odds, even as great as nine to one."

No branch caught Cormac's hair, nor did his foot pick up a thorn as he raced through the wood. No man could leap branches forehead high, and he swerved to avoid them, knowing that none among his pursuers could jump so high either. The other nigh-impossibility, that of stooping—while at the run—under a knee-high branch, had been ruled unnecessary.

He did bound one thick yew branch, which was half fallen and both the height and thickness of his waist; he was able to continue running without falling. His pursuers were four; he lost two of them then, for one tried to roll beneath that same obstacle and was caught by a wrist-thick branch thrusting downward from the main one. Another man jumped not well and fell to lie moaning and whimpering, clutching his genitals.

Cormac mac Art ran on. Behind him, two of the appointed pursuers followed.

They wore soft-soled buskins, all of them, for it had been decided that to race thus through dense woods without some sort of footgear was unnecessarily dangerous. Cormac limped several steps after coming down, on the arch of his foot, on a twig thick as his thumb and hard as lead. But he gritted his teeth and fled on, reminding himself that this was after all far better than riding a horse . . . .

He did not look back at another cry from behind, just after he had leapt a little stream as wide as his height. No backward glance was necessary; the shout was followed by a mighty splash and a wet thrashing about.

Cormac grinned wolfishly. Racing on without pause, he grunted when a branch gouged up his forearm as he passed it too close. Since he felt only the stinging, not the ooze of blood, he did not look down or raise his arm. To do so would have been to jeopardize himself in his running, for he needed his full attention and the constant full use of his eyes to avoid falling or slamming into a tree. He assumed an inch or so of the outer skin had merely been rolled back; such was not worth glancing at.

He bounded a fallen, half rotted bole, and came down on fat-stalked plant. His foot skidded on the moist green stalk. He fell, rolled, thrashed, hurled himself up by main force of will, and plunged on.

Around an oak with a bole thick enough for the building of two houses Cormac swerved. Thence he ran along a thick, waist-high growth of some weed he knew not, and dived into it when he sensed, as much as saw, a little opening within the bushes.

While his heart pounded in him and his breath came cold in his chest, the exile went absolutely still.

His pursuer raced noisily past, breathing hard.

After crawling out the other side of the little natural hedge, Cormac went running back the way he had come. And on, and on. Too soon he heard the noises behind him—well back, now—and he knew his last pursuer had discovered the strategic deception and was once again like a hound on the scent.

Cormac mac Art ran.

And ran. Across the stream he leapt again, with a grim smile for the bedraggled man lying on the bank, panting. He cursed as Cormac rushed by—and grinned. A tree seemed to arrange itself in the racing quarry's path, and in dodging it he slipped and fell.

Thus was his life saved. He *heard* the wicked little bee-song of the arrow that wizzed through the space where he should have been, and then he heard too the cry of shock and pain, from behind.

Floundering about, taking cover, crawling through thick weeds and shaking down a cloud of the pollen of some late-blooming wildflower, Cormac ascertained that he no longer had any pursuit at all. The fourth man rolled on the ground, with an arrow very high in his left thigh.

An arrow aimed for my heart, then, Cormac thought, *and so well calculated that it ranged down enough, fifteen or twenty feet behind me, to take him just below the hip!*

Cormac had no pursuit behind. But now there was an enemy ahead, and him bow-armed, and skillful at the aiming of his shafts! As for Cormac—like his pursuers, he was totally unarmed.

With great rapidity and far more noise than he'd have preferred, he crawled back on a ragged course that paralleled his twice-run path. Then he was staring into the wide eyes of the man who had fallen into the stream; he squatted beside his fallen comrade.

"Over here, and quickly," Cormac bade, in a loud whisper. "That arrow was meant for my heart. An he wants me dead badly enough, he'll not hesitate to slay the both of you as well."

"My Jesus mercy," the wet man said, looking forward. "Who?"

"I have no idea. But *get over here.* And pull him—if he faints from pain, it's better off he'll be!"

The other man came unfrozen to obey with sudden alacrity.

It was long the three of them waited, in what cover they could manage. But they heard no sound, nor came other feathered wands seeking their life's blood. The phantom archer had melted away in the thick wood.

At last, not running, Cormac and the wet man made their way through the woods, and out. Presided over by a marshal appointed by the High-king, a crowd of people heaved a cry. Then they went silent, for pursued and pursuer came together, and grim-faced.

Soon another sort of cry was rising, and angry voices muttered and stormed, for the two men had told of the treachery and of the fallen man who awaited succor, back within the wood. The two pursuers who had first been forced to give up the fight went in quest of him, along with the wet man, for all his being winded.

Much apology was made to Cormac mac Art, who stared impassively through it all. Dark was his tunic with sweat; more ran shining down his body. When the Ard-righ's picked marshal had ceased his apology and assurances, Cormac spoke, with his teeth nigh together.

"My hair was uncaught. I avoided stepping on a thorn, though I fell more than once, bounded trees, and a brook. I broke no branch I stepped upon, and I have eluded four fleet pursuers—and an assassin. Be this over?"

"Uh, aye, aye," the presiding noble said, nodding nervously. "I—" He raised his voice. "I proclaim this test at an end, and the candidate having passed."

Cormac paid no attention to those who cheered or called out jeers. "Then show me those who will cast spears at me, and show me too the shield and stave I will bear," he said in that same tight-lipped way, "that I might inspect all, to see if I am to be murdered in the second of your damned tests!"

"Son of Art, I assure you—"

"I know man, I know, but expect me not to be less than surly—and more than apprehensive." He stepped past the man. "Now it's water other than sweat I'm wanting on me, and ale within me. Save assurances for when I have passed all—if I am allowed to survive!"

235

Even though it was Tigernach who gave him the quarterstaff, and his own at that, Cormac tested it well. The shield was a gift upon him from Cumal Uais, and a handsome one at that—but Cormac strove to break it over his knee. Bronze-bound, steel-studded wood hardened by fire and painted and enameled the shield was, and it broke not. His tools of defense, at least, were reliable.

The nine men who were to cast untipped spears at him Cormac insisted on meeting, one by one. He looked darkly into their eyes—and examined their spears. Every man, following the lead of the first, wished him well.

"Make your best cast," Cormac bade in return, and examined the weapons he must face. None was of anything other than rocky-hard wood, well tapered so that the untipped head would fly true as the aim and skill of him who made the cast.

"I am satisfied," Cormac said.

"I am not," the High-king's marshal said. Bedecked in scarlet and fawn, he introduced two weapon men, and them with sheathed swords, bucklers, and armour as well. These would flank the line of spear-casters. "Beware," he said to the spearmen. "One already has sought this man's life, and it's forfeit will be the life of him who might attempt it again!"

The spearmen looked insulted, but the two weapon men stayed.

A few feet away, also helmeted and armoured and under arms, stood Tigernach mac Roig of Rath Cumal. Nor did he look kindly upon any of the eleven—or the marshal either, for the matter of that.

The priest who passed along the line of spearmen pointedly ignored the man who was to be their target. But to him came a servant of Behl and perhaps Crom, a Druid in loose-girt white robe who leaned on his straight staff. He braced Cormac, and gazed into his

236

grey eyes from pale blue ones, and he nodded.

"Even in the teeth of the *others* with their Roman-hanged godling, son of Art, ye avowed yourself for Crom, watcher over Celts for more thousands of years than men have trod Eirrin's sod. Be well, and beware." The man's voice was quiet, and steady, and his eyes steady. "Beware the dark that hovers about ye, descendant of Celts, when the trumpet sounds."

Cormac felt a shiver run through him, and gave his head a shake. Then he lowered both lids in a long blink.

"My thanks, Druid. Be ye of Meath, or Connacht?"

The quiet, droning voice came back, and the eyes seemed to drill: "Well ye know that Druids have no such earthly allegiances, son of Art. Beware the dark that hovers about ye, son of Celts, when the trumpet sounds."

Nervous in spite of himself, Cormac showed the man a brief nod, and turned away. He jerked his head and blinked several times as he walked across meadowland to the trench prepared for him. Behind him, the Druid went to talk to each of the spearmen. The servant of Behl and Crom walked tall, and very stiffly indeed, a spear-straight line with his robe falling about him. Nor did he lean upon his sturdy staff.

Cormac stepped down into the trench. It was not designed to aid his maneuvering, but it was, the wise men said, as had been those of the candidates for the Fian. Not so long as Cormac's height, it was perhaps three feet wide. He stood in it to the knees—and not without having examined the ground beneath his feet. It was well packed; no treachery here. All seemed well, but he knew no shame for his caution.

Cormac looked about him. The meadow was long, and broad. Many people were gathered about, hundreds perhaps, to witness this very old and much talked-of rite. Behind them, tall trees brooded over the testing ground like solemn guards. The spearmen were not so close that he could not see their staffs a-coming, nor so far removed that good men should not make good casts.

Beware the dark that hovers about ye, son of Celts.

Again Cormac looked about himself. He saw no dark. Behl's disk was bright overhead, and brightly dressed were the men and women of Eirrin who looked on, waiting. *Wagering,* he thought, without rancor.

Wager on Cormac, he bade them mentally.

The marshal's voice rose, loudly, and across the meadow another, chosen for his great voice, repeated each sentence for all to hear. The spearmen were to make their casts as they saw fit, once the signal was given. By his agility and skill in using his stout staff of hazel and his shield the examinee was to defend himself, and without being struck full on. Nor was he to retreat from the trench.

"REPEAT!" Cormac bellowed.

The words were repeated, and again from the meadow's far side: the defendant was not to retreat from the trench; it represented his keep.

Cormac nodded. He would not *retreat.*

He was asked if he were ready.

He nodded.

He was asked again, and he bellowed that he was.

Beware the dark that hovers about ye, son of Celts, when the trumpet sounds.

Cormac watched the line of spearmen from slitted eyes. At either end of that well-spaced line of nine men stood one of the watchful weapon men, and there too stood Tigernach mac Roig. He stared at the spearmen, not at his friend Cormac whom he had tricked into contending for the championship. Well behind the spearmen waited the priest, and near

238

Tigernach was the Druid. A flutter of white cloth tugged Cormac's gaze to that man, who was moving both arms, staring at the man in the trench, gesturing. His robe flapped.

I see no dark hovering about me, Druid.

Only the sound of a bird, a disapproving jay, broke the absolute silence on that plain of testing. Unconcerned, fluffy white clouds sailed like great ships across the sea-blue sky.

Tugging his gaze from the Druid, Cormac watched the spearmen. They seemed closer, and he sneered at himself for his apprehension. *All at once,* he wondered, *or one by one? Neither,* he decided; *they have no one to order a concerted cast, but will not dally about it.*

The trumpet sounded.

Almost instantly the voice roared out: "THE DARK IS UPON YE, SON OF CELTS!"

. . . when the trumpet sounds . . .

Cormac blinked, but took not his gaze from the spearmen, who were lifting their arms, balancing their long shafts, staring at him, sighting.

Suppose they all throw deliberately high or wide, Cormac thought, and then the dark came upon him.

The spearmen became dark, and darker, and then they were shadows.

And then they vanished amid the general midnight that Cormac saw swallow the meadow.

He flared his eyes wide, strained them in his efforts to pierce the deep grey fog. His shield he held close before him, arm doubled behind it, and he crouched, suddenly feeling fear come upon him. He was a helpless target!

A spear swished through the air over his head. He heard it strike the ground well behind him. Well cast, and with strength.

Cormac bellowed his desperate words: "I CANNOT SEE! TIGERRRRRNACH—IS IT DARRRRK?"

Tigernach thought swiftly, for all his confusion and lack of understanding. He answered in seconds.

"NA-A-AYYY! *Cormac! The sun's bright*. . . DEFEND, DEFEND!"

Blindly, Cormac pushed his shield forward, ducked his head behind it, striving to encase it between his shoulders. He struck out viciously with his hazel staff. At nothing visible, for he could see nothing. He felt the heavy blow against his left arm, heard the loud impacts of two untipped spears on his shield. He felt and heard, too, when the stave he so wildly waved struck one of them—or a third. Enshrouded in blackness, Cormac fought panic. It sought to encase his mind, as the sudden dark did all else.

"THE DRUID!" Cormac mac Art shouted, and it was nearer a scream than any sound he had hurled from his lips in many years. "Tigernach, the DRUID!"

A spear whizzed past, curving, and its tail struck him a jarring rap on the left elbow. Had the shield not been a buckler with attached strap, he'd have lost it, for his fingers flexed without his wish and his elbow tingled maddeningly.

Then up ahead a man cried out, and screamed, and the darkness vanished as swiftly as it had come upon one man of the many on that plain.

Cormac roared out the loudest, throatiest, most savage battle cry he could tear up from chest and throat, and thus the two men who were just in the act of casting were affected. One spear rushed well over his head; the other, even though it was enough to his left that all he need do was step rightward, he met with a slashing blow of his shield. Already another was rushing at him, a streaking line in the air that seemed to extend its tail all the way back to its hurler, for the eye could not record so swift a rushing movement toward it.

Cormac swept his shield up before his face. It was

hardly there before the spear slammed into it. He was knocked back by the impact. The rearward lip of the trench caught the backs of his knees, and he sat very suddenly. The shield had gone heavy, and he knew the reason even before the shouts of horror and anger rose all about the field of his testing.

To the side he moved the shield, in order to see, and then Cormac moved faster than ever he had. Two spearmen were casting, simultaneously. In the seconds between their launching and their reaching him, Cormac saw that the rushing javelins would brace him. He could not dodge the one without intersecting the flight of the other.

Deciding in less than a second, he dodged rightward and swung his right arm with all his might.

The leftward spear only touched his shield and sped on past, hardly deflected. With a sharp rap of wood on wood like the crack of a sail in a sudden gust, Cormac's stave smashed into the other spear that sought him. All his eye could see was its tip, approaching directly. Then there was that great *crack* sound, and the jolt to his arm. And the spear was no longer coming; he had slashed it from him and saved his eye with centimeters to spare.

For a moment he was still panting, lying back on the sward with his legs in the pit. He quivered with the familiar battle-excitement.

Then he jerked up into a sitting position, and inspected his shield.

From it stood a long spear, down-slanting, aye, but deeply enough imbedded to remain there. The bright steel of its tip showed, and in the trench lay one shard of the false wooden tip that had been so painstakingly made to encase that deadly sliver of steel.

Cormac stayed the hand that would have yanked it forth, and stared with blazing eyes. Surely the clouds shuddered with the great wave of rising sound from the spectators, but he did not look up to see. Nor did he turn his enraged gaze upon the crowd that ringed him.

He stared at the spearmen. All had cast. All stared back.

"Haaa-YAAAARRRRRGHHHHH!" Cormac roared again, and launched himself up from that trench that had nearly been his grave. As though in a red berserker rage, he charged the spearmen.

They did all he expected. They stared to a man; they glanced at each other, and back at him; they broke. The weapon men, frowning and with hands on hilts, raised their bucklers and looked anxiously to the marshal in his fawn and crimson.

That burly nobleman was otherwise occupied; he crouched, with Tigernach, beside the Druid the latter had downed—dissipating the encircling darkness of ensorcelment that only Cormac had seen.

"A spear!" Tigernach cried, dragging it forth as he rose to his feet. "The Druid has an untipped SPEAR beneath his robes!"

The one he exchanged with one of those nine, for this one in my shield, his staff, Cormac thought, now scant yards from the spearmen.

And then one of their number broke and ran.

Those around him were too astonished to react. But the man had only *begun* to run, while there was another already amove. Seven steps the spearman took, and Cormac eleven in the same space. Cormac's buckler crashed to earth and the impact dislodged the spear. Its long tapering point of steel shone in the sun for all to see. Two more steps the fleeing man took, and two more his pursuer, through and beyond the other spearmen and the two guards. Then it was with both hands Cormac mac Art drove the tip of his hazel staff into the middle of the man's back. His body arcing, the fellow was hurled forward.

Seconds later he was on his back, groaning at the

pain in its center. Across his throat lay Cormac's stave; on one end of that slim staff he set his foot. With a feral fire in his dark eyes, the intended victim looked down at him he assumed was the intended assassin.

"The spear ye exchanged for the Druid's false staff, a war-spear, and none was to know who'd sped the deadly one. But it's caught ye are, and it's I who'll save ye from torture. Speak swiftly who promised you gold for my blood, or it's both feet I'll set on this stick, man, and it's your adam's apple ye'll feel squirting out of your mouth."

The downed man stared up at him. His face was pale and his eyes wide with the fear on him.

Cormac moved his left leg, and the other caught the movement.

"STOP HIM!" a voice bawled, from behind Cormac. But Cormac was preoccupied. He stared down at the treacherous spearman at his feet.

"B—" the fellow began, and licked his lips. "Bress o— of the Long Arm . . . spare me!"

Then his eyes went even wider. He was looking past the vengeful man who stood over him, and warrior's reflexes hurled Cormac aside without his knowing what danger he avoided. The fallen man's eyes were warning enough.

For the second time the steel-shod spear intended for Cormac mac Art missed him. This time it plunged into the belly of the man on the ground. The Druid who'd snatched it up had intended impaling Cormac from behind, but was unable to stop when his target moved. In and in went the steel point, and scarlet bubbled up around it.

Then Tigernach, racing in the Druid's wake, arrived, and struck. His sword sundered cloth and flesh and bone. Blood gouted.

The Druid fell across the body of his fellow conspirator, at the feet of the man they had sought to slay. Thus did Mogh, Druid of Leinster, receive his payment for treachery and journey to the realm of Midir, king of the land of the dead.

hapter Twenty-two: A Free Man of Eirrin

> *Until the shining sea is surmounted,*
> *Which the gods have created above all*
> *else,*
> *No man from north to south shall surpass*
> *CORMAC MAC ART, chief among*
> *warriors.*

—Cethern of Tara

Bress mac Keth, called Bress of the Long Arm,
as nowhere to be found in Tara. Nor did his royal
rd profess to know aught of the man's whereabouts
his plots.

"An he has returned to your demesne, my lord
ng," the High-king asked, "will ye send him back
nder escort to answer queries and charges?"

"Captain Bress is a Leinsterman, my lord king,"
eredach said. "It's in Leinster and by Leinstermen
e'll be questioned, be assured."

"He is accused of crime in Tara of Meath—and
he man he sought to kill was a ward of the Assembly
f *all* the kings, and of the High Throne!" Erca told
he other, with heat he sought but little to control.

"It is in Leinster," Feredach pointed out, "that
his *ward of the High-king* is wanted, my lord, on a
harge of murder twelve years old."

Two pair of royal eyes stared each into the othe and Erca Tireach ground his teeth together behin tightpressed lips.

"He is cleared, King of Leinster, by kin, assembled and by trials physical as well!"

"It is possible," Feredach said, leaning a b forward, "even for a High-king to go beyond himsel to get himself into water too deep for his ability tread it. Whoever Cormac mac Art is, *Partha m Othna* belongs in Leinster! And so, noble Lord, o Leinster's prince and princess."

"I can swim," Erca mac Lugaid said, and th bargain was rejected, the interview ended.

Leinster's lord left surly and returned to h demesne. Whether Bress accompanied him concealment or had gone before was not known. B none among those who discussed the matter in Ta thought Bress had fled elsewhere. They pieced together, the High-king and his close adviser Cether with Cormac and Prince Ceann, aye and Prince Samaire too, for in Eirrin women were not chatt chained to cookstove and distaff. Nor did she wear th primrose of Leinster on her.

The former champion of Eirrin had bee defeated by a returned exile, and had then p disgrace on himself by attacking the proclaimed victe in berserker rage. And after . . .

"It's not friends we were, in the long ago, Cormac said. "His rage must have been deep as th sea when he learned who it was had put defeat o him!"

"And shortly after that," Samaire said, "h learned that his king had no reason to love ye, and ha himself been defeated and humiliated at Feis Mor."

"And so Bress, or someone in Bress's pay, soug to strike you down in the woods," Ceann said, "wit an arrow from ambush."

"And missed," Cormac said.

"Because you tripped," Samaire reminded him.

Cormac gave her a look and received a smile that as sweetness itself.

Cethern saw but saw not; he was silent and thoughtful.

Erca Tireach missed their eye-play; he was looking with narrowed eyes at the wall opposite. "And o Bress somehow enlisted the aid of a Druid—a *Druid!*" he added with a jerk of his head, for if one could not trust the priests of the ancient religion, and even then with one who acknowledged their faith and not that of the new god, where was there left that in which to place trust?

"Aye," Prince Ceann said quietly, "a Druid. A man with the power of sorcery, or of influencing men's minds that their eyes see that which is not there—"

"Where's the difference?" his sister asked sensibly.

"Or to see nothing at all!" Cormac said, and almost he smiled. For now it was over, and he had both passed the test and survived the death-plot. He'd come far, to sit now in such high company.

"And they in turn found a man who liked the gleam of gold well enough to accept the steel-shod spear, and hurl it for them," Ceann was saying on. "Unfortunately, both are dead and we cannot question them further."

"We have it all," Cormac said. "What further is there to ask?"

The High-king of Eirrin looked at him. "That which it is unseemly to think or say," he said, in a voice so low as to be but a whisper.

"I will say it," Samaire told them all. "We might have asked the one or the other what we must now wonder about. Whether Bress acted on his own—or whether he was himself paid to murder . . . or ordered o do!"

Poet, judge, and adviser, Cethern spoke almost

247

in accusation. "It is of your own brother you speak my lady, and him king in Leinster as well."

Samaire met his gaze, looked into the eyes tha were said to have melted the knees of men. "Aye," sh said. "So it is."

That brought a sombre quiet down upon then like the fall of night. They sat in silence, poet an weapon man and royalty, reflecting upon a man wh had slain his brother for his crown and sold his siste and younger brother into the hands of the barbarou men of Norge.

Their dark reverie was interrupted by a apologetic page, who advised the Ard-righ that Ba the Druid wished to speak with him.

"I am occupied with guests," Erca said.

"I know of your guests, and their identity," a new voice said, and all looked up as the robed man entere on feet that made no sound. "It is apology I make, t all, and beg the High-king to hear me in the presenc of these others. What I have to tell you is of interest t all here—and particularly to Cormac mac Art." An the Druid astonished them still further, by bowing hi head to the man he named.

Erca sighed. "Bas, Bas," he said, shaking hi head. "I have allowed you much freedom of movemen because of my wife, and endured much from th priests who think it worse than unseemly that I an brother-in-law to a Druid." Nor was his voice wholl pleasant.

"With your leave, lord High-king," Cormac ma Art said, "I congratulate you upon it!"

Cethern turned away; Ceann and Samaire smile openly—as did the slim man who was brother to th High-king's lady, and him born to far more tha priesthood in a dying faith.

Erca sighed. "Speak, Bas."

"I shall be swift, my lord. It is simply this: it wa a Leinsterman called out that Crom demande

248

Cormac mac Art's trial by the twin fires of Behltain. It was a Leinsterman, too, sought his death by means both sorcerous and earthly. Both were Druids, and we stood disgraced. But the High Lord Crom has given us back our respect, for he showed all the right. At the same time, he punished one not worthy of his priesthood. Cormac mac Art was absolved and cleared in the eyes of all men when he passed the tests imposed on him and proved himself worthy even of the old Fianna. And he was absolved in the eyes of . . . others, when it was clear that Crom and Behl favored him even over a Druid!"

"I think I like what you are saying, Bas, but you have promised to be brief and have spoken at length."

"Apology, my lord—I was born to a father who held royal ambition for me. My message to you and to Cormac mac Art is that in our eyes the gods have shown clearly their favour, and none of us would dare presume to try him the more. There will be no trial by the fire of Behltain for Cormac mac Art, favoured of the gods themselves."

Bas the Druid left the room on soundless feet.

Samaire gazed at Cormac, and her face seemed afraid to smile, though it wanted to.

Into the silence the High-king of Eirrin said, "Cormac mac Art, you have been cleared and absolved of all charges by the Feis Mor, by virtue of your enduring the physical trials imposed on you, and now by the Druids themselves. Eirrin born and Eirrin returned, you are a free man of Eirrin . . . and with honour."

Still Cormac was unable to speak—neither, indeed, was either Ceann or Samaire, who looked at him with tears brimming on the green pools of her eyes.

And the High-king said, "Welcome home, Cormac mac Art."

249

GUIDE TO PRONUNCIATION

The Irish had a way of using many lettters when one or two would do. A fine example is *Rudraigh*—sometimes spelled with an *e* on the end! Too, spelling/pronunciation lack consistency. But then so does our English, or Amerenglish. (If *though* is pronounced "thoe," then *tough* is "toe," isn't it? If *scone* is "skone," then *scene* is "skeen," isn't it? Difficulty of language is all in the viewpoint.

Listed below are a few words and names used in this novel. To the list I add this: I have used an apostrophe now and again to indicate a throaty sound found also in German, Arabic, Yiddish, Turkce, and other languages. *Lough* is often transpelled "Loch," but it isn't really pronounced that way, not quite. It might best be rendered "LOcH"or "LO(c)H," with the "c" even smaller. But then that's not *quite* right . . .

Oh well. Barry Fitzgerald's accent was never quite right, either.

Ard-righ ....ARV-ree
BLN .... First three letters of the Old Alphabet
Cashel ....CASH-EL
Ceann Ruadh................... Ken-ROO-uh
Ceannselaigh........................ Kens-slee
Celt....................................Kelt!
Connacht ....Kuh-NAKhT
Cuchulain ....KOO-h'u-lun
Cumal ....KOO-mul
Dalriada ....Dal-ree-AH-dah

```
DE Danaan ....................... Day DOV-nan
dubh ................................. doob'
dun ............................... doon
Eogan .................... YO-wen (now Owen)
Feis ............................... Feess
Feredach ....................... FAIR-uh-dakh
Liagh ............................... Lee!
Lugh ............................ Loo;Lou;Lew
Meath ............................... Meeth
Mi Chuarta .................. Mee KWAR-tah
Milcho mac Roig .............. MILko mac Roh'
Norge ........................... Norje (norway)
Oisin ............................ WY-sun
Rudraigh ..................... Rury; Rory!
Samaire ...................... Sam-AIR-uh
Senchann ...................... Sen-chun
Sidhe ............................... Shee
Ua-Neill ......................... O'Neil!
```
Uladh: Call it Ulster. It is now; Padriagh's ugly legacy.

FRITZ LEIBER

FAFHRD AND THE GRAY MOUSER SAGA

POUL ANDERSON

78657	**A Stone in Heaven**	$2.50
20724	**Ensign Flandry**	$1.95
48923	**The Long Way Home**	$1.95
51904	**The Man Who Counts**	$1.95
57451	**The Night Face**	$1.95
65954	**The Peregrine**	$1.95
91706	**World Without Stars**	$1.50

Available wherever paperbacks are sold or use this coupon

120

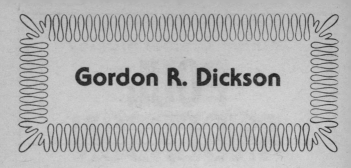

Gordon R. Dickson

☐ 16015	Dorsai!	1.95
☐ 34256	Home From The Shore	2.25
☐ 56010	Naked To The Stars	1.95
☐ 63160	On The Run	1.95
☐ 68023	Pro	1.95
☐ 77417	Soldier, Ask Not	1.95
☐ 77765	The Space Swimmers	1.95
☐ 77749	Spacial Deliver	1.95
☐ 77803	The Spirit Of Dorsai	2.50

Available wherever paperbacks are sold or use this coupon.

ACE SCIENCE FICTION
P.O. Box 400, Kirkwood, N.Y. 13795

Please send me the titles checked above. I enclose _____.
Include 75¢ for postage and handling if one book is ordered; 50¢ per book for two to five. If six or more are ordered, postage is free. California, Illinois, New York and Tennessee residents please add sales tax.

NAME_____

ADDRESS_____

CITY_____STATE_____ZIP_____

Ursula K. Le Guin